MW00829950

VOICE OF COMMAND

THE SPOKEN MAGE SERIES

VOICE OF COMMAND

THE SPOKEN MAGE BOOK 2

MELANIE CELLIER

LUMINANT PUBLICATIONS

VOICE OF COMMAND

Copyright © 2019 by Melanie Cellier

The Spoken Mage Book 2
First edition published in 2019 (v1.3)
by Luminant Publications

All rights reserved. Without limiting the rights under copyright reserved above, no
part of this publication may be reproduced, distributed, transmitted, stored in, or
introduced into a database or retrieval system, in any form, or by any means,
without the prior written permission of both the copyright owner and the above
publisher of this book.

The characters and events portrayed in this book are fictitious. Any similarity to
real persons, living or dead, is coincidental and not intended by the author.

ISBN 978-1-925898-05-7

Luminant Publications
PO Box 203
Glen Osmond, South Australia 5064

melaniecellier@internode.on.net
http://www.melaniecellier.com

Cover Design by Karri Klawiter
Editing by Mary Novak
Map Illustration by Rebecca E Paavo

For Sebastian Isaac,
who lights up my heart
All the waiting was more than worth it

ROYAL FAMILY OF ARDANN

King Stellan
Queen Verena
Crown Princess Lucienne
Prince Lucas

MAGE COUNCIL

Academy Head (black robe) - Duke Lorcan of Callinos
University Head (black robe) - Duchess Jessamine of
    Callinos
Head of Law Enforcement (red robe) - Duke Lennox of
    Ellington
Head of the Seekers (gray robe) - Duchess Phyllida of
    Callinos
Head of the Healers (purple robe) - Duke Dashiell of
    Callinos
Head of the Growers (green robe) - Duchess Annika of
    Devoras
Head of the Wind Workers (blue robe) - Duke Magnus of
    Ellington
Head of the Creators (orange robe) - Duke Casimir of
    Stantorn
Head of the Armed Forces (silver robe) - General Griffith of
    Devoras
Head of the Royal Guard (gold robe) - General Thaddeus of
    Stantorn

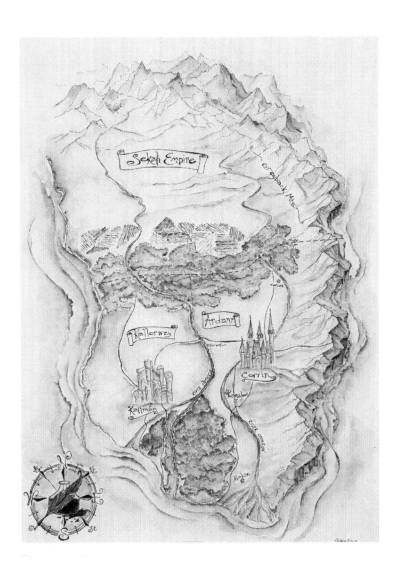

CHAPTER 1

"*E*lena! Elena! The mages are here!"

My hand spasmed, and I nearly cut off my finger. Putting down the knife I had been using to chop vegetables, I turned to regard my younger sister.

"Mages?" I tried to hide my consternation. For weeks now I had been so careful, not attempting even the smallest composition. Not giving even the slightest excuse for the Reds to descend on Kingslee. "Are you sure?"

Clementine rolled her eyes. "Of course I'm sure. I'm ill, not stupid. I know what a mage looks like. And the carriage is too fancy to belong to anyone else, anyway."

I narrowed my eyes at her. "You're right, you are ill. So what are you doing dashing around?"

She sighed. "I already have one mother, Elena. And I get sick of being stuck inside all day."

I winced in sympathy. I hadn't been studying healing for anywhere near long enough to understand why Clementine had been born with such a weak system, but she had always been that way. We had nearly lost her three times in her first year, and even now at twelve years old, she still contracted every tiny ailment that went through our village.

The winters were always the worst, but she was in the middle of a particularly bad summer cold right now and should have been tucked up in her bed. Every time I looked at her, I ached to try a composition. While I might not be able to heal her properly, I was fairly confident I could heal a simple cold. But her eager, innocent face always stopped me.

I couldn't draw on power here. Not in my family's home. It might not be exactly against the law—I wouldn't be reading or writing, after all—but I didn't intend to do anything that could even be looked at askance. I'd already done enough of that in my first year at the Academy—officially the Royal Academy of the Written Word. It was the same reason that I hadn't read a single word in the weeks I'd been home on summer break.

Common folk were forbidden to read, and while I had special permission to do so at the Academy, I wasn't willing to test just how far that permission extended. Only my position as a trainee under the authority of Lorcan, the Academy Head, had kept me alive so far. I had no desire to find out what would happen if someone felt I had transgressed while not under his oversight. I might have chosen to embrace my magehood, but that didn't mean the rest of the mageborn were ready to see me as one of them. I was a long way from enjoying the same freedoms and privileges they did.

But given my impeccable behavior all summer, I couldn't understand why red-robed law enforcement mages would be descending on me now, of all times. Especially when I had heard nothing from the mages since I returned to Kingslee for the second half of the summer. In fact, I would be back in the capital at the Academy in only a week.

Perhaps I should have known the peace and quiet of the past weeks had been too good to last. Especially given that a person, or persons, unknown had made three separate attempts on my life during first year. Despite the assurances the Academy Head had given me about my safety, I had spent the first two weeks at home in almost constant tension, waiting for some sort of attack. None had come, however.

"You get back into bed," I said to Clementine, hurrying toward the door. "I'll go see what they want."

Whatever they had come for, I didn't want them anywhere near my family. Especially not since I had every intention of defending myself if it came to that. And I didn't exactly have a great track record of control or finesse in those sorts of situations.

I hurried outside without waiting to see if my sister would obey me and return to bed. But no carriages waited outside. No one was in sight at all.

After a brief hesitation, I started down the dirt road toward Kingslee. Law enforcement knew where I lived, as did the gray-robed seekers, whose special role was to seek out any sign of reading or attempted writing among the common folk. Both had visited before. But perhaps it was possible they weren't in Kingslee for me at all?

My steps sped up. If someone in the town had been reading, we were all in terrible danger. Any attempt at writing by a commonborn—even a single word—could be enough to explode the entire village. I could only hope Clemmy would be safe enough in our house, given it sat outside the actual town. But both my parents were at work in the family store right in the middle of Kingslee, as they always were at this time of day.

If things went badly, I thought I could protect them. I hoped so, anyway. I couldn't do it from out here, though.

But even as the road flew past beneath my hurrying feet, I found it hard to believe. Kingslee prided itself on a long history without a single infraction. Even after the town managed to somehow produce me—the first and only Spoken Mage in recorded history—the watchers assigned by the seekers had left after only a few months finding nothing of suspicion.

I had returned home months after their departure, and yet I still hadn't heard the last of it. At least half of Kingslee blamed me for bringing the Grays down on them, and the local inhabitants were more vigilant about patrolling themselves than ever before. So how could there be trouble now? At least trouble that didn't center around me.

As I passed through the outskirts of town, I heard the distant murmur of a small crowd. It sounded like it was gathered in the square outside my family's store. I broke into a full run, even as memories washed over me. It had been while confronting an angry mob in front of that store almost a year ago that my powers had first manifested. Somehow I had composed a magical working without using written words. I had done it with a single spoken word, in fact. Even a year later, no one understood how it was possible.

I had proven myself, though, slowly gaining control of my ability to verbally compose. But now my skills were growing rusty from disuse. A part of me couldn't wait to get back to the Academy. Back to a world where words held power and unlocked untold mysteries.

I kept the longing to myself, though. It felt disloyal to my family to think of myself as a mage and to be eager to leave them. Especially to return to the world of the arrogant and entitled.

But still, I had to admit something more than anxiety lent urgency to my steps. I hardly wanted to acknowledge it, even to myself, but I wanted to see and talk to mages again. Any mages. As long as they weren't here to arrest me, of course.

One knot of tension in my chest eased when the crowd came into view. Whatever was happening, they weren't storming our store like they had been a year ago. The group was a small one, and even as I watched, it ebbed and flowed, some members slipping away while others appeared. This was the natural curiosity of villagers at an unexpected and notable arrival. One made all the more interesting by the fact that few in our village had ever been as far as the capital—despite it being a mere three hours' walk from Kingslee. While the occasional family went in for the festivals or to sell extra produce at the bigger markets, few villagers had spare goods, spare time, or spare coin that might drive them to seek out an unfamiliar place.

An expensive-looking carriage stood in front of the crowd. My short height meant I couldn't see past the interested throng to the small open space between the vehicle and our store, so I plunged in, elbowing my way through as needed.

Several people protested at my passage, but each one fell silent once they turned to see who it was. After weeks of my doing nothing out of the ordinary whatsoever, the local children had stopped following me everywhere I went, and the adults had stopped drawing away and muttering at the sight of me. But that didn't mean the people I had grown up with had become comfortable with my suddenly charged presence. Most of them didn't know quite what to make of me and vacillated somewhere between fear, pride, and resentment. Not exactly a comfortable combination.

The last few people fell away, but I faltered as I stepped out from the crowd. The two newcomers who stood beside the carriage were certainly mages. But there wasn't a dull-red or charcoal-gray robe in sight. Instead they wore the last color I had expected to see—purple. Healers.

Had they gotten lost and stumbled on Kingslee by accident? It was true that healers were the one discipline whose services were widely available to the common folk, but naturally their services came with a hefty fee. So we were too small and too poor to have ever had a healing clinic here.

The younger of the two mages looked around at the crowd uneasily, his eyes passing over me without recognition. He looked so young it was hard to believe he could have completed his four years at the Academy and two years at the front lines of our endless war with Kallorway. But if he had joined a discipline and received a colored robe, he must have done so.

"We should go into the store. Even if it's not the right one, they can direct us, I'm sure," he said.

"No doubt they could," said the older woman beside him. "But I'm sure one of these fine people could direct us as well. People in villages of this size tend to know one another."

Her calm, gentle voice washed over me, and I found myself leaning toward her unconsciously. Somehow she managed to sound wise, trustworthy, and experienced with just a few words. And that despite the weariness that emanated from her.

The young man looked around, his eyes latching onto me as the closest.

"You. Girl. We are in need of directions."

I stiffened at his arrogant tone. At seventeen I was hardly a girl—at least not to someone who couldn't be much more than five years my elder. But his next words effectively distracted me from my outrage.

"We are searching for the family of the Academy trainee, Elena of Kingslee. Can you direct us to their abode?"

My family. Not me. He claimed they were searching for my family. I had to remind myself these were healers and not Reds before my breath restarted.

"I apologize for my companion," said the woman when I didn't immediately respond. "He is young and lacks finesse. But we would indeed be grateful if you could direct us to Elena."

The younger mage flushed at her words and looked mutinous. But if he had objections, he kept them to himself.

Everything about this woman's bearing suggested she must be

a senior mage, but I had never met one with so much kindness and respect for common folk. Perhaps my friends back at the Academy had been right when they suggested that healers were a different breed.

My eyes fell on the man who was now scowling at the crowd. Some healers, anyway. I drew a deep breath.

"I am Elena. How may I assist you?"

"Elena herself! How fortunate." The woman smiled at me. "I am Beatrice, and my companion here is Reese. We've come to treat your...sister, I believe it is?"

I gaped at her, my mouth hanging open, unable to think of anything to say.

Beatrice frowned at me. "You do have a sister, do you not? An invalid of some sort?"

"Aye, she's a sickly one, all right," said a gruff voice from the crowd before someone else shushed him.

"Well, then." Beatrice smiled again. "It seems we're in the right place, after all."

"I...I don't understand," I managed to say.

"Is this indeed your parents' store?" Beatrice gestured at the building behind her. "Perhaps we might step inside to continue the conversation?"

I nodded, immediately aware of the interested crowd, and led them through the door. Inside it was cool and a little dark, full of a mix of smells that reminded me forcibly of my childhood.

My mother bustled forward, bowing to the two healers.

"My Lady. My Lord. It is an honor. How may I assist you?" Her eyes flickered to me, and I tried to assume a reassuring expression for her benefit.

"It is us who are here to assist you, I believe," Beatrice said with a smile.

"Assist us?" My mother turned openly to look at me, but I just shrugged.

"I don't know anything about this. She says they're here for Clemmy."

My mother drew back, sudden alarm on her face, so I hurried to reassure her, kicking myself for my thoughtless wording. I should know better than anyone the power of words and the need to choose them wisely.

"To heal her, I mean."

My mother's astonished gaze turned back to the healer. "Here to...heal...Clemmy? But we don't have..." She exchanged a concerned look with my father who had appeared from the back of the store to join us.

Despite all their hard work and their successful store, my parents had little spare coin. For years now, they had saved everything they could for my older brother, Jasper. They had started as soon as they realized exactly how smart he actually was, only slowed by the arrival of Clemmy and the need to nurse her and purchase what herbal remedies they could find and afford.

Even then, we might have scraped together the cost of a simple healing. But Clemmy's problem was complicated and difficult, and we had been told it would be vastly expensive to fix. And with me gone for the last year, unavailable to help with either nursing or the store, it had been an even leaner year than usual.

They had barely been able to manage the coin for another year's board for Jasper. He had won a position, along with a scholarship, at the Royal University two years ago—deemed one of the incredibly small number of common folk with memories good enough to keep up with mage students who had the advantage of being able to read and write. But the scholarship only covered tuition, and all the other costs of academic life added up to far more coin than my parents had to spare in any normal year.

It was part of the reason he wasn't here with us now despite

8

also being on summer break. He had chosen to remain in the capital both last summer and this one to allow him to continue to study but also to pick up what odd jobs he could find to help raise the necessary funds.

But no one in the family resented it. Jasper was our family's hope for a new and better life. Once he graduated, he would have his pick of jobs. With so few commonborn graduates, he would be able to secure a highly paid position, and then we would all move to the capital to join him. And once we were established there, with coin to spare, Clemmy would have access to the healing clinics. Or that had always been the plan.

Was it possible Jasper had found some unexpectedly lucrative job for the summer? It would have to be unimaginably lucrative for him to have hired these healers to come all the way out here for Clemmy.

"Did Jasper hire you?" I asked, and both my parents brightened at the suggestion.

"Lady Beatrice is one of the most senior mages in the healing discipline," said Reese, with a sour look at me. "Her services are hardly available for hire."

"Really, Reese." Beatrice shook her head at him before turning back to us. "Suffice it to say that it seems your family has some powerful friends." Her eyes crinkled with amusement. "And that there are some within my discipline who thought a quiet, relaxing trip like this was just the sort of thing I needed to keep me from over-extending myself elsewhere. Be at peace that I have not come with any request for coin."

My father frowned first at her, then at me, but her words had sparked a sudden realization in me, and it must have been visible on my face. He bowed and murmured his thanks and appreciation, accepting her presence without further argument.

Her use of the word friends had been the clue. While I was hardly the most popular person at the Academy—or at the

University or at the palace, or anywhere else I had been for that matter—I had managed to make a small handful of friends.

And one of them was Finnian. Son of Duke Dashiell of Callinos who just happened to be the Head of the Healers. Finnian must have somehow convinced his father to send Beatrice to heal Clemmy.

Part of me wanted to reject the offer as being far too generous, but the rest of me tamped down on that instinct. After everything I had endured—and all through no fault of my own—was it really too much to expect something back from the mages who had held all the power and wealth in Ardann for as long as anyone could remember?

Not that I wasn't grateful to Finnian. I would thank him profusely as soon as I saw him again. But in the meantime, I would let Beatrice heal Clemmy.

But even as my parents joyously closed up the store, ready to take Beatrice and Reese back to our home, a niggling doubt in the back of my mind made me shift uncomfortably. If there was one lesson I had learned in my year at the Academy, it was that I had far too little understanding of the subtle dynamics of power between the upper levels of mages. The royals and the four great mage families—Callinos, Devoras, Stantorn, and Ellington—created the laws, and the rest of us merely danced to their tune.

Even the minor mage families had little say by comparison. Not when only members of one of the great families ever possessed the necessary strength and skill to win a position as head of a discipline. And such positions came with more than just a lifetime rank of duke or duchess—or general in the case of the Armed Forces and Royal Guard. The ten heads made up the Mage Council, the body of powerful mages who assisted the king in governing Ardann.

I trusted Finnian—at least I thought I did—but did I really understand him? What price might be expected from me later if I accepted this unearned favor now?

But I thrust the thought aside. If there was a price, I would have to find a way to pay it. My sister was more than worth it. And every year longer that she had to wait for a healing might be her last. All it would take was one particularly bad illness to sweep through Kingslee.

I would choose life for Clemmy now and let the future look after itself.

CHAPTER 2

*W*hen we stepped out of the store, the crowd had dwindled, although several interested onlookers still lingered. The mages ignored them, moving toward their carriage, but a young woman pushed forward to accost them, her face frantic.

She held something bundled in her arms, and when she reached them, she thrust it out, revealing a tiny baby. I frowned. I recognized her and knew she had given birth only days ago. She should be home resting.

"Please!" she cried, tears in her eyes. "You are healers, yes? Please help me!"

Beatrice faltered, her eyes going from the woman to the baby and back. "Is there a prob—"

Reese cut her off, stepping between them. "If you wish to see a healer, the healing clinics in the capital are open to all. We are here on important business and cannot be disturbed."

I stepped forward to join them, speaking before I had thought it through, as always.

"Can't you see how young this baby is? Much too young for the trek into the capital, especially if she's ill. And no one in

Kingslee has enough spare coin for the healing clinics anyway." I turned to the woman. "What's wrong with her, Sara?"

Sara turned to me, pulling her baby back to cradle her against her chest. "She's burning up, and we can't get her temperature down. She's almost stopped feeding completely, and I'm so worried…" A sob slipped out. "She was born such a tiny thing to begin with."

Sara turned to look at Beatrice, still shielded behind Reese. "She's my first, and I don't know what to do. Please help her!"

Reese gave a long-suffering sigh. "Try seeping a tea from basil and ginger."

I put my hands on my hips and glared at him. "She's a newborn. How is she supposed to drink tea?"

He glared straight back at me. "She can suck it off someone's finger."

Beatrice shook her head and spoke softly. "You know that will not be enough, Reese. Not for such a small baby." She stepped around the young man. "Here, let me see her." She held out her arms for the baby.

Reese grabbed at her, trying to pull her back, and spoke quickly in a low undertone. "Beatrice, no. You can't help every-body—you know that." He gave her a significant look. "Or you should by now. That's why they sent you back from the front lines. Plus we don't know how complicated the healing with this sister is going to be. You'll exhaust yourself."

Beatrice shook off his restraining hand. "I will hardly need to write a new composition for a fever. I do have some stores, you know. So it won't exhaust me in the least."

Reese gave her a dark look. "Not now, perhaps. But later, when you have to replenish it…"

But she wasn't listening and had already received the baby into her arms. He turned to glare at me, instead, but I turned my back on him, giving my attention to Beatrice.

She sighed and clucked to herself, carefully examining the newborn with confident hands.

"A simple fever," she announced after a few moments. "The signs are clear. I don't even need to use a diagnosis composition to confirm." She looked at Reese, as if expecting him to be pleased with this news, but his sour expression didn't change.

"Great," he said. "Then there's no need for you to involve yourself in a simple case of fever."

"Don't be ridiculous," she snapped, sounding out of temper for the first time since her arrival. "The case may be simple, but in a child this young, it will still be deadly."

Sara gasped and reached out trembling hands to scoop up her baby, as if responding to some irrepressible motherly instinct. But Beatrice held firm to the child, refusing to relinquish her back to the villager.

"Elena, if you wouldn't mind?" she asked, calm returned to her voice.

I stepped forward, eager to help.

"In the carriage you'll find a small leather case. Inside you'll find a number of colored pouches. Please open the red pouch and retrieve a composition for the treatment of fever." She paused. "You can read, can you not?"

I nodded, and several of the interested villagers drew back, muttering to themselves. They knew my status had changed, but old habits still gripped them, and the thought of a Kingslee resident able to read violated all our most important laws.

The crowd had grown somewhat, word no doubt spreading that a healing might be about to occur. But for all their curiosity, fear also lingered in the air, and none of them had pressed too close.

Reese stepped forward, his face flushed. "I'll fetch it, Beatrice. We don't even know her."

"Will you, Reese?" Beatrice regarded him coolly. "Very well. But not because I don't trust her."

She turned to me. "He knows something of my system and will be able to put his hand on the right one faster."

I nodded, trying not to let my disappointment show. I would have liked the chance to get a look at her healing case. As Reese disappeared into the carriage, I regarded Beatrice with curiosity.

"You're clearly a senior healer," I said. "What family are you from?" It had to be one of the four great families.

She smiled at me. "I'm a Stantorn."

My eyes widened in surprise before I could force my face into a neutral expression. The Stantorns had set themselves against me from the beginning, and I had never seen one show compassion or care—particularly for someone commonborn.

Her smile didn't fade at my reaction. "I am something of a black sheep in my family, I'm afraid. Thus why they feel the need to hem me around with minders, such as my young cousin."

Now Reese being a Stantorn I could well believe.

The young healer reappeared, a curl of parchment held lightly between his fingers, reluctance in every line of his body.

"I've never seen it looking so empty," he said, his focus on Beatrice.

She merely shrugged, but I saw something almost like discomfort flit across her face.

Without stopping to think through the wisdom of it, I snatched the parchment from Reese, unfurling it and quickly reading the words. I recognized it. It wasn't a composition I had memorized, but I had read it before in my beginner level healing studies.

I looked up at Beatrice as Reese pulled it back from me with an outraged cry, launching into an angry speech that I ignored.

"I could do it. Under your supervision."

"What?" Reese stared at me, his speech bitten off mid-word.

A spark of interest lit in Beatrice's eyes. "I heard you've showed some interest in our discipline."

I nodded. "I studied it last year."

15

"But you were only a first year." Reese regarded me with narrowed eyes. "Discipline studies don't start until second year."

I just shrugged. I didn't feel the need to explain my reasoning to him. In fact, I had never explained it to anyone. But I would turn eighteen in the spring. And once I turned eighteen, I would be forced to leave the Academy.

One in our family must enlist with the Armed Forces between their eighteenth and nineteenth birthdays, and my brother had already turned twenty. My family rarely talked of it, but we'd always known that between my brilliant brother, my weak younger sister, and me, there was only one candidate to fulfill our family's conscription requirement. And my position at the Academy was precarious. All last year there had been those—particularly Stantorns—who had advocated I was too dangerous to be allowed to live. So as soon as I turned eighteen, I was enlisting. Once it was done, Clemmy was free. Even if I ended up executed.

If I had been the youngest, I would have taken my chances. I could only imagine Lorcan would put up a fight if the Reds came to drag one of his trainees away to be conscripted into the Armed Forces. But the Reds only came to drag away the youngest child. The older ones were under no obligation to enlist, unless they chose to take on that burden for their family. Which meant no one would come to drag me away.

My eighteenth year would pass, I would turn nineteen, and any future enlistment of mine would be considered separate from my family's responsibilities. By the time I made it to the front lines as an Academy graduate, it would be too late for my service to help my family. And then, on Clemmy's eighteenth birthday, as the youngest in the family, the Reds would turn up for her.

No, it wasn't even worth considering.

So, with all that in mind, studying healing as soon as possible had seemed like an excellent idea. I couldn't imagine a more helpful discipline if I ended up serving a three-year term on the front lines.

"I could heal the baby, and then you wouldn't need to use up your composition," I said to Beatrice. Sara's child might not be Clemmy, but I itched to use my dormant power to help someone.

And just the idea of composing again sent excitement coursing through me. I hadn't realized just how much I missed feeling the rush of controlled power, of speaking and feeling my words bend reality to my will.

It was a risk, of course, composing outside the Academy and in front of two Stantorns. But if I did it with Beatrice's permission, and under her supervision, how could her family turn around and complain?

"I would love to see a verbal composition," she said softly, her focus now wholly on me. "It seems like a fairy story, but I am assured the rumors are true."

She didn't pose it as a question, but I could hear the query all the same. I was used to this reaction. I was the first Spoken Mage in history—at least as far as anyone knew. Power could not be accessed by spoken words, let alone shaped and controlled. Only written words unleashed power. And only those born to mage families had the inherited ability to control that flow. Anyone else who tried unleashed an explosion of uncontrolled power that had been known to level entire villages. There was a reason none of the common folk were allowed to read or write. Writing was unimaginably dangerous, and everyone knew that reading led to writing.

On top of this, only the strongest and most skilled of mages—always from one of the great families—had the ability to compose a controlled working with a single phrase. Compositions of a single word were the stuff of legends. Everyone else had to use binding words to hold and contain the power until they had composed all the necessary parameters.

So when I—a commonborn girl with no known mage ancestry, unable to read or write—had composed a working with a single spoken word, I had turned the mage world upside down. And that world, in turn, had upended my life.

Necessity had forced the verbal composition out of me, and it had taken me many long months of training—and a second near disaster—for me to even unlock how I had achieved it.

The mages had taught me to read in that time, but I was still forbidden from writing. At least after my single attempt had exploded a chunk of the Academy. In some ways I was still very much a commonborn—writing remained out of my reach, too dangerous for me to attempt again.

So no matter how trustworthy the sources, every new mage I encountered seemed to harbor a seed of doubt. As if only the evidence of their own eyes could truly convince them.

"I'll believe it when I see it," Reese muttered, as if to confirm my thoughts.

"Well, how fortunate that here is your opportunity," said Beatrice. "If you're sure you can manage it, Elena." She looked down at the baby in her arms with her first hint of doubt.

I swallowed. Did I really want to experiment on a fragile newborn? But I recognized the composition, and it really was a simple one, well within my capabilities. I had worked more complicated healings before.

I nodded. "I can do it. But I'll need your composition. Just to refresh my memory of the words. You can have it back afterward." Until someone tore the parchment, her composition would remain intact. And if she was as skilled as I suspected, she may well have included a binding in her composition that allowed it to be accessed only by her. I would have to watch for any wording I didn't recognize and be sure to leave it out of my own working.

Beatrice nodded, and Reese handed over the scrap with exaggerated reluctance.

I took several moments to read it through, not wanting to risk getting anything wrong. But I couldn't see anything outside of the standard composition for the reduction of fever.

I took a deep breath and spoke the words slowly and clearly. It didn't work unless I first called up a mental image of the written words—the reason my ability had remained hidden, even from me, for so long. But it was easy to do with the parchment before me. Usually I tried to practice without a written prompt, since I couldn't rely on always having one to hand and couldn't produce them for myself. It made this working even more simple than I had expected.

"End binding," I said, reaching the final words. I flicked my fingers toward the baby in Beatrice's arms as I had seen healers do before when directing their healings. Power expanded out from my fingers, flowing in the direction I pointed. Normally I would have included more specific instructions as to the subject, but I hadn't wanted to risk changing Beatrice's words, and she had crafted the composition to work on any subject.

The power settled over the baby like a mist, recognizing her raised temperature and instantly working to lower it. The tiny girl stirred, opened her eyes, and then began to scream.

I stepped back in alarm. What had I done?

"Excellent! Well done, Elena!" Beatrice examined the baby again before passing her back to the anxiously waiting Sara. "Her fever is gone."

She quietly explained to the young mother what steps she should take to rehydrate and recuperate the baby while I sucked in several deep breaths of relief. The baby continued to cry, her tiny mouth searching blindly for her mother's chest.

Sara thanked Beatrice and me with wide eyes before hurrying away toward her home. As the crowd parted before her, I noticed how many uneasy looks were being directed at me. I bit my lip. I should have suggested we move back inside before I attempted the healing. All the work I had done in the last weeks to appear normal and non-threatening had clearly just been undone.

The villagers—my old neighbors—viewed me as a threatening curiosity. Although I should be used to it by now since many of the mages who I lived and studied the rest of the year with felt much the same way. I was an oddity who belonged neither with mages nor with common folk. And the more time I spent back in Kingslee, the more I realized that any hope of fitting in among the commonborn had passed. If I wanted to find a place for myself, it would have to be among the mages.

Beatrice followed the direction of my gaze and then hustled the three of us into the carriage. As we drove off, I caught a glimpse of my parents out the window. They were following in our wake, but their expressions made me more uncomfortable than those of the rest of the villagers combined. I might no longer belong with the commonborn, but surely that didn't include my family. With them I could never be out of place. With them I would always belong…Wouldn't I?

I tried to reassure myself that it had not been fear and mistrust I glimpsed in their eyes. I knew they felt that way about mages, but they could never feel that way about me. But somehow I couldn't quite convince myself.

CHAPTER 3

$\mathcal{W}$hen we reached my home, I ushered the two mages inside and offered them cups of tea. For a brief second I felt embarrassment at our humble house and limited hospitality. But the feeling was immediately overwhelmed by shame. My family worked hard, and our house was neat and clean. I had nothing to be ashamed of except for the change in me that had allowed for such a thought in the first place.

It was an uncomfortable reminder that it wasn't the villagers, or even my family, who had changed—it was me. And if I wasn't careful, I might change into someone I didn't want to be.

I had expected Clemmy to greet us with high excitement, but there was no sign of my younger sister. And when I climbed into the loft where she and I slept, I found it empty too. Frowning, I looked around, trying to hide my concern from Beatrice and Reese. My sister was sick and should be in her bed. Where could she be?

But it didn't take much reflection to know where she must have gone. And when my parents pushed open our door, Clemmy trailing behind them, all doubt was erased. I smiled at the three of them even as I scolded my sister. My words came from habit more than anything—my heart wasn't in it. Not when I was too busy searching her eyes for any sign of fear. If Clemmy had been hidden in the crowd and had also seen me compose…

But she greeted me with the same clear smile and eager words as always, and my heart lightened. I should have known nothing would ever make my sister turn from me. I had been her protector for almost as long as I could remember—it had always been Clemmy and me against the world.

"Is it true?" she asked breathlessly, wide eyes fixing on the two purple-robed mages. "Are you here to heal me?"

Beatrice nodded and smiled, putting down her cup of tea.

"You must be Elena's younger sister. I can see the resemblance."

Clemmy nodded. "I'm Clementine."

"Is there somewhere comfortable you can lie down, Clementine? The healing could take a while."

A brief flicker of alarm crossed my mother's face, and Beatrice directed her next words at the whole family.

"It won't hurt, I assure you. It's just that in complicated cases such as I believe this one to be, we must spend some time first diagnosing the problem. And that may take a number of compositions to achieve to our satisfaction. Once the diagnosis is complete, there is every possibility we will need to compose a new working specifically for Clementine. And that may take some time as well."

I hoped they meant to let me watch. I had never seen such a complex healing, and the process fascinated me.

In the end, Clemmy was settled on my parents' bed, and Beatrice, Reese, and I all managed to squeeze into the bedroom to join her. Reese had grumbled a little at my inclusion, but Beatrice overruled him. For all he had apparently been sent to mind her, there was no question as to which of them held the authority.

Beatrice took the time to explain the process as they

completed each step, and she even allowed me to work a simple diagnosis composition to assist. Reese grumbled the whole time that I was only a first year, and that he for one wasn't going to look after me if I overextended myself and fainted, but I ignored him.

Regular mages expended energy when they composed rather than when they released a stored composition, and they spent their four years at the Academy gradually building up their stamina. Most new mages exhausted themselves all too easily. So mages tended to assume that since I had no way to store compositions, I must have a severely limited ability to compose.

Only a very small handful knew the truth. I had always had stamina far beyond a typical first year mage and could work simple compositions for hours without coming anywhere near collapse.

In fact, I had only overextended once—and that after doing multiple major workings in a row, several performed in a life or death scenario where I had rattled them off without sufficient limitations.

Once the diagnosis was complete, however, it was my lack of medical training rather than any weakness that held me back from further participation. Reese had finally become absorbed in their task, seeming to forget who they performed it for, and he and Beatrice descended into a long and involved technical discussion.

I remained, sitting quietly on the bed and squeezing Clemmy's hand, but I couldn't follow what they were saying. And when it came time to actually compose the healing, I had nothing to contribute. They debated for almost as long again over the specific wording, Reese hovering over Beatrice's shoulder and giving constant suggestions and recommendations. I didn't know how she bore it, but she remained patient, accepting his input with good grace.

I didn't need to understand everything to recognize that she was far more experienced and skilled than him, however, and when she had pulled out the long sheet of parchment to begin the actual composing, he hadn't argued that he should do it in her stead.

She took her time, and I began to wonder if there was a reason she showed such patience for his input. She moved slowly, her pen constantly pausing, and I was watching closely enough to see her growing visibly more weary as she worked. Did she need the small breaks more than she needed his suggestions?

I remembered his earlier allusions and felt the creeping fingers of guilt. Beatrice might be a great mage, skilled and experienced in her discipline, but clearly something had exhausted her. And now she was draining herself further for my family.

What did it take to exhaust a mage like Beatrice? Reese had mentioned the front lines—had she been there long? How many healings had she done? And how exhausting must they have been to leave her still like this now?

I wanted to ask her, but good sense reasserted itself, and I knew I had already pushed things as far as I dared with these two. Beatrice, at least, appeared to have more compassion for common folk than I had yet seen in a mage, but I couldn't allow myself to forget they were both Stantorns.

The Devoras family didn't seem to like me much either, but it was the Stantorns who had led the campaign against me, as far as I had been able to tell. Certainly my Stantorn composition instructor had loathed me from the first time he laid eyes on me.

Finally the composition was completed, and Beatrice handed it over to Reese to complete the actual working. Clemmy's hand spasmed inside mine, and I murmured to her reassuringly as I felt the first stirrings of Beatrice's power break free of its binding and settle like a mist over my sister.

She twitched, each of her limbs jerking, although she made no sound, and then her eyes drifted closed, and she went still. I leaned closer to her in alarm.

"Don't worry," said Beatrice, her voice soft and strained. "It has worked as it should. She is sleeping now as her system finishes healing itself. It was a complicated working."

She ripped a much smaller parchment in front of her, flicking her fingers toward the bed. While I felt her power, I could see nothing, but she nodded her head in satisfaction.

"It has worked. When your sister awakes she will be as strong and healthy as any other twelve-year-old."

A soft sob sounded from the open doorway, and I looked over to see my father enclose my crying mother in an embrace. I slipped off the bed, gently detaching my hand from Clemmy's.

"We cannot thank you enough," I said to Beatrice. "Both of you," I added reluctantly.

"We didn't do it for you," snapped Reese, although he kept his voice low, at least.

I itched to ask who they *were* doing it for, wondering if they knew Finnian was behind the duke's request, but I managed to hold my tongue for once. Beatrice's visible exhaustion was a reminder of what I owed them.

My mother recovered enough to offer them a meal, and although Reese clearly wanted to be gone, he glanced at Beatrice, who was sitting back in her chair, her face slightly gray, and accepted for them both. My parents hurried away to prepare, and I turned back to Clemmy. How long would she sleep for?

I was about to ask, when Reese pulled something from a bag and approached the bed. He pulled out my sister's arm and was about to press a long needle into it, when I rushed forward.

"What are you doing?"

He jerked, pulling back just before he made contact, and glared at me.

"My job. What are you doing?"

When I didn't move away, he sighed.

"I'm just taking a vial of her blood. For testing. This is how we learn and expand our capabilities. It's the price of a complicated healing—and most are more than happy to pay it." He gave me a significant look.

I turned to Beatrice for confirmation. She was watching Reese with somewhat narrowed eyes, but she made no attempt to refute his words, so I sighed and stepped back.

He worked quickly, drawing her blood and then stoppering the vial and placing it in a small, padded bag. From the cold air that rushed from it when opened, clearly one or more compositions had gone into its crafting.

Reese barely spoke or ate during the following meal, but Beatrice had considerably recovered by the end. Unlike her young cousin, nothing in her manner suggested she would rather be elsewhere, and if I ignored Reese, it was actually quite a pleasant meal. Although both my parents and I tried to hide how often we glanced with eager interest toward their open bedroom door.

Beatrice commented that the Academy year was to start soon and offered me a place in their carriage to ride back to the capital, but I wasn't ready to leave home yet. Not that I had much to pack, but I couldn't leave Kingslee before Clemmy woke up.

Beatrice seemed to understand, and she assured us as she left that my sister would wake at any moment. I alternated between wild joy and a lurking sense of dread. It was all just a little too good to be true.

But Clemmy did wake—a bare few minutes after the departure of the healers—and woke full of energy, too. There was no sign of the illness that had been plaguing her before their arrival, and while it was too early to be sure if all their claims were true, she certainly looked to be healthy, strong, and full of life.

The next two days she proceeded to bound around with more energy than I had ever seen, and I began to believe that our worries for her might be truly over. I had planned to stay with my family until the last possible day, but the visit of the healers had put the thought of the Academy firmly in the center of my mind, and I found myself constantly itching to compose again.

Plus, the more I watched Clemmy, the more I wanted to thank Finnian for what he had done for us.

Finally, I gave in and announced to my parents that I planned to leave the next day. I had expected protestations and pleas to stay just a little longer, but neither made any attempt to dissuade me. Contrarily, I immediately wished they had been a little less amenable. Were they so eager to get rid of me?

But when it actually came time for our leave-taking, they embraced me warmly and gave no sign of any discomfort. I hugged them all back—Clemmy longest and hardest—and set off down the dirt road in the opposite direction to the village.

The road would join the great paved South Road soon enough, and the walking would be a little easier after that. But it was still only the beginning of autumn, and the dirt had yet to bog into mud, so I made good progress.

I had packed light, and my few possessions were easy work for the new muscles I had spent the previous year developing. All trainees spent their mornings on combat classes, so I had returned home for the summer far stronger than I left. Several of the village boys—those who expected to fulfill their family's conscription responsibility—spent large portions of their days on makeshift combat practice of their own, and I had made sure to join them regularly over the summer. They had been afraid to spar with me at first, but when I dumped a few of them on the ground—and showed no sign of composing while doing so—they had begrudgingly let me practice with them. They had always remained wary, however, and it had been nothing like sparring with my friends at the Academy, but I persisted anyway. I had spent far too much of the last year at the bottom of my class, and I had no desire to return to that position again.

I joined South Road, walking along the edge of the paving where I would be out of the way of passing wheeled vehicles. My first and closest friend from the Academy, Coralie, lived in Abalene, a southern city near the mouth of the Overon River.

Her journey home had started on the South Road, and she had dropped me at the Kingslee turn off at the start of our break. It meant this was the first time I had made the full trek into Corrin on foot.

As one hour turned into two, I had to admit that my light pack had begun to feel somewhat heavier. I had brought home none of the practical outfits given me by the Academy, leaving them locked in my room instead, alongside my white robes.

Damon, the head servant at the Academy, had explained that I could leave what I liked in my room. The top floor of the Academy held rooms for first years on one side and second years on the other. I had assumed I would have to change rooms, but he explained that the incoming trainees would take the side vacated by the second years, and that consequently I was welcome to use the storage in my room over the summer.

In truth, the clothes I had left behind were finer quality than any I owned in the village, but I had known I would already stand out among the villagers and had no wish to further highlight the changes in my life. Fitting back in had been a hopeless task, however, and I resolved to bring my clothes home with me next summer. Right up until I remembered that I wouldn't be completing second year at the Academy and returning home for the summer. In spring I would enlist in the Armed Forces, and I had no idea what my future might hold beyond that.

I pushed the thought from my mind. My birthday would come soon enough and thinking of it would do me no good now.

As the third hour wore away, and I began to approach closer to the capital, the traffic increased slightly. We were nearing the hottest part of the day, however, and I passed an increasing number of people stopped by the side of the road for a midday meal and rest.

Many of them called cheerful greetings as I trudged past, and I relished the sense of anonymity. None of these people knew me and, dressed in my own Kingslee clothes, I looked just like any other commonborn girl.

My parents had been concerned about it, in fact—unhappy that I would be traveling alone. But I had reminded them that the road was well-traveled, and that, if it came to it, I was hardly as defenseless as I looked. I hadn't told them the full story of my previous year—not wanting to cause them worry—but they had taken me at my word anyway.

But walking alone now, I felt a great deal less confident. Not that I doubted my ability to protect myself, but somehow the knowledge that I could do so didn't abate the creeping feeling of discomfort that had been steadily assailing me. It seemed my instincts had yet to catch up with my new mage status. I had spent far too much of my life as an unremarkable common girl, and they were reminding me of it.

Attempts to remind myself of my new powers did little good. I might be able to defend against attackers, but I hardly wanted to find myself in a situation where I had to do so.

I focused on my surroundings, trying to identify what had alerted my subconscious to potential danger. None of the travelers around me looked threatening, and none approached uncomfortably close.

But as the next mile passed beneath my feet, I noticed that those traveling near me changed. Some who had just joined the road fell away, moving at a slower pace, while others moved faster and soon passed me. A couple even managed to hail a ride on a passing wagon. Still others found a pleasant looking place to stop for a midday break.

I pressed on, however, the prospect of stopping on my own unappealing, and I soon noticed that two men behind me continued on also. They kept pace with me, although they kept their distance, and now that I had focused on them, I thought I had first seen them soon after I joined South Road.

I slowed my steps, forcing my body to move counter to the

wishes of my now wildly beating heart, and waited for them to pass me. They did not. After a sufficient tense interval, I glanced backward and saw that they maintained the same distance behind me as they had since I first spotted them.

Biting my lip, I changed strategy, increasing my pace instead, the weight of my pack forgotten in the rush of energy and fear that I couldn't entirely suppress despite my best efforts. I didn't wait as long this time before glancing surreptitiously back.

I told myself that the men would have fallen away, the distance between us increasing, and I would soon be laughing at my folly. Plenty of people might have a reason not to stop for a meal, just as plenty might travel at the same pace as me.

But when I peeked backward, my heart sank. The two men chatted to each other, neither watching me, but there was no denying the gap between us remained the same. As I had increased my pace, so had they.

I was being followed.

CHAPTER 4

I considered turning and confronting them but hesitated. They didn't wear the robes of mages, but then neither did I. I had composed my way free of both of my attempted abductions the year before, so whoever my enemy was —and I strongly suspected they were a combination of Stantorn and Devoras members—they were unlikely to make the mistake of underestimating me again.

But perhaps they didn't mean to attack at all. There had been plenty of opportunity for them to do so, and surely it would have made more sense to do it earlier when there were far fewer witnesses—or even passing mages who might intervene.

My tense nerves didn't like that conclusion, but I couldn't risk courting a confrontation when none might be necessary. Not when I didn't know who was following me or what they wanted.

Instead I kept up my faster pace, the last couple of miles flying away as I soon reached the outskirts of the city. The traffic here was much heavier, and for a while I lost sight of my pursuers. I had almost begun to calm down, when I caught a glimpse of them again. Still behind me, but closer this time.

I ducked and dodged through the street, weaving around

carts, wagons, carriages, horses, and pedestrians. The last time I had walked these streets I had been wearing my white robe, and the crowds had parted before me. I briefly wished I had it on now, but quickly rejected the idea. It would only make me a clearer target and easier to follow.

The simpler houses on the outskirts of the capital grew taller and closer together, sagging against one another with age. Only the free-standing buildings of red sandstone—healing clinics, law enforcement stations, and other public buildings—stood alone.

The window boxes on the houses were mostly colorless at this time of year, doing little to lighten the drab impression of gray stone. But I knew that in spring it would be different. The small parks had color at least—the reds and oranges of autumn brightening the trees—and the markets I passed were sprinkled with bright stalls.

The lower part of the city, home to common folk, gave way to fancy store fronts with wide, clear windows that sold goods only mages and the richest of common families could afford. These shops held only a passing resemblance to the general store of my parents back home in Kingslee.

And at my fast pace, even the stores quickly disappeared, replaced by mansions that each stood alone in their own grounds, protected by railings and gates and surrounded by fountains and greenery. No weathered gray stone here. Only red sandstone or white marble.

I had never been inside any of these dwellings, and yet the sight of them gave me an unexpected feeling of homecoming. The Academy was built of white marble, and I could hardly believe how accustomed I had grown to the daily sight of it.

As I walked uphill toward the crest of the mound on which Corrin had been built, I let my attention dwell briefly on the enormous building which filled the summit. The royal palace.

It soared above the rest of the city, all glistening white marble and elegant towers. Although I couldn't see them, I knew that its various outbuildings flowed down the other side of the mound, only ending at the northern city wall. And flanking the palace on either side, were two more tall, white marble buildings. The Royal Academy of the Written Word and the Royal University.

If it hadn't been for my pursuers, I would have considered turning right, into the University, to surprise Jasper. But the solid walls of the Academy called to me, and my whole focus narrowed to getting safely inside them.

I didn't breathe a sigh of relief until the gates closed behind me, and I paused, my back against the inside of the Academy wall. For almost a minute, I blindly watched the fountain in the center of the courtyard. I no longer had even the smallest bit of doubt those men had been following me, but it seemed they had not been doing so with the intention to attack.

As my breathing slowed and calmed, a new idea took hold of me. Those in power believed the attacks on me the year before had come from our perpetual enemy—our western neighbors, Kallorway. But I had seen one of my attackers—supposedly deceased while in prison—in a Stantorn retinue.

If no one believed me, then no one was even investigating the possibility. Which meant, if I wanted to protect myself, I needed to do some investigating of my own.

Being inside the Academy grounds had already had an effect on my nerves. I was no longer a solitary traveler—I was once again a mage trainee. And I was once again free to compose. A composition I had read the year before during my voluntary discipline studies on the Armed Forces sprang into my mind.

I had thought it a foolish composition at the time. What use was a working to turn someone invisible when mages could sense the use of power, even if they couldn't tell exactly what shape it was forming? How invisible would you be if a swirl of discernible power enclosed you?

But I had been picturing the composition at work while on patrol in the woods and plains of the river region that made up the front lines in our ongoing war with Kallorway. Or perhaps used by a spy while sneaking through the halls of some important Kallorwegian building, such as their palace. Here in the city, if I kept to the busy streets, it would be another thing altogether.

If my followers were indeed mages, they might feel the use of power, but they would have no way to know it was me. Or even that it was a concealed person. Too many mages roamed this part of the city, and too many compositions were in constant use for all manner of purposes, including in the buildings themselves.

I didn't hesitate. Speaking quietly, I said the binding words, and then as much of the composition as I could remember, improvising when the specific words didn't spring to mind. I took special care to build in limitations—I didn't want to end up pouring everything I had into the working only to spend the first few days of my new year at the Academy unconscious.

"End binding." I looked down at myself and grinned. I could no longer see my body. I held up my arms in front of my face but could see nothing but the courtyard and fountain.

Almost running now, I threw open the gate and slipped out. Glancing up and down the street, I began to worry that my pursuers had already departed. But, no. I found them lounging against the outside of the University wall, talking quietly to themselves, their eyes on the gate of the Academy.

For a moment, I panicked, before remembering that they couldn't see me. A hint of confusion crossed their faces when the gate closed again with no one having gone in or out, but neither of them moved or called a challenge.

I took up an opposite position, leaning against the Academy wall, and waited. Time seemed to pass slowly, but in reality it couldn't have been more than ten minutes before they pushed themselves off the wall and started back down the street.

This time I was the one to follow them.

Turning the tables in such a way gave me a thrill. Right up until the first horse nearly trampled me. After that I kept my attention on the road, dodging the traffic while trying not to lose the two men who were moving faster now than they had been while following me.

I was just starting to worry that they might be heading for the back warrens of the lower city where my use of power might actually stand out, when they slowed. One of the larger mansions, built of the same white marble as the palace, stretched along the eastern edge of the road. They paused in front of a small gate, a short way down from the elaborate main gate that was no doubt used by the mages who lived here.

After the men exchanged brief words with a bored looking guard just inside the smaller gate, it swung open, and the men disappeared inside. It swung closed again before I could even contemplate following them, which was probably just as well. I wasn't equipped for exploring a hostile mage mansion, even with my composition in place.

But I couldn't bring myself to return to the Academy, either. Not when I had no idea who lived there.

I crossed the street and took up a position against the railing that protected the mansion on the western side. I had time. I could afford to wait a little and see if anyone recognizable came in or out.

But as the minutes ticked by and became an hour, neither gate budged, and no one approached the home. My stomach started rumbling, and I began to think I would be better off finding someone to ask rather than just waiting here.

"Elena!" The call made me jump and stare wildly around.

"Elena!" It came again, a simple carriage pulling to a stop in the road just past me.

I glanced down at myself and realized with a shock that I was visible again. How long had I been loitering here, visible to anyone who passed?

I was still kicking myself when a familiar figure jumped down from the carriage and rushed over to embrace me.

"What are you doing here?" Coralie smiled, clearly happy to see me, so I forced myself to pull my mind away from my mission and smile back.

"Have you walked all the way back today?" Coralie rushed on without waiting for my answer. "I bet you're exhausted. No wonder you were having a break. I wish we'd known. We could have picked you up." Her face fell. "But I suppose you had no way to get a message to me. Drat this no writing thing!"

I shrugged and smiled apologetically, not wanting to correct her misconception about my reason for standing here.

"Well, you can come the rest of the way with us, at least," she said. "Although it isn't far now."

As she tugged me toward her carriage, I glanced over my shoulder at the mansion across the street. Coralie might come from a minor mage family, but she had still grown up in the mage world.

"Coralie, whose house is that? The big, fancy one?" I pointed at it.

She turned to look, her face immediately souring. "That's one of the Stantorn mansions."

My heart sank, but she kept going.

"Home of General Thaddeus, Head of the Royal Guard." She said his titles like an insult rather than an honor, and I appreciated the sentiment. The general had been one of my staunchest enemies the year before.

Her words confirmed all my worst fears, until she continued to speak, muddying the issue.

"As you know, he's cousin to the queen herself." Coralie rolled her eyes at me. "Apparently he's been hosting a summer house party for the last week. General Griffith is back at the front lines, but his three children are there." She gave me a significant look, and I grimaced.

Their older brother had been at the University the year

before, rather than the Academy, but the Devoras twins were year mates of ours and no fans of mine.

"Natalya and Calix—my favorite people," I muttered, and Coralie grinned.

"And don't forget Weston and Lavinia. Naturally as Stantorns, they've been there too."

The two cousins made up the rest of the group who had most fiercely resented my presence in first year at the Academy. Lavinia and Natalya were best friends, so it was no surprise they would be together at this event.

Coralie cast me a quick sidelong look as she started to step into her carriage. "I heard Lucas was there too. The general being his mother's cousin and all."

She disappeared inside before I could respond which was just as well since I couldn't think of anything to say.

Of course Prince Lucas of Ardann would be at such an illustrious event, hosted by a family member no less. It didn't have anything to do with me, and really I couldn't care less. That's what I told myself, anyway.

The prince had disliked me since I first appeared at the Academy, and I had spent a large portion of my summer break reminding myself that nothing had changed between us. He had always been an arrogant, entitled royal, and we had always hated each other.

But when the nights got too hot, and I tossed and turned in my bed trying not to wake up Clemmy, I all too often found myself reliving the feel of his lips pressed hard against mine, and the feel of his arms wrapped around me, catching me as I fell.

For a brief moment at the end of last year, I had thought something changed between us. I had begun to wonder if perhaps, under all his royal manner, Prince Lucas and I might have become friends. Because even in my imaginings, I couldn't really believe we could ever be anything more than friends.

But even friendship had been an illusion, apparently. At least based on his behavior when I emerged from the healing rooms after draining my power. I was a commonborn—worthy of interest and study as the first and only Spoken Mage, but not worthy of respect as a person.

Which brought me back to the fact that it made no difference to me who Lucas chose to spend his summer weeks with. No difference at all.

I pulled myself into the carriage after Coralie, and then nearly fell as I stumbled my way to a seat. The interior was more crowded than I had been expecting.

"Are you sure…" I glanced at Coralie. "I can walk, you know."

"Don't be silly."

She squeezed closer to a boy beside her, making just enough room for me to fit next to her on the bench seat. I dropped into the position she indicated and smiled awkwardly at the other occupants.

"This is my mother and father," she waved at the middle-aged couple across from us. "And this is my brother. Everyone, this is Elena. Who I told you about."

I nodded at them all.

The boy leaned forward to see around his sister, gaping at me.

"*The* Elena? You're the Spoken Mage?" He looked with excitement between Coralie and me. "Can you show us? A verbal composition, I mean?"

"Arthur!" His mother frowned at him. "Don't be rude."

"She's not going to do one right here." Coralie rolled her eyes. "Really!" She turned to me. "Excuse Arthur, he gets a bit overexcited. My family weren't going to come to drop me off this year, but he starts at the Academy next year, and he begged for us all to come up."

Arthur, who didn't look fifteen to me, flushed and slouched in his seat.

"I didn't beg," he muttered.

Coralie opened her mouth, no doubt to correct him, when the carriage slowed and began to turn, distracting them both.

"Oh, we're here!" she said at the same moment as Arthur said, "The Academy!" in reverential tones.

I watched him out of the corner of my eye as he gazed eagerly out the window. What must it be like to be raised in a mage family, looking forward to the day when you would join your year mates and begin your studies?

By law, all mages attended the Academy the autumn after they turned sixteen. No one could attend sooner—a mage's ability to fully control power only matured at sixteen—although in exceptional circumstances it could be delayed. This had been the case with Lucas who had started at seventeen, delayed after he was required to travel with a royal delegation to the northern Sekali Empire the year he turned sixteen. I had often wondered if he resented being forced to wait, but he had never mentioned it in my hearing.

Passing the Academy was as mandatory as attendance. A mage without control was a danger to everyone. And unlike a regular mage, my failure would have resulted in my execution rather than imprisonment, since they had no way to safely contain my ability to verbally compose. Given that, I had expected my enemies to attempt to manipulate my first year exams. If they could ensure I failed, it would take away the problem of me once and for all.

I had not expected to be abducted part way through, however, and I still couldn't quite believe I had been given a passing grade. It helped that the Academy Head Lorcan was highly invested in my remaining at the Academy. After all, if I was executed, he and the University Head, Jessamine, wouldn't be able to study me like some sort of academic curiosity.

I had been terrified the first time I arrived at the Academy, with no idea how I had managed to compose and no idea what my fate was to be. I had felt none of the wonder, awe, and excitement I saw in Arthur's face.

A sadness crept over me, and I turned quickly away from him. The Academy had become a second home of sorts for me, a place I felt—if not safe, then safer, at least—than I felt most anywhere else. And that would have to be enough.

When we came to a stop in front of the huge square block of the Academy, so different from the elegant lines and towers of the palace, I hurried out of the carriage. Coralie and her family would want time to make their farewells.

"Thank you for the ride." I nodded at her parents who smiled kindly back at me.

"I'll see you inside," I called to Coralie, and then launched myself up the front steps and into the large entrance hall of the Academy.

For a second I thought it was empty, and then I managed to collide headlong with the only occupant.

I stumbled and would have fallen if strong hands hadn't steadied me. For a breathless moment, Lucas and I stood face to face, a mere breath apart. And then he released me and stepped back, his face expressionless.

"Elena. You're back."

CHAPTER 5

"*A*re you surprised?" I glared at him. "I am a trainee here, remember?"

His usual mask cracked, a grimace briefly crossing his face as he ran a hand through his hair.

"I just meant…"

I raised both eyebrows. "Yes? You just meant what, exactly?"

He sighed. "As belligerent as ever, I see."

"As rude as ever, I see." I told myself my anger now had nothing to do with our kiss. It had obviously meant nothing to him, and it meant nothing to me either.

He glanced around at the still empty entrance hall. "I just meant that I saw you arrive earlier. And leave again. And I saw you work that composition."

He gave me a significant look, and I flushed. I had been in the Academy grounds at the time. I hadn't broken any rules by composing—had I?

He continued to look at me expectantly, and I felt myself weakening. Lucas might not be a friend, but he knew more about the attacks on me—and my theories about them—than anyone else. And I was bursting to tell someone what had happened.

"I was followed."

"Excuse me?" Clearly that hadn't been the answer he was expecting.

"I walked in from Kingslee today, and someone followed me."

He frowned. "So you decided to follow them back."

I nodded. For all his stubborn refusal to consider that Stantorn and Devoras mages might be behind the attacks on me, he wasn't in general stupid.

The thought of the final destination of the men I had tracked reminded me of something else.

"What are you doing here, anyway?"

"I am a trainee here, remember?" He drawled my words back at me mockingly.

I narrowed my eyes at him. "I thought you were at some important mage house party at General Thaddeus's mansion. With Natalya and her lot."

His face quirked into a half smile. "What? Have you been tracking me, Elena? I didn't realize you cared so much about my movements."

"What? I don't…" I spluttered to a halt, feeling a flush creeping up my face and cursing it.

"I left early to return to the Academy," he said, apparently taking pity on me. "I wanted to get started on my study."

I barely refrained from rolling my eyes. Like he wasn't already ahead of the rest of us in every class. Well, maybe with the exception of Dariela. Perhaps he was determined to pull ahead of the distant Ellington girl this year.

I took a deep breath and gathered myself together. "No, I have not been *tracking* you. Coralie mentioned it. And only when I asked her about a particular house—which turned out to be the general's mansion." I gave him a loaded look. "I asked, of course, because it was the house where my pursuers ended up."

Lucas frowned. "You don't still think the general is involved in some sort of treasonous conspiracy against you, do you? I've already told you—the Council of Mages ruled you are to continue at the Academy, and he might disagree, but he wouldn't cross them."

"What then?" I put my hands on my hips. "Why was he having me followed?"

Lucas looked away from me, his face sliding back into its usual careful mask.

I narrowed my eyes and stepped forward, closing the gap between us.

"Oh no, you don't. Tell me the truth. What do you know?"

Lucas looked back at me, and something that looked like guilt flashed briefly through his eyes. He paused a moment more before sighing and speaking.

"As you said, the general is hosting a house party at the moment. Those men could have been reporting to almost anyone." He took a deep breath. "And they were most likely your official watchers, not anyone nefarious."

I took a step back. "My...what?"

Lucas sighed. "Did you really think we would just let you go off alone to some small village for weeks? Right after Kallorway attempted to abduct you? You've had two mages keeping watch—from a distance—the whole time. They were there for your protection."

I knew my mouth had fallen open, but I didn't care.

"My...protection? Are you serious? Then why not tell me about them? Why force them to hide away for weeks?" I barely resisted the urge to start pacing, wanting to let off some of my pent up energy. "You mean they were there to watch me. To make sure I didn't step out of line, or attempt to compose without supervision, or break any of your precious laws."

"The laws are there to protect all of us, Elena." Lucas sounded weary.

"Perhaps. And yet I can't help but notice some seem to get more protecting than others."

He shrugged. "Think what you like. The council rarely agrees on the motives for something. You learn to settle for agreement on the action itself. And if Kallorway had come for you again, you would have been grateful for their presence."

"Would I?" I stared at him. "That's funny. Because I seem to remember rescuing myself previously."

"Elena."

I looked away, knowing I was being difficult and obstinate. After all, I had thought the same thing—that if my attackers came again, they would come with more force. Only the irony was that it wasn't Kallorway who was likely to attack me. So Lucas had sent me *protection* in the form of my enemies.

Maybe it had actually saved me, though. No doubt they had been unable to act while they were tasked with watching over me. It would have been far too suspicious.

The clatter of steps sounded, and then Coralie burst into the hall.

"Elena! There you are!" She faltered and slowed when she saw who I was with, looking back and forth between us. "Oh, I'm sorry. Am I interrupting…"

"No," I said hurriedly. "Not at all."

Lucas's eyes lingered on me for a moment, his face impassive, and then he nodded at us both and strode away.

"What's he doing here?" asked Coralie. "I thought he was off partying with the rest of them."

I shrugged. "He's already started studying, of course. Our prince wouldn't want to miss an opportunity to get ahead of us all, Coralie."

My friend regarded me with narrowed eyes, but I turned toward the stairs, and she trailed me without further comment.

We only made it up one flight before her natural buoyancy returned, and she started chattering about her summer, about the changes she had found in her home city of Abalene, and about our upcoming classes.

Her anxieties were all centered around combat—the class that was set to change drastically in second year. In first year we had trained in one of the dirt squares at the back of the Academy, slowly graduating from unarmed combat to staffs to swords. But we had never set foot inside the small arena that stood at the back of the Academy grounds.

The arena was used by the senior years who rotated through on different days. And in the arena we dueled with more than just blades. We dueled with a mix of weapons and compositions. Coralie wasn't the only one who was nervous about it.

After we checked our rooms and dumped our bags, she dragged me along to the storeroom that supplied basic provisions for the trainees. The servant on duty there laughed and joked with her about trainees that wouldn't stop growing as she collected a new set of white robes. Unlike the court, the Academy had a relaxed culture, and titles were rarely used.

Apparently it was the reason we were all supposed to feel so fortunate that despite having an unusually small intake in our year level, we had a number of year mates from important families. This time at the Academy was our chance to bond and form connections that would advantage us in the years ahead. A laughable concept in my case, of course, for too many reasons to count.

The servant turned to me with a questioning look, and I shook my head.

"I'm finished growing, I think—sadly. My old robes still fit."

The woman made a sympathetic noise as she eyed my small stature.

"Never mind," said Coralie, looping her arm through mine and tugging me out of the room. "You don't need height to make an impression."

At the meal that evening, the dining hall was half empty, many of the trainees not yet returned. But two welcome faces sat at our usual table.

"Finnian! Saffron! You're already here!" Coralie bounced over and embraced them both.

Given the status of Finnian's father, I had expected him, at least, to be at General Thaddeus's mansion.

"Don't tell me you've abandoned this fancy house party early, too," I said, as I slid into a chair and looked around for the servers. I was ravenous.

"Are you surprised?" Finnian gave an exaggerated shudder. "It was full of Stantorns."

Coralie chuckled, and Saffron wrinkled her nose.

"And don't forget the Devoras twins and half their family. I wish we'd stayed up north instead of coming down early for it." Saffron's caustic comments surprised me, and I grinned at her. She had been withdrawn the previous year, only friendly with us because she seemed to follow Finnian's lead in everything. But apparently she had opened up over the summer.

The two cousins came from the Callinos family, like both the Academy and University Heads, and had the dark gold skin and black hair that marked them as northerners. I had learned enough about the four great mage families during first year to know that Devoras and Stantorn were usually allied, but that Callinos was currently in a period of ascendancy—holding four of the ten positions on the Mage Council. It meant they equaled the combined voting might of the Devoras and Stantorn members—much to those two families' disgust.

I got the impression the fourth family, Ellington, rarely held a strong position among the others. A pity since they seemed by far the nicest house—with the possible exception of the aloof Dariela. Hopefully the Ellingtons were enjoying holding the current balance of power with their two head positions, a situation I was more than happy with, since they had voted in my favor the year before.

And I had more to be grateful to them for than just their votes. The Ellingtons working at the Academy—including the

Academy healer, Acacia, and the head of the Academy library, Walden—had been kinder to me than the average mage. Walden, in particular, had spent untold hours assisting me to access and control my power.

While it had been Callinos who gave me their full support from the beginning, working tirelessly to protect me, they had done it in their quest for knowledge, not out of kindness. Finnian and I had only become friends part way through the year, and he was the first Callinos to view me as something other than a fascinating test subject.

I tried to remind myself I should feel grateful for their protection at least, but the thought sparked an entirely different gratitude.

"Oh! Finnian! I have to thank you."

"Thank me? For what? Gracing you with my presence?" He winked at us, and I shook my head.

"No, for sending Beatrice, of course. Honestly, my family couldn't be more grateful. I never dreamed—"

"Beatrice?" He looked at me curiously. "I heard she had a job just outside of Corrin, but it didn't have anything to do with me."

I frowned. "But surely it was you. Who else could it have been? She mentioned my having important friends, and I thought..."

The others all exchanged bemused looks.

"Were you sick?" Saffron asked.

I shook my head. "Not for me. For my younger sister, Clementine. She has...*had*," I corrected myself with an amazed shake of my head, "...a weak system. She always came down with every little thing and got it worse than everyone else, too. Ever since she was a baby. It seems like a miracle she survived this long, but we didn't have the coin for such a complicated healing. Not yet, anyway..."

I trailed off as Finnian shook his head. "I wish I'd sent her, but

I'm ashamed to admit I didn't even know you had a sick sister. It wasn't me."

"But…" I bit my lip. Who had known about Clemmy, then? Phyllida, the Head of the Seekers, had questioned my family last autumn after my powers first manifested. Perhaps someone had mentioned it…

But while Phyllida was a Callinos and had voted for me, we had never even spoken. Not really. Perhaps she had mentioned it to Lorcan, and he had…But it didn't seem like the kind of thing the Academy Head would do. Not when half the time I was fairly certain he forgot I was a person at all.

"Ooh, a mystery." Coralie grinned. "But a happy one, if she healed your sister. You must have more friends than you realize, Elena. Do tell us if you work out who it was."

I forced a smile, and the arrival of the food distracted the rest of them, but I couldn't match her optimism. It had been one thing to be beholden to Finnian, my friend. It was another thing altogether to owe an unknown price to an unknown person. A powerful person.

I shivered and reminded myself that Clemmy was worth it.

But my eyes fell on Lucas, and the memory of the way he had brushed aside my concerns came flooding back. I was far too new at this game of intrigue and power—and if someone was trying to play me, I had little doubt they would succeed.

The prince ate in silence with only Dariela for company, and I let my eyes linger briefly on the two of them. Since the tall girl was not only an Ellington, but also brilliant and head of the class, I wasn't surprised she hadn't been included in this exclusive party. Natalya and Lavinia saw her as a rival—and for more than class rankings.

But I could see nothing of romance between Lucas and Dariela. Little even of friendship—although they didn't show any outward signs of rivalry or dislike either. But then perhaps I didn't know how to read those signs, either. Perhaps Natalya and Lavinia were right.

Once again, I reminded myself that nothing Lucas did mattered to me. But for some reason I found it hard to laugh at my friends' jokes for the rest of the meal. I had a mounting headache behind both temples, and all I wanted was my bed.

CHAPTER 6

I considered starting study early myself but going to the library would likely mean running into Lucas, so I let my friends convince me to laze around with them until classes started instead. We wandered the grounds and lay in the gardens in the autumn sun as much as possible. The new first years had started to arrive, and we watched them with interest, assuring each other we had never looked so young, anxious, and naive.

Of course, I had arrived downright terrified rather than merely anxious and had known nothing about anything—I couldn't even read. But it felt good to pretend with my friends, so I refrained from mentioning it.

Coralie in particular had a morbid fascination with the arena, and we spent many conversations guessing at what our new combat classes would look like. We even poked our heads in when no one else was around.

I could see the structure from my window, but it had looked small from so high up. From the inside, it looked bigger than I had imagined. Sloped seating ringed the oval floor—far more than was needed for a single year level. How many spectators would be observing our bouts?

We strolled away in unusual silence, no doubt each contemplating standing in the middle of that floor facing off against one of our year mates. I looked back at it over my shoulder.

"It sort of shimmers. The air around it. And I can feel power. I don't know why I haven't noticed that feeling of power around it before."

"That's the shield," said Finnian. "Since it's used for training, they want to contain any uncontrolled bursts or poorly crafted workings."

"We're only supposed to be able to kill each other in there," said Coralie glumly. "Not anyone else."

Saffron patted Coralie's arm. "No one has ever died training in the arena, Coralie."

"There's always a first." Coralie sighed.

I felt an icy trickle down my spine. If the first trainee to die in the arena was going to come from our year, then I didn't think it was likely to be Coralie.

The same thought filled my mind when I actually stood in the center of the arena a week later. Our first couple of days of lessons had been completed in one of the regular training yards, giving the other trainees time to compose a series of stored combat compositions in our afternoon composition class.

Redmond, our composition instructor, taught the basics of several simple workings, but I could tell that most of the trainees had been preparing for this moment and wouldn't be relying on his examples.

Thornton had explained the parameters of our arena bouts in our first combat class. We would face off one against one, with both a sword and three prepared compositions. For a moment I had thought this might give me an advantage, but he had sternly informed me that I would also be limited to the use of three verbal compositions.

"As if she could do more, anyway," muttered Natalya.

I stayed quiet. I had kept my strength a secret the year before as much as I was able, and if I was going to be limited in the bouts, then I didn't see any reason to reveal it now.

"Why only three?" asked Calix, Natalya's twin brother. "I certainly wouldn't be foolish enough to go into battle with only three compositions. If we're strong enough to prepare more, we should be allowed to do so."

Thornton narrowed his eyes at him. Our instructor might be Devoras, and willing to weight the class against me, but he took his duty of training young mages to fight seriously. Something that had made a lot more sense to me after I discovered that while one child from every common family was forcibly conscripted into the Armed Forces, it was considered the duty of every mage graduate from the Academy to serve a two-year term at the front lines. According to Lucas, it was the only way we had succeeded in holding back the never-ending Kallorwegian attack for thirty long years.

"No doubt you would not enter battle with only three compositions," Thornton said, addressing his words to the whole class. "But battles can be long, and your stores can be depleted. Thus why you need to be proficient with ordinary weapons as well. And sometimes attacks can come at unexpected moments, when you haven't had a chance to rebuild your stores. These training bouts are not an opportunity for you to destroy each other, they are a chance for you to work on developing strategy. You need to learn to use the best tool in each situation, and to conserve your compositions for the optimal moments."

Several of the students nodded thoughtfully while I told myself that it had been my imagination that his eyes lingered on me when he spoke of us destroying each other. The thought returned, however, when I looked across the arena floor at

Natalya. Of course I would be facing her in my first bout. And of course we would have been chosen for the first bout of the class. I really shouldn't have expected anything less.

Finnian had even assured me in a cheerful whisper that I should be grateful. It could have been Calix or Weston, who were both stronger and more skilled than Natalya. Strangely enough, I didn't feel particularly reassured.

"Remember the purpose of the bout," said Thornton, in a bored voice. It was the first time we had seen him since he had given us the information about the bouts at our first combat class of the year. No doubt he had been busy with the first years since then, our standard combat exercises overseen by several junior combat instructors instead. But apparently our first set of bouts in the arena were worthy of his attention.

"This is going to be fun," Natalya said in a low voice, clearly not paying attention as Thornton continued his short speech.

"No lethal compositions are permitted. Even if you're confident your opponent will block it. This is an exercise in strategy, not a duel to the death."

I glanced over at my friends, and Coralie gave me an encouraging smile. I straightened my spine. I had fended off four separate attacks with my words the year before. I could do this.

"Begin," called Thornton, and I let everything else fade away as I focused in on Natalya.

We both held our swords loosely in front of us, but at Thornton's announcement, I tightened my grip and lunged forward. To work one of her compositions, Natalya would need to extract and rip a piece of parchment. I, on the other hand, only had to speak mine. If I could keep her busy defending herself, it might give me the extra edge.

She whipped up her blade equally quickly, parrying my attack and falling back several steps. I pressed forward, attacking again. This time I spoke as I came, panting out the binding words to begin my composition. I wanted to end this quickly, but I didn't want to give anyone fuel to say that I was out to punish mages—a theory that had been suggested by my enemies in the past. So I had decided on a literal binding working—I would attempt to bind her arms and legs. With no way to compose or wield a weapon, she would have to yield.

But I got out no more than three words of the actual composition, thrusting forward with my sword as I did so. Even as she blocked my attack, Natalya's free hand disappeared up into the sleeve of her robe and reappeared with a small scroll.

She had little trouble doing so since my lunge had been wild due to the concentration required to both attack, call up a mental picture of the words I needed, and speak all at the same time. And as soon as she had the composition free, she gripped part of the parchment with her teeth and ripped.

Fire roared up from the ground in front of her and raced toward me. Abandoning my sword, I threw myself to the side, landing hard on the ground, just beyond the flames. They continued across the floor of the arena until they hit the barrier on the far side with a loud sizzle and dissolved.

I panted for breath, forgetting all about the fire as I felt my own power—held in place by my initial binding words but then abandoned when I reacted to Natalya's fire—stretch and snap, washing over me in a formless backlash like my very first composition in front of my parents' store. I had lost focus and control before I could complete the working or end the binding, and my hold on the power had broken.

For the second time in the bout, the breath was knocked out of me as the solid wave of power made my bones shake.

Natalya paused for a second, thrown apparently by the unexpected release of my power, before jumping toward me, her sword point reaching for my neck. I scrambled out of the way just in time.

Pushing to my feet, I ran back toward my own weapon. But

when I bent over to scoop it up, I yelped and dropped it again. The fire had swept over it, and it still burned too hot to touch.

Growling in frustration, I did the only thing I could do. Run.

"That's right! Run!" taunted Natalya.

I went to speak the binding words again, but hesitated before any sounds actually emerged. A quick glance over my shoulder revealed that Natalya already had a second parchment in her hand. Without a weapon to distract her, I had no hope of composing more quickly than she could release her own working.

So I bit back my words, unwilling to face a second backlash when every muscle still ached from the first. I would have to try good old-fashioned dodging as I had done with the fire.

But to my surprise, she withdrew a third composition without tearing the second. For a brief moment, our eyes met across half the arena. She smirked at me, and then tore both at once. I barely had time to recognize the bubble of power that sprang up to shield her, before the entire arena floor began to shake.

The arena shield protected the stands and the rest of our year mates, and Natalya's own shield protected her. Leaving me the only one to stagger out-of-control across the pitching ground. Several large cracks appeared in the dirt floor, and as I attempted to leap over one, another one raced toward me.

I landed on the edge of it, tipping forward and twisting, my ankle giving way with an audible snap. I fell, hard, screaming with pain. But it wasn't over.

As I lay there, chunks of the now broken ground rose up and began to catapult themselves through the air. Several careened straight toward me, and I threw up my hands to protect my face. Responding on instinct, a short phrase formed in front of my eyes.

"Shield me!" I screamed across the arena.

A bubble of my own power formed around me a scant second

before the first of the chunks collided with it, pulverized into dust by the impact.

I collapsed back onto the ground and closed my eyes, breathing through the pain in my ankle as several more chunks hit my shield. Then the ground stopped shaking, and silence descended. My bubble of power burst and fizzled out. Cautiously I opened my eyes.

Thornton strode into the middle of the arena, his face livid.

Oh good, said my exhausted brain. *For once he's actually going to reprimand one of them. He did say no lethal compositions.*

But he turned toward me, not Natalya. "I never want to see that again, Elena!"

CHAPTER 7

*W*ait. What? I pushed myself up on my elbows and glared at him. He was reprimanding *me?*

He stopped several steps from me, ignoring the fact that I was still sprawled on the ground, my ankle twisted unnaturally.

"This is not a game! I never want to see you compose without restrictions like that again. You're fortunate Natalya's attack didn't have more force, or you could have burned yourself out completely."

"It felt forceful enough to me," I muttered.

He leaned in close, his words quiet. "I can assure you if that had been my composition, it would have carried a great deal more force than that of a second year."

Looking at his angry face, I believed him.

"But better burned out than dead," I snapped back, too angry to let it go. I knew the more power that was thrown at my shield, the more of my own power it would drain holding itself in place, but surely it was worth the risk. At least in the face of a potentially lethal attack.

This time he answered loudly, no doubt for the benefit of the rest of the class. "Burning out could very well mean death. When a mage crafts a composition, he is careful to put only as much energy into it as he has available in the moment. That finite power in the stored composition then costs the mage nothing upon its release. With a careful accumulation of stored compositions, the limits to a mage's power can be endless. And there is good reason we do it that way."

He glowered around as if someone had disputed him before continuing.

"There are some who have composed workings in such a way that, when released, they would draw further from the mage's strength. Many of them died. Some compositions will continue to drain you of energy even after you lose consciousness—as you nearly did, Elena."

I frowned at him, and then remembered how I had closed my eyes and sunk back against the ground. My movement had been due to my ankle, not exhaustion, but it seemed Thornton didn't realize that. Did he think I had burned out, and that my shield was drawing from my unconscious body? Had he thought for a moment that his class had killed one of his students—a trainee valued by the Academy Head and various other people of importance for her research potential?

Reluctantly I felt a small burst of understanding for his anger. I was all too aware of how strong an anger fueled by fear could be. It had driven far too many people to seek my death the year before.

Thornton kept speaking, clearly continuing to lecture the class as a whole.

"When composing a shield, you need it to carry enough strength to be effective. Otherwise a strong attack will burn through its stored power, causing it to fail and leave you defenseless. Since you cannot build endless power into it, you can build in various limitations to achieve your aims. For instance, you can shape it to ward only lethal blows, conserving its power for when it is most needed."

His volume lowered as he looked down at me. "It could also be made to shut off at a single word, so that you can collapse it as soon as help arrives. There are any number of ways to protect yourself from both attack and burn out. I suggest you learn them. And don't try a trick like that in my class again."

He turned to stride away while I was still grasping for words. It was the first time an instructor in one of my classes had actually given specific advice to me. Advice that only really applied to a verbal composition, since there was no advantage to shutting off a stored composition to save power. With the composition released, the power could not be retained and re-stored.

I didn't know quite what to make of it. But I did know that his fear didn't make what had happened here all right.

"I thought you said no lethal compositions," I yelled after him, loud enough for everyone to hear.

He paused mid-stride, although he didn't turn back to me. After a second of silence, he nodded once.

"You will limit yourself in future, Natalya." His gaze swept over the small cluster of second year trainees in the stands. "That goes for all of you."

And then he resumed his progress back to his seat.

I slumped back down. I guess I would have to be happy with that. At least the smirk had disappeared from Natalya's face as she resumed her own place beside Lavinia and Calix.

Coralie and Finnian raced across the now uneven ground of the arena, kneeling down beside me.

"Are you all right?" Coralie's face looked as white as mine felt.

"Well enough." I sighed. "It's my ankle."

Finnian grimaced down at the appendage in question. "I'm going to be honest. It doesn't look great."

"Thank you for that wisdom." I groaned. "Are you going to help me up or not?"

They each took one side, heaving me to my feet, while I carefully kept my injured ankle suspended above the ground. It still hurt like anything, and I had to bite back a scream.

"There's good news," he said as they helped me hobble off the arena floor. "You don't need to go all the way back to the Academy building. Apparently old Thornton knows to expect trouble on the first arena day. Either that or he just knew you were going to be in class."

"Smile at me one more time, and I'll poke your eye out," I growled at him.

He just laughed, helping me to sit on a section of seating some way around the arena from the rest of our year mates.

"With that foot? I'd like to see you catch me."

Acacia popped up beside us, looking almost as cheerful as Finnian, so I growled at both of them.

"Cheery as always, I see, Elena," she said, bending to examine my ankle. "Why am I not surprised to find you're my first patient?"

"Because Thornton and half the class have it in for her?" My ever-loyal friend glared at both of them.

"What she said." I gestured weakly at Coralie.

Acacia just shook her head and withdrew two separate curls of parchment from her purple robe. I eyed them greedily, wondering which was the pain-numbing one.

Two rips sounded, and then a cool mist settled over me.

"Ahhhh…" I closed my eyes and let the absence of pain wash through me, ignoring the unnerving pop from my ankle as it shifted back into place.

When I opened them again, she was watching me with a rueful grin. "Anything else that needs attention?"

I shook my head. The pain-numbing composition had dealt as effectively with the rest of my body as with my ankle.

She shook her head. "I don't know how you do it. You have far more energy than seems natural."

I shifted uncomfortably. Had she been watching the bout, then?

"Funny," I said, "you didn't say that when I was out for two whole days at the end of last year."

She gave me an odd look. "You were out for two days because I worked a sleeping composition. I knew you would have been up on your feet too soon otherwise."

"Oh." I avoided her eyes, not sure how I felt about that.

She shook her head and told us to return to our year mates, and the three of us trudged off. Araminta and Clarence, two of our year mates from minor mage families, had already begun their bout. Araminta was the weakest trainee in our year, and Clarence was useless with weapons, although with the amount of time he spent with his nose in a book, he was significantly better at composition. I had no doubt he would be attending the University after his stint on the front lines—on track for an academic position, no doubt.

Their bout was far from impressive, with none of the dramatics of my own. Araminta managed to produce a wind to push Clarence back, and he responded with an effective shield. Since Araminta wasn't prepared for that, he managed to knock the sword from her hand, forcing her to yield.

Thornton made some comments about being prepared for our opponent to respond to our compositions and not being thrown off when they did so, but I wasn't really listening.

"Hey," I said quietly to my friends, "the arena's been fixed."

Finnian glanced over at me. "A lot of power goes into maintaining the arena. At the beginning of every year the instructors all work together to refresh the shield around it. And again later in the year, if it's taken enough of a beating to need it. And every senior mage in the creator discipline is expected to contribute at least one composition a year to restore the arena to its pristine condition. Old Thornton has a whole stash of them, ready to be whipped out and used at need."

"Well, that's good to know," I muttered. Just how many times was I going to be expected to bout like that?

Both Dariela and Lucas went for subtle, tricky compositions, rather than showy ones, and both easily won their bouts. There were no lightning storms, or earthquakes, but a frozen sword arm and legs that collapsed at just the right moment had disabled each of their opponents just as effectively. Especially when the other trainee hadn't seen it coming.

Thornton praised them both highly, pointing out to us that we should strive to achieve our goals with a minimum use of power. He didn't mention that the more finesse the composition required, the harder it was to compose in the first place. I doubted many of my year mates were up to producing the compositions Lucas and Dariela had used.

Which put me in mind of something that had been bothering me. As I wandered back up to the Academy for lunch, I asked my friends about it.

"Did those compositions seem rather powerful to you?"

"Which ones? Dariela's was impressive, I thought," said Saffron. "The timing was so exact."

I shook my head. "I mean Natalya's. That was a lot of brute force she used. I can't see her replacing them in a hurry."

Finnian grimaced. "She might have gotten them from someone else, but she would get herself in a lot of trouble if she did that and the instructors found out about it."

Mages could choose to craft compositions so that anyone could work them or so that they could only be worked by the composer.

Finnian sighed and rubbed the back of his neck. "You're probably right that she didn't compose them this week, though. No doubt she's been receiving extra training throughout our break. She's probably come back with a store of combat compositions ready to go. Everyone knows we bout this way in second year."

My shoulders slumped. Of course she'd been working on

them for weeks. I had tried to keep up my combat conditioning, not wanting to return to the position of last in the class again, but my efforts had been useless. And even if I'd had a tutor and opportunity, I had no way to store my compositions. Having unnatural strength to compose did me little good if I didn't have time to get the words out.

~

The only good thing about the arena was that it was only allocated for use by the second years once a week. The rest of the week we would spend doing our normal exercises under the same set of junior instructors who had watched us the past few days.

The one other bright spot was that our arena day fell directly before our rest day.

"So I'll be able to recover after each pummeling," I said to my friends, as I poked at my dinner. "Which is something I suppose."

All three grimaced at me, and even Finnian didn't offer any upbeat words. No doubt they had all realized my fatal limitation. They certainly spent the rest day doing their best to cheer me up, and eventually their efforts succeeded. After all, I still had six more days until I had to face the arena again.

On the first day of the second week, Redmond announced the beginning of our discipline studies. Discipline studies happened in the second afternoon session after composition—the one first years had free. The three higher year levels all studied two disciplines of their choice out of the eight options—law enforcement, seeking, healing, growing, wind working, creating, the Armed Forces, and the Royal Guard.

Trainees worked in the library, largely on their own but under the supervision of the head librarian, Walden, and his assistant, Jocasta. Plus the occasional visiting lecturer from the discipline in question.

Since trainees were permitted to either change disciplines every year or study the same ones for more than one year, the classes were mixed, with beginner and advanced assignments given based on how long the trainees had been studying the discipline.

My friends seemed to alternate between dread at the extra work and interest in their potential choices, and Finnian and Coralie had spent the last week debating which two disciplines they should choose for second year. I had expected Finnian to be firmly set to follow in his father's footsteps, but he intended the same as Coralie—to change his studies each year to cover as many disciplines as possible.

"You never know where my aptitude may fall," he told me when I asked him why. "I wouldn't want to limit myself."

All trainees were required to do at least a year's study in healing plus a year's study in the armed forces discipline as preparation for the front lines. I had chosen those two for my voluntary studies during first year with exactly the same reasoning. I hadn't actually studied for the whole year, though, so I wasn't sure my previous studies would exempt me from needing to do them again.

And on reflection, they still seemed the most practical two for me to continue with. After all, I could be facing the front lines much sooner than my year mates.

Like me, Saffron declared her intention to start with those two, and I was again surprised to see her speaking out so decisively. I had expected her to wait and follow whatever choice Finnian ended up making.

In the end, it went the other way. After a great deal of debate, both Finnian and Coralie decided to stick with Saffron and me. And when we arrived in the library for our introductory lecture on discipline studies, we discovered that most of our year level thought the same way.

Walden beamed around at us all as he explained how the

studies worked, and then invited us to sign up for the two disciplines of our choice. My year mates all filed up and filled in their names on two of the eight sheets which already held lists of third and fourth year students. I lingered until last, wanting a private word with Walden.

His eyes held extra warmth when I finally approached, and he smiled broadly at me.

"Ah, Elena! I've been wondering where you were hiding yourself away."

I smiled apologetically. "Just easing in slowly." I had practically lived at the library last year, so I could understand his confusion. But I was hardly going to admit I'd been avoiding Lucas.

I asked him to add my name to the healing and armed forces discipline lists for me and noticed as he did so that the healing list held all twelve second year names, and the armed forces list held over half. It seemed that most of the class wanted to get the required studies over and done with. Although some apparently would do them one at a time. No doubt these were the students who wished to follow another discipline all the way through.

Walden noticed my interest.

"We usually get a high uptake in healing from the second years, but the whole lot of you is somewhat unusual. Mayhap it's because you're a smaller year."

I smiled back at him. I had spent a lot of time with the friendly librarian when he had given me private tuition as a first year, helping me to unlock and then hone my capability for verbal compositions. And now, with the final day of the week already looming in my mind, I was hoping he might be willing to do it again.

"Walden," I started, and then paused, aware I was asking a great deal.

His face immediately fell. "I'm afraid we can't resume our practice sessions, if that's what you were going to ask, Elena.

While I would be most interested, of course—an opportunity to study and develop your powers is once in a lifetime for us all—it just isn't possible. Jocasta has yet to return for the year, and with the full load of supervising the discipline studies, I'm afraid I just don't have the time."

He looked genuinely disappointed, so I tried to swallow my own chagrin.

"Oh, well, in that case..." I shrugged, forced a smile and turned to leave. But I paused before I'd gone far. "Where's Jocasta?"

The assistant librarian didn't have the same friendly attitude as Walden, but she had helped me at the beginning when I was still learning to read—and had received a less than desirable reward for it when I subsequently lost control. I hoped I hadn't chased her away from the Academy.

"She was needed at home, I believe," he replied. "But I'm sure she'll be back among us soon enough, never you fear."

I nodded and hurried away, already wondering what I was going to do without Walden's assistance. I didn't know if I could work out how to fight in the arena on my own.

We wouldn't start proper studies until the next day, but Coralie, Finnian, and Saffron had found a small table tucked into a corner of the library and were already discussing their thoughts on our new disciplines. I slipped in beside them, but didn't really listen to what they were saying.

"Coralie," I said when a lull came up. "You're from the same family as Jocasta, right?"

"She's not from my immediate family, or anything," she replied. "But she's a Cygnet like me."

I remembered her telling me about the connection with pride when I first started at the Academy. Positions here were prestigious, it seemed, and it was an honor for a member of such a minor family to be selected.

"Is she also from Abalene?" I asked.

"A smaller town just south of us, I think," said Coralie. "Why?"

I shrugged. "She isn't here, that's all. She hasn't returned for the year yet. I just wondered if you might know why."

Finnian leaned in slightly, lowering his voice.

"South of Abalene did you say?" For once none of his usual joking good-humor showed in his eyes.

Coralie nodded, and he frowned.

"I overheard something about trouble down that way. Just before Saffron and I returned to the Academy. The king came for an evening reception at the general's mansion, and he and my father were off in a corner talking about it."

"Trouble?" Coralie's mouth twisted. "Near Abalene? How near? And what kind of trouble?"

"If the king was talking to the Head of the Healers about it, then I don't imagine it was the good kind."

We all exchanged unhappy looks. Just the faintest hint of the threat of an epidemic had always terrified me. I had to remind myself several times that Clementine had been healed now. My family was in no more danger than anyone else's.

"I'm sure if both Uncle and the royal family are overseeing the situation, she'll be back at the Academy in no time," said Saffron quietly, and we could only hope that she was right.

CHAPTER 8

*W*hen my next bout was against Calix and the one after against Lavinia, I found it hard to believe it could be a coincidence. The only good thing to be said about either confrontation was that they had listened to Thornton's warning, and no longer unleashed quite such deadly compositions.

I still ended up with a broken arm after the first one, however. And when I limped out of the arena after the second, a long gash on my arm bleeding sluggishly, I couldn't bear to look in the direction of my year mates. I didn't want to see the satisfaction on the faces of Lavinia's friends. So far I had done nothing but prove all their low opinions of me.

I ground my teeth as Acacia tended to me with a number of weary sighs. Out in the real world, I could save myself. I'd proved that. But I'd done it through brute force every time. And Thornton was right, though I hated to admit it. If I was going to serve at the front lines—in constant danger of my life—I needed to learn finesse. Otherwise I would end up burning out at some inopportune moment only to end up with my head chopped off.

But I hadn't worked out how to distract or disable my opponent quickly or effectively enough to give me time to actually complete a working. I kept trying, and the backlash from my disrupted attempts only made my collective injuries worse. I had started to let myself believe I was a mage—someone special in fact—but now I had weekly evidence that while my powers might be strong in some ways, I couldn't hold my own against true mages.

I felt eyes on me as I sat to one side with Acacia, and my head turned despite myself. But it wasn't one of the Stantorn or Devoras trainees watching me. It was Lucas.

He had seen me save myself more than once and was one of the few who knew the truth about my strength. It stung more than I liked to admit that he was now seeing the truth about my weakness, too. No doubt it merely confirmed his perception of how inept I was, how unfitted for his world and a position among the mages.

My chin came up, and I glared at him, unwilling to look away first. His expression didn't change, and I had to admit it looked coolly thoughtful rather than mocking. Was he mentally composing his report for his parents?

Despite early promise, the Spoken Mage is now consistently demon-strating considerable disadvantage against a regular mage.

Eventually he blinked and looked away, and I let my own gaze fall. I had to think of something because despite his contempt at the idea, it couldn't be more clear that the Stantorn and Devoras families still had a vendetta against me. Even our Devoras instructor was assisting them since there was no way I was randomly being allocated to bout only those with a desire to hurt me.

Later that evening, when my friends had already withdrawn to their rooms, I slipped into the library in search of a book. I had fallen behind on our latest healing assignment—too busy worrying about the combat bouts.

When I saw a lone familiar light at the back of the library, I briefly considered walking straight back out again. But instead my feet carried me forward, along the well-worn track I had taken so many evenings during first year. Back when I studied most evenings in the circle of that light.

But when I stood in front of the only occupied desk, staring at the lone trainee, no words came.

Lucas looked up at me, and something crossed his face that I couldn't interpret. "I was wondering if you were going to come back this year."

His words unleashed my own, and suddenly I was talking without thinking, as I all too often did.

"Do you still think there's no way that the Stantorn mages could wish me harm despite the council's ruling? And the Devoras ones too. Have you been watching those bouts? Do you really think it's coincidence that our Devoras instructor keeps assigning me to duel them?"

I stopped to take a shallow breath, and he sighed.

"There's a difference between abduction and attempted murder and disliking someone."

I raised an eyebrow. "That first bout sure felt like attempted murder to me."

His lips tightened into a thin line. "That got out of hand. Thornton should have stepped in earlier. But Natalya has always been on the vindictive side. That doesn't mean her father—or anyone else—put her up to it."

He paused. "The truth is that a lot of mages don't like you, Elena."

I raised an eyebrow, and he actually looked faintly apologetic.

"What I mean is that they don't like the thought of you. A commonborn who can wield power they can't? It seems dangerous to them. They want to bring you down, if they can. Prove to themselves they have nothing to be afraid of."

I deflated, sinking into a chair as all my righteous indignation seeped away. It was all I could do to keep the tears out of my eyes.

"Well, it seems they're right. Clearly they don't."

Lucas leaned across the desk, a fire in his eyes that made me draw back a little. I'd been burned by that fire before.

"No. You're wrong, Elena. I've seen you in action. I've seen what you're capable of."

"Reckless power, the kind that's going to kill me one day? Yes, I can do that. But I can't keep doing it forever."

He sat back in his chair, his eyes growing distant and thoughtful.

"You have the power," he said. "Your problem is time. You don't have the time. Your opponents might have spent an hour on the actual composing, but you only get seconds."

"Thank you for that. I didn't realize." I gave him a flat look, but he ignored me.

"So you need to be better than them. Much better."

"If this is supposed to be an encouraging speech, you're terrible at them."

He ignored me again.

"You passed your composition exam at a second year level, as you well know. You're already ahead of most of our year mates. They're building up their stamina and energy levels, but you've never needed that. You need to start working on the next level. Shortening your compositions."

I regarded him dubiously. "Not all mages are even capable of that."

"Elena." He shook his head. "No one can do what you can. No one. Twice now you've produced a controlled working with only two words—and effectively shielded yourself with them."

"You heard Thornton. Controlled might be stretching it," I muttered, suddenly uncomfortable.

He shrugged. "Maybe, but the shields did what you needed them to. And they didn't blow up in your face."

I winced. "Mostly."

He gave a tiny smile. "They were controlled enough. I just

don't think you realize how rare that is." He watched me in silence for a moment. "Thornton told you no more compositions without restrictions, and he's right. But that doesn't mean they can't be short. You just need to learn the necessary finesse."

"That's easy to say. But how exactly am I to do it? You may not have noticed, but the instructors here aren't exactly falling over themselves to actually instruct me." I looked down into my lap, trying to keep the bitterness out of my voice. "Apparently I'm the sort of curiosity that's supposed to be observed only, not trained."

Lucas sighed. "It's not that simple. I thought you knew that. You still have enemies, Elena, even if they're being held in check for now. Lorcan is the Academy Head, and what he does is closely watched. If he was seen spending his time building your strength—turning you into a weapon, even—well, that would have consequences. Devoras and Stantorn don't like the idea of you as a rogue commonborn wielding untold power. But they also don't like the idea of you in the hands of Kallorway. How do you think we convinced them you needed mage guards during your break? And on top of all that, they don't like the idea of you as a Callinos pet all that much more. Lorcan is keeping the distance he needs to keep and hoping for the best."

I snorted. "Am I supposed to be grateful? Walden didn't seem to feel the same restraints."

Lucas narrowed his eyes. "Yes, well, he's an Ellington. No one tends to worry as much about them. And he's also only a librarian. He doesn't have nearly so many eyes on him." Something in his voice told me he was uncomfortable with this idea. As if he didn't like the idea of anyone not being sufficiently watched.

After a moment of silence, he spoke again. "And even he's not volunteering to help you now, is he?"

My head shot up, and I stared at him.

"Jocasta is away. He can't afford the time."

Lucas just watched me in silence, knowing he had made his point. No one thought it safe to help me.

After a moment I threw up my hands.

"So I need to outstrip all my year mates and learn advanced composition. But at the same time, I need to accept that none of my instructors are going to help me in that task. So what, exactly, are you suggesting, oh Wise One?"

He actually grinned at my mockery, and I felt a sudden urge to punch him in his too-perfect face. Just once I would like to see the dark, almost black, waves of his hair disordered, or the brilliant green of his eyes dimmed. Although no doubt a black eye would only bring out their color.

"I don't think I like you looking at me like that," he said. "I feel like I'm going to have to defend myself at any moment."

I rolled my eyes, trying to hide my embarrassment at being so easily read. "You're a prince of Ardann, Lucas. I'm not going to attack you."

"Well, that might be your only option."

"Excuse me?"

"You need someone to train you, don't you?"

My mouth fell open. "You? *You're* offering to train me?"

"Don't sound so shocked."

"And why not?" I challenged him, scrambling for time to process his words. "You're only a second year like me. Why would you be able to train me?"

He raised both eyebrows. "Didn't you just say it? I'm a prince of Ardann. And I turned sixteen nearly two years ago. I'm not just naturally strong, you know. Although I am that too." He gave me an infuriating smirk. "I've been receiving private tuition since my sixteenth birthday."

"I knew it," I muttered. Such a practice was frowned on from what I'd heard—unless you were royalty, and then the rules didn't apply.

"Anyway, Walden may have helped you focus. Provided some guidance, even. But you were the one to work out how to unlock your power. And you were the one who worked so hard to hone and control it."

I looked at him in surprise. Had it all been me?

"Well, weren't you?"

I thought back over my lessons with Walden. "Yes…I suppose I was. But that doesn't mean I could have done it on my own."

He leaned back in his chair and spread his arms wide. "And here I am. Ready for you to hurl combat compositions at all night long."

"All night?"

The grin fell off his face. "If I'm going to help you, Elena, then it has to be a secret."

My eyes narrowed. Ah. Now we came to it.

"First of all, as you so rightly said, I'm a prince. And there are a great many people who will not like the idea of you repeatedly attacking me without supervision."

I raised an eyebrow. "You don't seem worried."

He gave me his smuggest grin yet. "Don't flatter yourself, Elena. I said you're ahead of *most* of your year mates. You might have raw power, but I'm not worried."

"Ugh. Of course you're not."

He laughed. "Don't take it personally. There's a reason there are laws about who royalty can marry. Other royalty or a member of one of the great families only. We've been carefully cultivating our line, breeding strength and control for generations. It's why you won't find a weak royal."

"Ugh," I said again. "You make it sound like you're a herd of cattle."

He shrugged, the laugh dropping from his eyes. "I've told you before that being royalty doesn't give me any more choice in my life than you."

I looked away, discomfited by the reminder.

"So you're proposing secret nighttime training sessions. For me to learn to shorten my compositions."

"I guess it's up to you." He shrugged. "Do you want to keep getting destroyed in the combat bouts?"

I stood up. "Of course I don't. And I'm up for training any time. Just name it."

My eyes challenged him, but his challenged me straight back.

"Tomorrow night. An hour from now. In the arena."

"The arena?"

"Officially speaking, we're not really even supposed to be in here at this time of evening. So we push the boundaries a little further."

I said nothing, and he seemed to think I needed convincing.

"Besides, we need that shield. And not just to prevent you destroying the Academy. If we're really going to keep this a secret, we need it to shield all the flashes of power we'll be using."

"Fine," I said. "The arena. Tomorrow night. I'll be there."

I turned to leave and then paused.

"Why are you doing this, Lucas? Why are you helping me?"

A crease appeared between his brows. "Elena, I know you think—" He broke off, apparently rethinking his words.

"Training you might be a political danger no one else can afford. At least not right now. But you have so much potential. Your ability..." He shook his head. "You might save us all. And I, for one, don't like to see any potential advantage squandered."

"Because we're in a war. One we don't seem able to win."

His eyes met mine, and their intense gaze seemed to be trying to communicate something I couldn't quite understand.

"Among other things."

When I slipped into bed minutes later, I had a lot to think about. But foremost of them was hope. Maybe I could learn to hold my own in combat, after all. And if I could do that, maybe I truly did deserve a place among the mages. And maybe I actually had some chance of surviving my three years of conscription, whatever they might bring.

~

The next night I called good night to my friends and entered my room, feeling like a fraud. The minutes stretched endlessly, and my attempts to study turned into pacing instead. But finally the time arrived.

I slipped carefully back into the corridor, looking around for any sign of other movement. All was quiet. No doubt the rest of the Academy were fast asleep—the far more sensible thing for me to be as well.

But I didn't hesitate as I hurried down the stairs and quietly exited through the front doors. The walk through the gardens and training yards felt long, and I kept twitching at shadows. Several times I glanced back at the blank windows of the square Academy building. Was anyone gazing out into the night? And, if so, could they see me?

But no one else appeared, and no shout sounded to call me to account. At last I stood inside the arena. For a moment I thought I was alone and wondered if this was all some elaborate prank. But then a shadowy figure rose from the stands, and Lucas crossed the floor of the arena to join me.

"You came." His eyes were shadowed in the darkness.

"So did you."

He pulled two pieces of parchment from his robe and held them out to me. I took them but kept my eyes on him. He gestured for me to read them, and I angled them to catch the moonlight.

Both appeared to be compositions for calling a brief spot fire to a particular location that would be indicated by a pointing finger. But one took up half a page, and the second one only two lines, leaving out many of the specifications of the first one.

"You'll need to get yours even shorter than that." He pointed to the two-liner. "Especially given the need for the binding words as well. But it gives the idea. Go on and release them both. One at a time."

When I hesitated, he prodded me again, so I shrugged and tore the long one, pointing at a small clump of grass some way away from us. A bright light split the night as flames erupted on the spot. They burned without fuel for a full minute and then winked back out of existence.

"And now the other one," he said.

I ripped the remaining parchment and pointed again at the same spot, now a charred piece of dirt. The same light filled the space around us as identical looking flames winked into being, burned merrily, and then disappeared again.

I handed back the four half-sheets, and he stuffed them back into his robe.

"Did you notice any difference between them?"

I shook my head. "No, they seemed to last the same amount of time and burn to the same height."

He nodded. "Exactly. The limitations and restrictions were there in both, I just had to describe them less fully. That's the basic idea behind shortening your compositions. Rather than using a large number of specific words, you shape the power within a smaller number of words as you're composing. It's all about the way you form and channel the power as you send it through the words."

He ran a hand through his hair. "This is harder to describe than I thought." He grimaced apologetically. "I've never tried to teach anyone before."

"No, I think I know what you mean." I chewed on the inside of my cheek. "It sounds hard, though."

When he gave me a challenging look, I shrugged defensively. "I don't mean that I thought it was going to be easy. But it's one thing for you to work on shaping the power while you're calmly sitting at a desk, slowly writing out some words. But I have to visualize the words, speak them at regular speed—or faster if I'm in the arena—and shape the limits of the power all at the same time. While also potentially fighting someone with a sword and possibly dodging fire balls. Or some such."

"Fire balls?" He laughed. "I don't think I've seen that from any of our year mates."

"Sheet of fire, fire balls, it's all the same to me. Dodge or get burned."

He nodded slowly. "In all seriousness, you're right, of course. It is harder for you. But that's why we're here now. So you can practice slowly. Without swords. Or fire—in any format. You're going to need to be able to do it without much thinking. We should probably pick a couple of useful compositions and start on those. Even if you can only hone a small handful, that will make a difference in your bouts."

I sighed. "Like you said, I'm going to need to get them down much shorter even than your example."

"I know. So let's get working." He raised an eyebrow. "Unless you want to give up now?"

I stiffened. "Never. I'm ready when you are."

A smile spread across his face. "And there she is," he whispered, almost too quietly for me to hear.

CHAPTER 9

*D*espite my motivation, I couldn't train for half the night every night. And despite his superior attitude, neither could Lucas. We still needed sleep.

We fell into the pattern of meeting every third night, the weather surprisingly staying warm enough to allow our night time exertions, despite winter creeping in on us. In the meantime I still got flattened in my bouts, but I no longer felt so dejected about it. Slowly I was getting better, and soon I hoped to be able to hold my own.

Lucas was a good teacher, and once when I made a break-through—building an unspoken limitation into my shield—I almost forgot myself and embraced him. But at the last second I remembered and saved myself the embarrassment of his rejection.

Sometimes, particularly when his eyes lit up with excitement and victory at some mark of our progress, it was hard to remember he was doing this to help Ardann, not me.

But outside of our training I had reminders of what might be motivating him. Rumors had begun to filter into the Academy, and every time I saw concerned faces and pinched expressions on huddled groups of trainees, it helped remind me. There was a war going on.

Of course, there was always a war going on. It had been slowly burning along the border regions for almost twice my lifetime. But this felt different. Something was changing.

My brother Jasper dropped in to see me early one rest morning, his face pale and drawn.

"What is it?" I asked, scrambling from my bed.

"It's Torkan. He's been killed."

I sank back down onto my mattress. "But he had less than a year left to serve," I whispered.

"I guess the Kallorwegian who speared him through didn't know about that," Jasper replied harshly, before rubbing a hand across his wet eyes.

I swallowed and tried to take in the news. Torkan had been Jasper's best friend back in their days at the Kingslee school. And even when they had finished there at age ten, they had remained friends. Torkan had always joked about what an unlikely pair they made—the scholar and the soldier. He was the second of only two sons, with four much younger sisters, so he had known he would need to conscript ever since his older brother won a valuable apprenticeship at age twelve.

He had spent so many years training—with the same dogged persistence my brother had always shown at his own studies— that I had fallen into the habit of thinking that he was sure to survive his term in the Armed Forces.

"I'm sorry," Jasper said after a long silence. "I didn't mean..."

I shook my head and moved forward to embrace him. "I know. I just can't believe..." We fell silent again.

"What are you going to do?"

Jasper swallowed, clearly trying to pull himself together. "I'm walking home. I should be going now in fact. They've sent back his ashes, and his family mean to hold the ceremony today. I want to be there."

"But…" I hesitated, trying to think how to say it. "You'll be back?"

"Of course. Life must go on, right?" He ground out a humorless laugh.

"Do you want me to go with you?"

He shook his head quickly. "I'll be moving fast, and there's no reason for you to exhaust yourself." He paused, and I could see him weighing up whether he should say what was on his mind.

"Just say it," I said softly.

"Clemmy has been healed now. And she's young. She has time to train. Have you considered…"

I shook my head before he could finish speaking.

"No. Nothing has changed. Clemmy might be healed, but she's never going to be big. She's never going to be a soldier."

Jasper eyed my own short frame and raised an eyebrow.

"But you're forgetting. I have other ways to defend myself now."

A ghost of relief crossed his face. "You've been preparing? I didn't like to ask…"

I nodded. "As much as I can. Every day."

He pressed his lips together. "And they'll let you go? Let you enlist?"

I shrugged. "I don't intend to ask permission."

For a moment we stood, eyes locked, a weight of understanding and history hanging between us, not needing to be spoken. And then he wrapped me in another embrace and was gone.

I couldn't concentrate for a full week after that, until Lucas finally snapped, and sent a fire ball at my head in training. I reacted on instinct, calling up a shield to deflect it. I spoke only a single limitation, as we had been working on, instructing it to fizzle out of existence as soon as the threat had passed. But as I pictured and spoke the word shield, my mind overlaid it with the phrase I had used in the past to limit my shield to a small flat sheet.

It took less time than having to speak all the words, and when the shield appeared, it was small and flat rather than a complete bubble. My first true success in days.

I put my hands on my hips. "A fire ball? Really?"

Lucas winked at me. "I've been saving that one for the right moment."

"Did you just wink at me?"

"No. Princes don't wink."

He winked again, and I raised an eyebrow. "Did you hit your head or something when I wasn't looking?"

The humor dropped from his face. "I'm just glad to see you back." He hesitated. "What happened?"

I turned away slightly, a lump rising in my throat. For a second I considered not answering, but then I couldn't hold it back.

"I found out a friend was killed. On the front lines. He had nearly served his three years, too."

"Oh." For a moment neither of us spoke. "Was he...a special friend?"

My eyes flew to his, but Lucas had also turned slightly, placing his face into shadow.

"He was my brother's best friend. And yes, he was special."

Something changed in Lucas's posture, and honesty compelled me to add, "But not special like that. Not that it makes a difference. He didn't deserve to die."

"No, I'm sure he didn't."

The grief poked at my anger, and I stepped toward him. "And he was one of the more prepared ones. Not that you lot did anything to help him. He trained himself. And he still died. Many of those conscripted are far less capable."

"Us lot?" Lucas shook his head. "Do you mean mages or royals?"

"I don't know. Both?" I gestured around us at the dark and deserted arena. "Mages—already born with every advantage—are trained exhaustively for four years before being sent to the front lines. And then they only have to serve for two years. If Torkan's term had been two years, he would be safely home by now."

"New recruits receive training," said Lucas. "Every new soldier goes through basic training."

I stepped closer again, pointing accusingly at him. "Yes. Basic is right. It's what? Two weeks? A month?" I took another step. "Jasper went home for Torkan's ashes ceremony. He heard what happened. He was trying to protect two new recruits. Eighteen-year-olds fresh from this so-called training. Small, unprepared. Neither of them had been expecting their conscription, apparently. All three of them died."

I was close enough now to see a wince cross his face despite the shadow. He made no defense, but neither did he offer any sympathy. We just stood there in silence, my chest heaving as I tried to control my breathing.

His eyes fastened on my face, and this time he was the one to step forward. We were far too close now, but I didn't step away, not willing to be the one to draw back.

"Elena." My name was half breath, half word, and his eyes dropped to my lips.

My breathing, which had slowly begun to calm, hitched again. He swayed toward me, and for a moment I couldn't see anything but his eyes.

But then Torkan's face rose in my mind, and I stepped hurriedly back.

"Good people are dying, Lucas. And what is your family doing about it?"

His head snapped up, and I thought I saw a faint flush on his face, although the darkness made it hard to be sure. He stepped back as well, and his arms swept up and around in a broad gesture.

"Everything we can. We want this war to end, too, you know."

For a second my eyes followed his waving hands in confusion, and then I remembered. Me. I was what he was doing. Honing my skills for combat. Seeing what could be gleaned from my new ability. Seeing what new capabilities could be learned and fed into the war effort. I drew even further back.

"I'm done."

I turned and strode away, but his quiet voice sounded clearly through the night.

"For tonight? Or in general?"

I didn't slow. "I don't know."

The next morning I carefully avoided looking in the prince's direction as I slid into my usual chair for breakfast. But one look at Coralie's tear-streaked face drove all thought of Lucas from my mind.

"What is it? What's happened?"

Finnian answered for her, he and Saffron looking grim, although their own eyes were dry.

"We were right about an outbreak in Jocasta's hometown. And the healers haven't been able to contain it. It's reached Abalene."

"Oh no." I put my hand up to cover my mouth. Abalene was a large city. An outbreak there would spread quickly.

"It's green fever. They're using the word epidemic," said Saffron quietly.

I swallowed. Abalene was far to the south of Kingslee and Corrin, but such a disaster touched everyone. And Coralie's family lived in Abalene. Although I could only imagine mage families had ways to protect themselves from epidemics that commonborn did not.

I was still absorbing the news when the meal finished. Lorcan appeared in the dining hall before anyone could leave, and a hiss of whispers spread across the trainees. I tried to remember if I'd ever seen him at a meal before.

"Second years, please remain. The rest of you can continue to class as usual."

The first, third, and fourth years filed out, their curious gazes jumping between Lorcan and the twelve of us. But one glance at my year mates was enough to see none of them had any more idea what was going on than me.

Except possibly for Lucas. It was hard to tell with him since his face was generally impassive, and I didn't let my eyes linger to look for any signs of greater knowledge.

When only the twelve of us remained, Lorcan crossed over to stand closer to where we all sat in the second row of tables.

"As you have no doubt heard by now, the healers have declared an epidemic in southern Ardann. Your year is in a somewhat unusual situation, as not only are you particularly few in number, but you have all signed up to study the healing discipline this year. Given these factors, your instructors feel that this will be a valuable teaching exercise for you."

I could see my own disbelief mirrored on Coralie's face. Teaching exercise? Were they seriously referring to an epidemic as a teaching exercise?

"With that end in mind, you will temporarily suspend your other studies and travel down to Abalene to observe how the healers manage the situation."

"Excuse me?" From her voice, Natalya shared our disbelief, although I suspected it was for different reasons. "You want us to travel into an epidemic region?" Her eyes scanned the tables. "Even Calix and me? Even Lucas?"

Lorcan's eyes hardened. "All second year trainees are expected to participate. You can consider it required coursework if you wish to pass second year."

Natalya gaped at him.

His gaze swept over the rest of us. "Any further objections?"

No one said anything. Everyone knew the price of failing the Academy.

"Our parents will have something to say about this," muttered Natalya, obviously intending her words to be too low for Lorcan to hear. She misjudged, however.

He sighed. "You may relax, Natalya. No trainee will be in any danger. As well as our own Academy healer, Acacia, you will be traveling with two healers—including one senior healer. Between the three of them, they will travel with enough healing compositions to deal with the first hint of sickness that might arise in any of you. They have been given clear instructions that these compositions are not to be used for any other purpose."

Now I was the one gaping at him. Three healers? They were going to waste three healers and a whole store of compositions on the chance we might get sick? When we could just stay here? Would twelve commonborn victims die because those compositions were being withheld?

My eyes traveled involuntarily to where Lucas sat at Natalya's side. She had suggested the trip should not proceed because of their status. But perhaps it was the opposite that was true. We were taking this trip precisely because we had so many trainees from powerful families in our year. These were the future leaders of Ardann, and what were a few commonborn lives compared to their training?

I gritted my teeth, fighting to keep my outrage inside. I, least of all, could afford to fail the Academy.

Lorcan surveyed us all again, and then nodded once. "You may take the rest of the day off to pack. You leave in the morning." He hurried from the room, leaving shocked silence for a half-second. And then several conversations broke out at once.

"Home," said Coralie, not looking like she'd taken the news in yet. "I'm going home."

Finnian still didn't look his cheerful self, but I could see a new spark of interest in his eyes. He was excited to have this opportunity.

I frowned across at him. "Doesn't it bother you? That they're treating this like some sort of excursion when people are dying? Those compositions they're holding for us could be used to save lives."

Finnian shrugged uncomfortably. "The healing discipline would never allow all their healers to be exhausted by a single epidemic. It would be too dangerous. So if they're sending healers with instructions not to assist, then those are healers that would have been kept in reserve anyway. Lorcan mentioned a senior healer, so they're most likely sending someone with administrative expertise. Someone whose knowledge is too valuable for them to exhaust themselves on healing. I don't see much harm in us joining them. Honestly, we're not likely to get sick anyway, since I'm sure they'll take precautions not to overexpose us. Plus, if we pick up the signs of any illness early—which we would—they'll probably have us practice healing each other."

His words made sense, and my discomfort eased a fraction. But it didn't disappear. There were still those stored compositions being held back. And somehow he had too many explanations. It all sounded just a little too convenient, too much like the kind of excuses that always accompanied injustice.

Coralie stood up abruptly. "Let's go talk to Acacia. Lorcan said she'll be leading us." She started off without waiting for our agreement, and we all followed obediently behind.

We found Acacia's rooms in unusual disorder, the young woman rushing around between open drawers muttering to herself, her face drawn and tired. She looked up at the sound of our arrival but immediately returned to what she was doing.

"Oh, it's just you lot."

"How bad is it, Acacia? Really?" Coralie's voice trembled slightly, and the healer froze.

Slowly she turned to face us. A silent look passed between her and my friend. I suddenly remembered that Acacia also came from Abalene. She and Coralie had known one another before the Academy.

"They're saying it's bad. But they still hope they can prevent its spread further north. So that must mean they have it at least partially contained. And they're sending new healers down. Ones who haven't exhausted themselves yet. That's why I asked for permission to go. My new assistant could do with the experience here, and I know they've already given Jocasta leave to remain down there until this is over, despite not being a healer. But I didn't expect Lorcan to want to send all of you as well."

I could see the frustration on her face. Clearly she had hoped to help, not babysit twelve trainee mages.

"Perhaps we'll be able to help," I said quietly.

Acacia glanced at me briefly before returning to her previous flurry of activity. She appeared to be sorting through rolled parchments, storing them in pouches like the one Beatrice had described having inside her case.

"Perhaps," she said. "Although this isn't a simple disease. It wouldn't have spread this far if it was."

That explained Coralie's fear. Mages usually treated themselves in simple cases—or within their families at least—only calling healers for cases too complex to be touched without additional training.

Although surely the healers would prioritize the local mage families. I immediately reprimanded myself for the ungenerous thought. Coralie surely feared for the commonborn locals as well —including, no doubt, her family's servants.

"I have a lot still to do," said Acacia. "And you should all be packing yourselves. Be off with you."

We left without further comment, each busy with our own thoughts.

$\mathcal{W}$e were a quiet group when we met in the front courtyard of the Academy the next morning. If the twins had protested to their parents, it had done them no good since they waited silently with their bags, just like everyone else.

Lorcan had come to see us off, and Acacia and all twelve of us trainees had arrived on time, but still we all waited. I was just getting impatient enough to ask what we were waiting for, when the great gates of the Academy swung open.

A small group of young people entered, accompanied by several black-robed mage instructors from the University, Jessamine leading the way. The University Head crossed immediately to Lorcan and began to speak quietly to him, while the rest of us eyed the newcomers.

"Jasper?" I rushed over to embrace my brother who looked equally pleased and surprised to see me. "Clara." I nodded at the petite young woman by his side. She was the only other commonborn scholarship student at the University, and I had met her a couple of times before. "What are you both doing here?"

"The same thing you are, apparently," said Jasper. "Being sent to observe the crown's response to an unfolding tragedy." I could hear in his voice that he felt much the same way about our instructors' attitude to it that I did. "The offer was put out to all the students, but I'm sure you'll be astonished to hear there weren't too many of us eager to take the risk."

So that was why the two commonborn scholarship students—surely the bottom of the University ladder—had been included. A persistent tugging at my elbow made me spin around. Coralie stood there, her face white.

"Edmond's here, too."

I scanned the rest of the group and spotted the tall young man who I had met once before. He and Coralie had danced at the last Midwinter Ball, and she had been taken with him ever since. Hopefully his presence would distract her from her worries rather than adding to them.

"Oh, yes, I heard about your dance." Jasper grinned at my friend, before waving across at his fellow student. "Oy! Edmond! Over here."

Edmond joined us with a grin and an elaborate bow.

"Ah, the fair Coralie. I didn't expect our group to be so graced with your presence."

Coralie flushed and giggled, but I caught Finnian rolling his eyes.

"What's the matter?" I whispered to him. "You two could practically be brothers. You'd both have made good Players, at any rate. If you weren't already busy being mages."

He just shook his head and continued to look on with an unimpressed expression as Edmond flirted outrageously with Coralie. I glanced over at Saffron, and she met my eyes before giggling.

"It will do him good to have some competition," she whispered to me.

But all conversation ceased when a stream of carriages began to roll through the gates. The first stopped in front of Lorcan and

Jessamine, and two purple-robed figures stepped down. To my surprise, I recognized them both.

"Beatrice."

Finnian turned at my soft exclamation. "That's right, you've met her, haven't you? Lorcan did mention a senior healer. Come on." He gestured for me to follow him as he moved toward the cluster of senior mages, and I followed with some reluctance. Beatrice I was perfectly happy to see again. Her young cousin, Reese, a great deal less so.

Beatrice greeted Finnian with affection and me with friendly recognition. Reese on the other hand just narrowed his eyes at me.

"You. I should have known you'd be here."

"Yes," I said, meeting his gaze. "Since I'm a trainee and this is the Academy, you should have."

Finnian snorted, quickly turning the sound into a cough. Reese transferred his disapproving look to him.

"Finnian. My day just keeps getting better and better."

"Please excuse Reese," said Beatrice with a soft smile. "The poor boy is still stuck on babysitting duty, and it's put him in a perpetually bad mood."

Reese spluttered, temporarily bereft of words, which I took from her smile to have been her intention.

"Trainees and students," called Lorcan, distracting us all. "Please find places for yourselves in a carriage. You will at all times obey the instructions of the healers traveling with you and conduct yourselves as is befitting members of the Academy and University. Do not give us reason to be shamed by you."

He gave us all a hard stare followed by a single nod.

As well as Acacia, a black-robed University academic joined Beatrice and Reese in the front carriage, leaving the trainees and students to find their own places in the other vehicles.

I followed Jasper, Clara, Edmond, and Coralie into one of the last ones in line, Finnian jumping in after us at the last moment,

Saffron close behind him. It was tight with seven of us, but no one protested, and the journey had soon begun.

~

Despite our somber goal, it seemed it was impossible for seven young people to travel together in such close confines without some joking and laughter. At least not when both Edmond and Finnian were part of our number—each seeking to outdo the other.

But I held myself a little apart, watching out the window, until we passed the turn off to Kingslee. When the dirt side road flashed past, Jasper reached over and squeezed my hand. For a brief moment, our eyes met. We were now further south than either of us had ever been before.

I couldn't deny the smallest flash of excitement, although I wished we were traveling for a different purpose. A visit to Coralie's family, perhaps. Although there would be no reason for Jasper or Clara to accompany us on such a journey.

And the brief feeling of elation was soon swallowed up by memories of Torkan. How many families in Abalene, and further south, were holding such ashes ceremonies for their loved ones now? Or were whole families being wiped out—with no one left to celebrate their life or mourn for them?

I leaned my head against Jasper's shoulder and tried not to look at Edmond or Finnian who were joking on the other side of the carriage. Jasper leaned down to whisper in my ear.

"Don't blame them. We all respond to tragedy differently. Some need the release of tension that a laugh can bring."

I sighed and smiled. It was nice to be with someone who knew me so well. It had been too long.

And as the hours continued to roll on, I had to admit he was right. I didn't think I could have borne such a long journey if the mood had been somber and grief-filled the whole time.

We had a short break for lunch just after crossing the broad bridge which spanned the River Overon. The large inn, located in a prominent location on the road, had clearly been warned of the arrival of such a significant group, and a decent meal had been prepared.

We soon moved on, however. An even larger inn hosted us for the evening meal, rooms already prepared for our stay. We would spend the night here, Acacia informed us, before splitting off from the South Road to follow a smaller one toward Abalene.

All of the students and trainees were expected to share bedchambers, much to the disgust of some of our number. But Coralie and I were both happy to gain a roommate for the night, Coralie in particular being eager to discuss the day's company in the privacy of our room.

The mention of a smaller road turned out to be somewhat misleading since, unlike the Kingslee turn off, only a slight decrease in width seemed to separate this offshoot from the main road. A reminder that Abalene was a significant city. It sat in the southeastern corner of the kingdom, on the southern reaches of the Overon, just above the delta at the river mouth, and it was a center of trade. Which must mean the city was hurting in more ways than one right now, since all travel into and out of the region had been restricted.

We encountered our first road block when we branched off the main road, a group of bored looking soldiers who talked briefly to someone in the front carriage before waving us all through. We passed two more before we reached Abalene, however, the soldiers manning them looking increasingly more alert and nervous. They weren't wearing face masks, however.

"What do we know about green fever?" I asked the carriage. We hadn't had enough time before our departure for me to look it up in the library.

The mood had already dropped after the last road block, but my question depressed it even further.

Finnian sighed. "Not enough. Which is the problem."

Jasper looked across at him measuringly. "You're Dashiell's son, right?"

If Finnian was offended at Jasper not using his father's title, he didn't show it.

"Yes, that's right. He's been staying up at the palace, coordinating the response to the crisis. So I went up to see him the night before we left."

I straightened on the seat. This was news to me.

"Green fever hits southern Ardann every year. It comes down from the Graybacks." He named the mountain range that ran along the eastern coast of Ardann. "Usually it only comes down in the warmer months, when the mountains are covered in green —that's where the name comes from."

Some of this rang a vague bell, although I had never paid much attention to the disease. Not when it never made it up as far north as Kingslee.

"Bloodsucking insects carry it, and then they breed like crazy in the river delta. But usually by the winter months they're gone. And while it's not the most pleasant of diseases, it's not usually a big killer either. Only the very young, the very elderly, and the already ill are at risk."

I winced at his words and felt Jasper shift beside me. We were far too used to classifying Clemmy in that category, and it was still hard to believe she no longer fit.

"Which is the problem." Finnian sighed. "Healers have to pour a great deal of energy and research into a disease before they can learn how to compose a true cure. Sometimes it's the work of generations. We don't tend to waste the time on something like green fever. Healers treat the symptoms, if it's a bad case, or an at risk patient, and their body does the rest."

"So what's different this time?" Clara asked.

Finnian shrugged, his face sad. "We don't know. It's been an unseasonably warm winter, for one. We've felt it up in the capital, but not like it's been down south from what my father tells me. It hasn't gotten cold enough to drive off the insects. And, somehow, with the longer fever season, the disease has mutated into a far more dangerous strain. This one's a killer—and not just for babies and the elderly."

Coralie gave a little whimper, and Saffron put an arm around her shoulders.

"What are the symptoms?" I asked.

"Normally it's a fever—obviously—along with aches and pains and some vomiting."

"And this new strain?" asked Jasper.

Finnian grimaced. "It starts out like normal, and after a couple of days, the patient seems to get better. But less than a day later, it hits again. Only harder this time, with more severe symptoms. Some fight it off and make a true recovery. Others start vomiting up blood." He paused for a moment, but we all remained silent. "If the blood appears, they don't last much longer from all reports."

"But they're working on a cure, right?"

Finnian exchanged a glance with Saffron over Coralie's head, and I knew I wasn't going to like his answer.

"Now that it's become truly deadly, the healers will, yes. Once this epidemic is past."

"Once it's past?" I stared at him. "But they need it now!"

Saffron responded, her voice quiet. "Yes, they need it now, but cures don't come that quickly. For the moment, the healers must allocate their available resources to treating patients and preventing its further spread. They don't have enough healers to work on a cure as well."

Just as she finished, the sound of the cobblestones under the wheels changed. We all looked out the windows to discover that we had reached the outskirts of Abalene.

The city rolled past the windows, a collection of mostly single-story buildings with large windows and flat roofs. Bright material had been strung between many of them to create covered walkways, and I could easily imagine it as a vibrant and cheerful place.

But a strange quiet hung over everything, and few people were out on the streets. Those who we did see hurried about their business, their heads down and walk purposeful. And a light haze hung over everything, carrying the faint smell of smoke.

"They'll have bonfires on the outskirts of the city," said Finnian, in a dull voice.

I didn't ask what they would be burning. I didn't want to know the answer.

Coralie didn't look out the window for long, burying her face in Saffron's shoulder instead. The northern girl looked across the carriage at me, sharing a pained look as she patted Coralie's arm. But there was nothing either of us could do to change the new reality of Coralie's home.

The carriage rumbled past several market squares, but no stalls were in sight. Instead large canvas tents filled the empty spaces.

"Makeshift healing clinics," murmured Finnian.

"And supply centers," added Saffron, as we watched a trickle of people emerge from one of them with packages clasped against their chests. "Since neither trade nor the markets are functioning."

No one said anything else until the carriage rolled to a stop. We were deposited in front of a long building, larger than many we had seen and with a second story. Presumably the small southern campus of the Royal University where we were to stay. The top level was dorm rooms—our new home for the duration of our visit.

Servants emerged to unpack our baggage, although far fewer than I would have expected under normal circumstances. The task would take them a while.

In the meantime, we were all ushered into a large room on the ground floor, filled with familiar looking tables. A dining hall.

No one but our group was here, despite a mouth-watering smell emanating from a side door. We sat together in our usual groupings, although here the individual tables were much longer than the ones at the Academy. Jasper, Clara, and Edmond joined us, as they had in the carriage, and the black-robed academic supervising their group took a seat beside Edmond, somewhat to my surprise.

A moment later Beatrice took another seat at the table. Apparently here, unlike at the Academy, trainees and supervisors were to eat together. Perhaps no one wished to make extra work for the reduced number of servants.

The food arrived, a delicious but spicy curry that left a burn in my mouth, and for a brief span there was only the sound of spoons scraping against bowls and murmurs of appreciation. But my thoughts kept returning to the interrupted conversation in the carriage.

"So the healers may not be trying to cure the green fever, but they can treat people at least? Right? Save them from dying."

I directed my words at Finnian, but he hesitated, glancing at Beatrice.

She put down her spoon and sighed, rubbing the back of her neck.

"They're doing their best," she said. "The problem is that the only sure way we've found is to completely treat each separate symptom during the initial, weaker phase. The healers down here have worked out that if the patient can be completely cured that way, then the second phase doesn't develop."

"That sounds good," said Clara, but her voice suggested she knew a qualification was coming.

"Yes and no," said Beatrice. "Too many are coming down with the disease. Far more than the healers can treat at the early stage. Not without burning themselves completely dry, which would help nobody. We've already sent down most of the stored compositions we had in the north for fever, muscle aches, and vomiting, but it's still nowhere near enough."

She paused. "What they need is a way to work out who will be able to fight it off on their own, and who will start vomiting blood. Then we could treat only those who need it at the early stage. Because by the time they show the signs that they're not going to make it, it's already too late. We don't know enough about what internal systems the disease is destroying at that second stage, and only a very great expenditure of power, broadly applied, could save them once they get there."

Realization shot through me.

"That's why you're here. To develop some simple way to test the patients."

Beatrice paused for a brief second and then nodded. "That is the task assigned to Reese and me. We have been expressly forbidden from doing any direct healings. Unless one of you should fall sick and need us, of course."

She looked sad, and I remembered the concern on her face when she held Sara's newborn in her arms back in Kingslee. Beatrice was a rare being—a mage with true compassion for everyone, regardless of their birth. I could only imagine how such a stricture would grate against her in a situation like this. But what she had come here to do was important. It would save many lives in the long run.

I immediately resolved to do what she could not. I would find a way to heal some of the ill—even if only a handful. I hadn't been forbidden to do so, and if I could save even a few lives, it would be worth it.

CHAPTER 11

*O*ur rooms were more basic than at the Academy, but we each had one to ourselves. At first it made me a little queasy, wondering if the usual occupants of the rooms were now lying in one of the white tents—or worse. But a moment's reflection reminded me that the students must be mages, as were the ones at the main University campus in Corrin.

Conversation over the meal the next morning confirmed it. The majority of the students had fled Abalene at the first sign of the infection spreading into the city.

While I didn't wish them dead, such cowardice disgusted me. I had been mulling over Beatrice's explanation, and it had occurred to me that while some parts of the healing situation were complex, other parts were actually simple. Second year simple, even.

Acacia came down the long tables, stopping at each trainee and student to inquire about their well-being.

"If you get a single symptom, I want to know about it," she said to us. "So much as a twinge in your back, and you come straight to me." She gave us all a stern look. "Understand?"

We all nodded obediently. She had reached us last, so she

turned to leave the room, but I called after her, gesturing to an empty seat beside me. She gave me a wary look but slid into it without protest.

"I've been thinking," I said.

"Why do I have the feeling we should all be afraid?" asked Finnian.

Jasper, sitting two seats down, leaned forward to give my year mate a cold look. I shook my head at them both. It was sweet of my brother, but he would soon get used to Finnian's joking ways.

"We're here to learn, right?" I said to Acacia. "About healing. And surely that should mean practicing."

Acacia raised an eyebrow. "What does that mean?"

"Well, I know we don't have the skill or training to help with Beatrice's task."

Acacia gave me a questioning look, and I shrugged.

"She told us about it last night. Obviously we can't help her. And I don't think there's much any of us could do for someone in this new second stage of the fever. But Beatrice said that the best chance of treatment is in the first stage anyway. But that each of the symptoms has to be fully healed separately and completely, and the healers' stores of the necessary compositions have been depleted."

Acacia nodded slowly, as if reluctant to agree to my logic. Finnian on the other hand had fixed me with a look of dawning interest, clearly seeing where I was going.

I shrugged again and tried to keep my voice cool.

"It just occurred to me that compositions for things like healing basic fevers, aches and pains, and vomiting are probably within most of our capabilities. Or they're simple enough that we could learn them, anyway."

Acacia shifted uneasily. "The Academy sent you here to observe and learn, not to help heal. None of you are healers."

"But we're healing students," said Finnian, leaning forward across the tables. "Elena is right. It would be a good lesson. And then, of course, we would need to practice." He winked at me, and I grinned back at him.

"I don't know…" Acacia frowned.

I lowered my voice. "I know you want to help. That's why you came. Not to babysit us. Well, here's how you can help. If you teach us, we can produce far more compositions than you could on your own. Even if we can all manage only one of each type per day, that's twelve people who could be saved. Surely that's worth it?"

"Thirteen," said Edmond from next to Coralie. "I did two years of healing studies at the Academy and got a fair bit of practice on the front lines. I'm a bit rusty these days, but I'm sure it would come back to me fast enough. One of each type of composition a day shouldn't flatten me or prevent me pursuing my own studies."

Coralie beamed at him, and I couldn't help but wonder if he truly wanted to help or was just trying to impress her. Either way I would take it.

"Well…" Acacia looked into the distance while I held my breath. "I suppose we could spend today learning about the necessary compositions. We'll have plenty of time to study the logistics of epidemic management the rest of the week."

I didn't try to hold back my grin. "Thank you, Acacia."

She sighed and stood to her feet. "Just don't make me regret it. Let the other second years know, and any of the University students who wish to join us. We'll meet in an hour in Lecture Room 4."

I watched her leave the room and then turned back to find the others all staring at me.

"Why are you looking at me?"

"You heard her," said Coralie. "She wants you to tell the others."

"Oh no." I held up both hands. "Not a chance. I'm sure you can all imagine how that would go down. Finnian, you can do it. They're more inclined to keep their claws sheathed with you."

Coralie rolled her eyes, but she didn't actually protest. Edmond beside her continued to regard me with interest until his eyes suddenly flicked to my brother. Given he studied with Jasper and Clara, he no doubt knew exactly the sort of dynamic I was referring to.

"Well, go on, Finn," said Saffron. "Let them know so we can get out of here."

Finnian heaved a dramatic sigh but stood to his feet.

"You owe me for this, Elena."

"You wish," I said, as he meandered away.

I watched his progress at the other tables as he stopped to chat with each cluster of people. But mostly I tried not to look at Lucas. It had been three days now since our last disastrous training session, and we hadn't exchanged a single word.

What would he think of what I had done? Would he disapprove of important mages expending their energy to heal common folk? Did he see this whole trip as wasted time from his quest to weaponize my ability and defeat Kallorway?

I had challenged him in our last conversation. Told him people were dying and asked what his family was doing about it. Well people were dying here, too, so now was his chance to show me his true colors.

I studied his face as Finnian spoke to him and the group around him. As usual, it gave little away. His eyes flicked to me, and I looked quickly back at my food, fighting a flush at being caught staring. But when I risked another peek, he had focused back on Finnian.

"What?" Natalya's screech came clearly across the room, although I hadn't been able to hear Finnian's words. "They want us to drain ourselves on endless healing compositions? The same ones over and over?"

Finnian's own voice carried more loudly this time, although it held none of her heat. "Well, repetition is a time-honored method of learning. I'm sure next time you get a back ache, you'll appreciate the expertise."

"I'm not seventy, Finnian. I don't get back aches." She glared at him.

He just shrugged. "Then you must be in a different combat class from me."

She flushed and looked away, scanning her friends for signs of support.

Her twin, Calix, gave an exaggerated sigh. "It seems half the Academy is going soft. But I, for one, am not going to fail second year over a few compositions for fever."

"Indeed." Lucas sounded bored. "And I can't imagine myself *drained* by three minor compositions."

Natalya flushed again, pushing to her feet. She directed her glare at Finnian. "Fine. We'll be there. But only because we don't want to fail."

She dragged Lavinia to her feet, and the two of them hurried from the room, heads close as they whispered furiously.

Calix stretched slowly to his feet and yawned.

"I guess I'll be seeing you in lessons." He nodded at Weston, Lucas, and Finnian, and then strolled after his sister.

Weston rolled his eyes. "I can't see the value in bringing us out here just to lock us in a room to study composition. Surely we could have done that back in Corrin."

When neither of the others said anything, he shrugged. "I suppose I can extend my stamina as well here as anywhere else." And he, too, left the room.

"It's truly touching to see how much they all care," I muttered.

"You were expecting something else?" Jasper gave me a warning look, his eyes reminding me who it was we were dealing with.

I sighed. He was right, of course, but that didn't stop the sting. And it was different for him. Despite his studies, he could still regard them as other. Still disdain them as we had always done.

But I had become one of them. Of sorts. And I couldn't help wanting them to be different—better. To be a group that I could be proud to be a part of.

As the rest of the room trickled out, I moved slowly, my earlier pleasure somewhat soured.

"An interesting idea, Elena."

I froze, giving myself a moment before twisting to face Lucas. I glanced at Finnian's retreating back as I did so, but Lucas shook his head.

"Finnian didn't have to mention your name for me to know where this idea came from."

I raised my chin defiantly. "If you ask me, every mage in the kingdom should already have been asked to do it. It's not like they would need to be here personally." I pursed my lips. "They don't have my limitations."

Lucas regarded me with narrowed eyes. "Yes, you won't be able to do much good with this plan."

"Wow, thank you for that."

He sighed. "I just meant don't do anything stupid."

I couldn't help a slight smile at that. "It never occurs to me it might be stupid until afterward, I'm afraid."

"Yes, that's what I'm afraid of."

Silence fell as I realized we were the last two in the room.

"It is an interesting idea, though," he said. "You might even be right about getting other mages involved. But…"

I gave him a long moment before prompting him. "But?"

He ran a hand through his hair, the locks somehow falling back into their ordered perfection.

"That's not how we work. Not how we're used to working."

"You mean mages aren't used to being expected to expend their precious energy unless it benefits them somehow."

He grimaced. "That's one way of looking at it."

I put my hands on my hips. "And what's another way?"

His eyes grew distant. "You've only experienced the Academy, where mages are prepared not only for life but also for the front lines. We learn broadly across disciplines, so that new mages will have at least a basic understanding of everything they may need for the future. But after the Academy, we become locked into disciplines. A wind worker may know how to fix their own child's fever or relieve the ache in their back after a day on their feet, but they would no more be expected to provide a healing composition for the healers, than a healer would be expected to assist in dissipating a hurricane or bringing rain to a drought-stricken region. It's not how we do things."

"So change how you do things, then. This is an extraordinary situation, it's not like you're asking them to take a shift at a healing clinic."

He sighed. "It's not that simple."

I shook my head. "What's the point of having a king if he can't change things? Surely you of all people can bring change."

"It's just not that simple."

This time I was the one to sigh. "No, I don't suppose it is. Not when you've let yourselves go for generations, becoming more and more ingrained in your insular and self-focused attitude. The real wonder is that there's anyone like Coralie and Finnian and Acacia left."

Lucas raised an eyebrow. "Don't hold back, Elena. Tell me how you really feel about us."

One side of my mouth quirked up despite myself. "Haven't you noticed? Holding back isn't exactly a strength of mine."

He regarded me for a long moment.

"You can try to change the world, Elena. I'll wish you luck, even. Just don't be stupid about it."

"No promises," I said before striding out of the room.

I struggled to focus on Acacia's instruction, still fuming over Lucas's attitude. He might be better than Natalya and her lot, but it wasn't enough. He had the power to bring change, and not opposing it wasn't the same as supporting it.

It took the whole day, but by the time we broke for the evening meal, everyone had managed to produce one composition to heal fever, one to heal aches and pains, and one to prevent nausea and vomiting. Everyone except me, of course.

Acacia checked them all thoroughly to ensure they were of a sufficient level to heal the first stage of green fever, and then collected them into her colored pouches. As she left the room, following the majority of the students who had rushed toward the dining room, she paused beside me.

"These are thanks to you, Elena. Don't think you're not contributing."

I smiled at her, grateful for the thought, but it didn't take away the sting. I had listened and memorized the relevant words, but I hadn't even been able to practice. It galled me to see my exhausted year mates so eager for their food, while I sat here full of energy with no way to usefully expend it.

The next morning Acacia announced we would compose for the morning only. After lunch we would be venturing out into the city.

"Remain aware of your energy levels, and don't push yourself too hard. I don't want you out in the city if you're run down and depleted. If that means only producing one composition, so be it."

I sat back and watched my year mates. Edmond easily completed the three compositions, as did Dariela and Lucas. Weston and Calix both completed two before exchanging a look and sitting back. I suspected they lacked the will rather than the capacity to go on.

Natalya and Lavinia both completed only one, along with Araminta. But Clarence and Saffron each managed two, and in their case it seemed to be a legitimate reflection of their capacity.

Coralie and Finnian both completed the three, Coralie casting a defiant look at Acacia's back. Sudden fear gripped me, and I resolved to watch both of them closely for the least sign of infection. This had all been my idea, and I didn't want to see either of them come down with green fever because they had pushed themselves too hard during the morning.

As soon as the midday meal was completed, Acacia gathered us all together.

"This afternoon we will tour some of the facilities provided by the crown for combating the epidemic. Later in the week, you will all have the opportunity to observe Beatrice and Reese as they research the mutation of the fever and experiment with ways to identify those most at risk."

Her eyes strayed toward me. "It's important work, so I hope you all know better than to disturb them in any way."

I bit my lip, my brow creasing. She should know me better than that. I could contribute nothing to Beatrice's work and would never consider interfering.

Before we left, she handed us each a small roll of parchment and instructed us to rip it. I scanned the words before doing so. A composition to ward off insect bites. I rocked backward.

This epidemic could be stopped in its tracks if these could be distributed to everyone.

"How long does it last?" I asked Acacia.

"Depends on the strength put into it during the composing. These will last a couple of days. We'll refresh them as needed."

She gave the still whole parchment in my hand a significant look, and I ripped it with a feeling of disappointment. The mages had neither the existing stores nor sufficient strength to heal those who had come down with the fever. At least not strength they were willing to expend. They would certainly not have enough to protect everyone who had yet to be infected from bites. Especially not when it needed such regular refreshing.

Although apparently they have plenty to keep us in a constant supply. I pushed the thought aside. Some things I could do nothing about.

Outside the wind felt cool against my exposed skin but, like further north, it didn't seem nearly cold enough to be approaching Midwinter. Now that I knew the part the unseasonable weather had played in the epidemic, I could no longer enjoy the unexpected reprieve. Would it turn soon? And, if it did, would it bring an end to this outbreak?

We walked this time, through nearly empty streets. Now that I was paying attention, I saw thin material over every open doorway or window, and everyone I saw seemed wrapped up far too well for the weather. Attempts to keep away the insects, I realized.

No one we saw talked to us, although everyone stepped aside to let us pass. I saw several sour looks. We didn't need our robes to mark us apart when we had made no effort to cover our exposed skin. We strolled through their streets—too powerful even to fear an epidemic.

Acacia took us first to a large white tent that held no taint of sickness. Supplies stood in ordered piles, and a small queue of locals waited in front of a large desk to have their names marked in a book and supplies allocated to them.

The majority of it seemed to be food, although I also saw stacks of thin material of the type covering all the building openings.

Two black-robed mages sat behind the desk, processing the applicants with bored expressions. Their robes—the same color as those worn by our instructors at the Academy—were a flash of familiarity in an unfamiliar place. But of course they were University academics rather than Academy instructors. I recognized neither of their faces.

The tail end of an altercation seemed to be under way, but the local man stormed from the tent before I could grasp the issue of contention. The mage who had been talking with him left the table to approach us.

"Common folk," he said. "Always so demanding."

I stared at him, and my mouth opened without my quite knowing what I meant to say. But someone bumped against me, sending me stumbling a step to the side, and the moment passed.

I glared at Jasper, but he looked unrepentant as he stepped away from me. My mood didn't improve when I caught a look of amusement on Lucas's face as he watched my brother and me. I turned back to Acacia and tried to put them both out of my mind.

She introduced the black-robed mage who turned out to have been sent down from the main university campus a couple of weeks earlier. From his comments he was expected to serve only a limited stint before being relieved—an event he was looking forward to with great anticipation. His companion, however, was from the local campus. He acknowledged us with a nod but didn't get up, continuing to process the queue which had grown a little longer now that the second mage had abandoned the task.

I tried to ignore the disgruntled looks and unhappy body language from those waiting as the mage made no move to return to the desk. Instead he took us on a tour of the large tent, explaining how they sourced and organized their supplies, and how they were allocated.

Twice I caught Lucas's eyes on me, and for once I had no trouble reading his expression. *Look,* it said, *see how the crown is providing for its people in a crisis. See how the mages are the ones dispersing the largesse.*

And I had to acknowledge that the supplies had come from the crown. But I also saw that while the two keeping records were, by necessity, mages, the other helpers in the tent were all commonborn. The ones sorting the newly arrived crates of supplies, the ones handing out the various items once the mages had allocated them, and the ones who now moved up and down the increasingly restless line with quiet words of calm.

And it could not be more clear that one at least of the mages working in this tent would rather be almost anywhere else. An unfortunate cost of a University position, as he called it.

By the time we had completed the tour, and the mage guide had answered the questions put forward mainly by Edmond and Clarence, I couldn't wait to get back out into the open air. But when Acacia turned us back toward the campus building, something in me rebelled.

We still hadn't even seen a sick person, and I couldn't bear to overflow with energy that could do so much good somewhere else. What good was being a mage if I couldn't use my powers?

I let my friends pull ahead of me, drifting toward the back of the group until we passed a narrow side road. I could see that it led into a small square, now filled with a white tent. With a quick glance at the group—now all ahead of me—I slipped away and down the road.

CHAPTER 12

*I*t was only a small square, so the white tent filled it almost completely. I edged around it, looking for the opening, which turned out to be on the opposite side. Two large flaps had been secured open, and no one seemed to be monitoring new arrivals, so I walked straight in.

The inside of the tent smelled like sweat and blood and vomit, and I gagged. Pausing, I forced myself to take a deep breath in an attempt to acclimatize to it. A breeze blew past my face, bringing fresh air, and I took an even deeper breath.

My eye caught on a single blue robe. A tired looking young mage—a wind worker from her colors—sat in a corner of the tent, her gaze on a small opening in the canvas near her feet. The breeze which had just sprung up flowed past me and through the gap back into the square. Not a natural wind, then.

I surveyed the rest of the tent. It had been divided into two sections, and a moment's observation showed the distinction between them. Just the noises were enough. In the front section, first stage patients lay mostly quietly, although some tossed and turned restlessly, and the occasional retching could be heard.

From the back section, however, a chorus of groans and cries mingled with a much more constant sound of vomiting.

Gratefully—and a little guiltily—I turned away from the opening that led to that section. I could do nothing for those poor people. A single purple-robed healer mage walked up and down through each section. Both of them wore leather satchels strapped tightly across their torsos—closely guarding the valuable compositions.

The other people who walked between the long rows of stretcher beds wore the purple-hued uniforms of commonborn nurses, who assisted healer mages with all the practical tasks associated with healing. Without exception, they looked harried and exhausted.

I briefly considered approaching one of them, or even the mage who was occupied on the far side of the tent. But I quickly rejected the idea. Explaining how I could help would involve explaining who I was—and I could only imagine the questions and confusion such an explanation would provoke.

Some of the patients watched me with curious expressions, but my robe kept me from any questions, and the lack of purple kept me from requests for assistance. I walked along the lines of beds, watching the faces, suddenly gripped by indecision.

I wanted to help them, but there were far more here than even my strength could stretch to. And now that I was faced with the people themselves, I didn't know how to proceed. If I could only heal some, how did I choose between them?

An anguished wail pierced the close atmosphere of the tent. Many heads turned toward it, but even more turned away, their expressions closed and eyes hooded. How many times had they heard similar cries?

But I was new here and could not ignore it.

Steeling myself, I stepped through into the back section. The wailing woman had broken down into sobs, still easily identifiable among the rows of beds. She wasn't lying in one of them, however. Instead she bent over a stretcher that looked tragically large for the small child lying on it.

As I approached, the young girl spasmed, her eyes glassy and unseeing, and vomited. A nurse moved quickly, wiping it away, but not before I saw the red. The woman clutched at the child, but when the nurse firmly moved her aside so she could continue attending the girl, the mother leaped to her feet. Running between the beds, she threw herself at the mage, clutching desperately at one of her arms.

The healer spoke to her in quiet, firm tones, attempting to detach her. I couldn't hear the words, but I could see the repeated shakes of her head. And when she glanced toward the girl, the weight of exhaustion and grief in her eyes told the story clearly enough.

"But the blood has only just started." The mother's voice rose into a screech. "Surely it's not too late. It can't be too late!"

I reached the girl and the nurse still attending her.

"Is it true?" I asked quietly. "Has she only just started with the blood and…"

The nurse looked up, her brow creasing briefly as she took in my white robe. But she didn't question my presence, the previous weary expression taking hold again.

"Yes. We had hoped she might be one of the lucky ones." She wiped the girl's forehead with a soft hand. "They try to prioritize healing the little ones, but her mother didn't bring her in until it was too late. She'd already hit the second stage."

"Why would—"

The woman shrugged. "Some don't trust us when we say it's not spread person-to-person. They think they'll be better off and safer in their homes. Others can't accept the truth that they or their loved one are ill. They close their eyes to the symptoms and don't believe they have it until they hit the second stage. And they don't realize it's too late by then."

"Oh, how sad." I looked down at the girl, tears stinging my

eyes.

"We try to spread the word, educate people as much as we can." The nurse shook her head. "But we already have our hands full here, and we can't reach everyone. The irony is that it would be different if it *was* spread person-to-person. Then they wouldn't have a choice. We'd have quarantines and door-to-door house checks. Anyone with symptoms would be dragged in whether they wanted to come or not."

The girl cried feebly, calling for her mother, but the woman was too far away to hear, still pleading with the healer. I swallowed.

"If it's only just started...the blood, I mean...if it's only just started, perhaps her organs are still undamaged. Or not too damaged at any rate. Perhaps it's not too late?"

The nurse shook her head. "It doesn't matter. The damage will be done soon enough. And we don't have the spare power it would take to burn her system clear at this point." Her eyes moved tellingly to the single mage who oversaw the whole section.

Determination gripped me. There was power enough here, I was sure of it. Inside me.

The girl had stilled, and someone on another stretcher had started calling feebly for the nurse.

"You go," I said. "I'll stay with her."

The nurse was already moving, nodding her thanks as she left. I sat on the stretcher and took a deep breath. Beatrice had said they didn't heal patients in the second stage because only a very great expenditure of power, broadly applied, could save them at that point. Not even the healers had the necessary knowledge to apply finesse to such a healing.

But brute strength was exactly what I possessed.

I could hear Thornton screaming at me in my head, but I pushed him away. I could do this. I knew I could. And some things were worth the risk.

Gathering the girl into my lap, I leaned down and whispered quietly. First the binding words, and then a general direction to heal the girl.

"End binding." I felt the rush of power streaming from me toward the small figure in my arms. It settled over her as a mist, and she twisted slightly, mewing like a kitten.

As I watched, breathless, her expression cleared, and her color dropped sharply from her fevered flush as she briefly turned pale and then returned to a normal, healthy color. Her shivers and shakes ceased, and she stilled in my arms.

Still I felt the power streaming out, sinking into every part of her. Now I was truly struggling to draw breath, my head spinning with more than anxiety for the girl. Still the power drew from me. I needed to cut it off. But if I did, if some part of her remained unhealed, it might all be for nothing. I could hold on a little longer.

The black closed in further.

And then abruptly it was over. The power cut off, and the girl opened her eyes and looked up at me.

"Who are you? I'm hungry."

I managed a wobbly smile as my vision slowly cleared, and my head settled.

"I'm Elena. Are you feeling better?"

She nodded. "Was I sick? Where's..." She trailed off as she looked around, presumably for her mother.

The woman, still latched onto the mage, looked up and gave another loud cry. Rushing over, she scooped the girl out of my arms. The healer trailed behind her, eyes fixed on me.

I stood and tried to look and sound far more confident than I felt. But I swayed slightly, not helping my effort.

"She's better now. I healed her," I said.

"*You* healed her?" The healer looked me up and down. "But you're a trainee. What are you even doing here? You shouldn't be here. Where are your instructors? And where did you get the compositions? That would have taken a lot of power."

"I did it myself."

"Yourself? Impossible. Now look here, this isn't a time for games—"

She broke off abruptly, her eyes flying to something over my shoulder. I whirled around too quickly and nearly fell as the light-headedness returned.

A strong hand steadied me, sending warmth pouring through my body. My head cleared.

"Your...Your Highness." The healer looked rapidly between Lucas and me. "I don't understand. This girl says—"

"This girl is the Spoken Mage, and if she said she healed that child, then no doubt she did." His commanding tone assumed her belief and left no room for questions. "But we need to be returning to the University."

"Of...of course." The healer dipped into a shallow curtsy, reminding me that only at the Academy was Lucas treated with informality.

The prince nodded to the woman and to the astonished nurse who had rushed back over at all the commotion. Then he tightened his grip on my elbow and hauled me out of the tent. I stumbled behind him, nearly tripping several times until we reached the outdoors and his pace slowed.

I pulled back against him, both of us coming to a stop.

"What are you—"

"What am *I* doing?" His voice thundered, although the volume was low. I had never heard him angry like this. "What are *you* doing, Elena? What were you thinking healing that girl? She was in the second stage. And you shouldn't have been in there at all. You are too valuable to risk yourself. When will you get that into your head?"

"How could I not?" I snapped back. "How could I come here to Abalene and do nothing? At least the rest of you can help from afar, but I can't. It's not as if this disease is spread person-to-person. I got the protection against insects just like the rest of you."

"Have you looked at yourself?" His voice was icy now.

"What do you mean?" I looked down at my once-white robe. "Oh."

Somehow I had gotten a dark smear of blood all across my front. From the girl, I supposed.

"It might not be spread easily person-to-person, but it is spread via blood. Thus the insects. There's a legitimate risk for those nursing second-stage patients."

"Don't be ridiculous. It's only on my robe. I don't have any open cuts. I'll be fine."

He narrowed his eyes. "You'd better hope so."

And then he let go of my arm only to pull off my robe. With two quick strides, he approached a barrel which sat just outside the entrance to the tent, a small fire inside sending up a steady stream of smoke. He stuffed my robe inside, the fire disappearing for a moment and then sprouting up higher than ever.

"Hey!"

He glared at me. "Really? You still wanted that?"

I glared straight back. "I want to be consulted and treated like an equal. But that's always been too much to ask from you, hasn't it?!"

He looked at me with confusion, as if he couldn't even process my words. "Like an equal?"

I snorted, shook my head, and took off toward the campus building. Lucas followed closely but didn't try to grab me again, or even to walk beside me—trailing a few steps behind instead.

When we arrived, I headed straight for my room, exhausted but not wanting Lucas to see it. I collapsed straight into my bed, but I wasn't able to stay there long. An insistent knocking on my door soon drove me up again.

"Lucas, I don't—" I flung the door open and choked off the

words.

Standing on the other side was Acacia, not Lucas. And she looked furious. She stalked into my room, carefully closing the door behind her before turning back to me.

"What exactly did you think you were doing?"

I opened my mouth, but she didn't leave me time to answer.

"That was foolish beyond permission. You could have caught the fever. You still might. And you're fortunate you've lived long enough to even worry about that. You might have collapsed right there. And then what would have happened? With no one knowing who you were and what you'd just done."

She stopped for a shuddering, anger-fueled breath, and this time I didn't even try to speak. I had never seen her like this.

"Whatever you were thinking, it was inexcusable. You have all been entrusted to my protection, and I will not have trainees going rogue." She fixed me with a hard stare. "If you do anything like that again—if you leave the group at all—I will put you straight into a carriage and send you back to Corrin. Do you understand?"

I nodded.

"Do you understand, Elena?"

"Yes. I'm sorry, Acacia. I guess I wasn't thinking..."

"No. You weren't." She snapped the words, and I winced.

"I just wanted to help."

The anger drained out of her, and she sighed. "I know you do, Elena. But please believe me when I say that the most helpful thing you can do is stay alive. And out of trouble. For now, at least. There will be time for everything else later."

"Will there?" I muttered, but too low for her to hear. I glanced up at her. "I can't believe Lucas told you, though."

"Lucas?" She frowned at me. "What does Lucas have to do with this? Don't tell me he was there too?" She held up a hand. "No, seriously, don't tell me. You I can deal with—the prince, on the other hand..."

"But then how did you know?"

"You're a trainee, Elena. And you just did something that healer thought impossible. She sent a messenger to me asking for answers as soon as you were gone."

"Oh."

"Lorcan is not going to be pleased," Acacia muttered before shaking her head and turning for the door.

She paused in the doorway. "I like you, Elena. I really do. For reasons I can't always fathom given you cause me more work than any other trainee. But don't think I'm not serious. You put another toe out of line, and I'll send you back."

"I won't. Honestly, Acacia. I'll be good, I promise."

Acacia laughed, the sound low and strained. "Good? It's not really about *goodness*, is it?" And then she was gone.

Somehow my friends had caught wind of what happened, and they demanded a full account of my escapade. Coralie seemed torn between approval and disapproval while Finnian, although impressed with my act of rebellion, shook his head over the risk I'd taken with the open composition. Edmond seemed mostly fascinated by the account of my ability in action.

Jasper, on the other hand, wasn't in the least torn in his response. He was as livid as Acacia and stopped speaking to me for a week. Since he combined this treatment with regularly pressing his hand against my forehead to check for a temperature, I had to use every scrap of my mostly non-existent patience to put up with it. I figured I deserved it, though, for scaring him so badly.

Jasper made two people who weren't speaking to me. But in Lucas's case, it was a relief. He might not have been the one to sell me out to Acacia, but that didn't mean I needed any more anger or condescension directed toward me right now.

The days passed, and I tried to suppress my chafing in each morning session when the others all spent time and energy crafting healing compositions. It was valuable work, whether or not I could participate. And Finnian and I had been right about its value as an exercise in stamina. Weston and Calix had stopped pretending they could manage only two of the compositions per morning—not wanting to appear weak, no doubt—and even Araminta had managed to increase her production levels.

The afternoons we all spent observing Beatrice, visiting the tents, or completing assignments on healing theory and epidemic management in the campus library. When we made our official visits to the healing tents—some of them far larger than the one I had stumbled on—Acacia stuck to my side like glue, glaring at me if I so much as opened my mouth.

So I had to content myself with sending dirty looks at Finnian who was clearly amused by my situation. But even he always left these visits with a depressed air, and I noticed that while Natalya and Lavinia looked disgusted at being there, they refrained from any offensive comments—to me or anyone else.

Unlike the University mage in the supply tent, the healers I saw looked universally strained, exhausted, and grieved. How could they not be when they spent each day in such an environment, knowing their resources were far too few to do what needed to be done? My admiration for the healing discipline grew, and I couldn't help mourning the impossible dream that I might one day join them. Even if they did leave all the least desirable tasks to the commonborn nurses, at least they seemed to care.

Midwinter approached. I received a beautiful invitation to a Midwinter celebration at Coralie's home and was glad to see my friend brighten a little at the prospect of hosting. She did apologize to me, though, once the invitations had gone out.

"My parents were so excited to invite the prince to our home, that I couldn't say no. But since he's not exactly a particular friend of ours, inviting him meant inviting the whole year." She grimaced before perking up. "I invited the University students, too, of course, so at least we should outnumber them."

I assured her I was excited to visit her home regardless of the company and even assured her I would let her pick a dress for me to borrow. I half expected all the trainees except our friends to decline the invitation, but she told me the next day that Lucas had already accepted. And the others soon followed.

We were to have two days off over Midwinter, as we had the year before, so I was pleased to have an activity to fill the otherwise empty days. But I still wished there was something useful I could do to actually help.

On the last day before Midwinter, we visited the largest of the healing tents. And for the first time, I actually saw empty beds. Not many, but the sight still caught my eye.

"Do you think we're past the worst of it, then?" I asked the healer in charge of the tent, in defiance of Acacia's narrowed eyes at the sound of my voice.

"Our forecasters think we should hit the peak of the epidemic soon," she said. "So we're nearly there but not quite."

"But the empty beds?"

She actually smiled, a sight I wasn't used to inside these tents. "With so many new compositions coming in, we've managed to increase our rate of first stage healings."

When I gave her a blank look, she shook her head.

"I suppose you all didn't hear about the request since you were already here helping."

"Request?" I glanced at Acacia, but she remained silent.

"The crown sent out an official request to all non-healing mages in the kingdom. Everyone with the capacity and inclination was requested to start producing compositions to heal fever, muscle aches, and nausea. Just one per day, or whatever they feel comfortable doing. Many have ignored the request, of course, since their energy is valuable, but some have responded. Enough to make a difference." She smiled again. "Fast messengers are traveling throughout the kingdom on regular routes to collect them and bring them here."

"That's…that's excellent."

She nodded. "It's wonderful seeing the disciplines supporting one another in such a way."

My brow twitched, but I kept my expression neutral. Of course she saw it as mages supporting mages and not as support for the commonborn victims. And she was most likely right. But it didn't matter why they were doing it, the important thing was that they were.

A raised voice called to her from the other side of the tent, and she disappeared off down the rows of stretchers.

"It came from your idea, Elena," said Acacia quietly. "With the trainees."

"Thank you for passing it on." I beamed at her. "And I don't in the least mind if you took the credit. In fact, I hope you did. It was more likely to win support that way."

She shook her head, looking a little guilty. "It wasn't me. To be honest, the thought didn't occur to me, although I can't imagine I would have had the sway anyway."

My eyes crossed to Finnian. Had he written to his father?

Acacia followed my gaze, but must have misinterpreted the target of it since Finnian stood talking to Lucas and Calix.

"Yes, it was the prince. He wrote to his father, apparently."

As if he could hear us, although the distance made that impossible, Lucas looked up just at that moment and met my gaze. For what felt like the longest moment, we remained like that, eyes locked. Then Finnian spoke, and Lucas looked away.

I tried to settle my thoughts, but they churned with too much confusion. Lucas had actually liked my idea? Had acted on it? He was the cause of these empty beds?

I shook my head. Would I ever work him out?

CHAPTER 13

*L*ucas still didn't approach me, and in the midst of Midwinter preparations, I had no opportunity to approach him. Coralie had invited me to spend the night before and after Midwinter at her house, and I had eagerly accepted.

Their house turned out to be a large and comfortable building on the outskirts of town with a generous garden and high fence surrounding it. While it was neither as large nor as lavishly appointed as the mansions of the great families in Corrin, it was still far larger than any home in Kingslee, and larger than the majority of the ones I had seen in Abalene.

"A branch of the Callinos family live in Abalene, and another of the Ellingtons," Coralie told me. "That's Acacia's branch. They have bigger homes, of course. No doubt they would have seized the opportunity to host a Midwinter celebration themselves with Lucas in town, except they all fled Abalene at the first hint of this new green fever spreading here."

"Which leaves the honor to us," said her mother, with a slight frown at her daughter's chatter. "And we are most pleased to have the opportunity."

I wanted to thank her for staying, as well as for contributing daily compositions, which Coralie had admitted when I asked her. But the thought sounded ridiculous—they weren't doing any of it for me. So instead I made do with thanking them for having me, and complimenting every arrangement they had made for the party.

Midwinter breakfast with Coralie's family was accompanied by an exchange of gifts that embarrassed me since Coralie gave me an elegant evening gown, and I had only a small wooden flower for her. Jasper had helped me carve it, and Coralie assured me that she loved the gift, and that the dress was an old one of hers, so it didn't really count as a proper gift anyway.

We were decorating for the party at that stage, busy converting a large receiving room into a ballroom that would be sufficient for the size of the event, although small compared to the Corrin mansions, let alone the scale of the palace.

"I keep growing, so half my old stuff doesn't fit me anyway," she told me as we hung garlands and arranged flowers. "And it will look better on you than it ever did on me."

Her words did make me feel a little better, and decorating turned out to be more fun than I had anticipated. It helped that there were actually flowers—an unusual thing for Midwinter. The sight of them gave me a pang, given the other results of the unseasonable weather, but I decided not to think about it. The flowers hadn't caused the epidemic and refusing to enjoy their beauty would do nothing to help fix it either.

Many of the trees and plants down south remained green all year round according to Coralie, so the flowers were interspersed with lush green garlands and arrangements.

The Cygnets didn't have their own colors, so Coralie's mother had decided on a red and green theme, with elements of both gold and silver woven in.

"To honor Lucas's presence," Coralie told me, "but without looking like we're pretending we're something we're not."

The reminder that Lucas would be here soon made me dive back into my flower arrangement, effectively hiding my face. Two days ago I would have been irritated and resolved to avoid him, but I didn't know what to think now. At the very least I would have to seek him out to thank him for sending my suggestion to his father. The thought made me exquisitely uncomfortable.

Somehow the day melted away, and Coralie and I were soon dressing for the evening in her large bedchamber. A maid helped us button up our gowns and arrange our hair on top of our heads. Gazing into her long mirror, I hardly recognized myself, I felt so elegant. The sight gave me a boost of confidence—much appreciated considering the ordeal before me.

At first I had thought the very small number of servants at Coralie's house was caused by a reduction in their numbers due to illness. But when I raised it sadly with Coralie, she assured me it wasn't the case.

"You're getting us confused with one of the great families," she had said with a cheerful grin. "We've actually hired three extra servants to help over Midwinter because of the party preparations. Thankfully they were more than happy to take up the positions on minimal wages, because my parents and both my aunts have been working together to supply our servants with protection from insect bites, just like the family members."

Several members of Coralie's extended family shared the home, including her grandparents, a single aunt, and the widow of the eccentric uncle she had once told me about.

Arthur, her younger brother, was clearly ridiculously excited about the upcoming celebration, and equally clearly trying to hide it and act calm. At least the act meant he had refrained from asking me to compose for him.

He still got his wish, however, because I asked Coralie to let me renew the insect protection on the servants and on her family to save her parents' energy for one round of compositions at least. I had been doing my own ever since the first compositions were handed out to the trainees—once Acacia had observed me and reassured herself my working had sufficient power and control, of course. It was the one thing I could actually usefully do.

So since I had plenty of practice, it had occurred to me as a way I could pay back some measure of Coralie's family's hospitality. And when the inhabitants of the house all filtered through the makeshift ballroom Midwinter morning to receive their protection, I noticed Arthur managed to linger for most of the workings.

"Sorry about him," muttered Coralie, but I just shrugged and smiled.

Secretly I rather liked his youthful enthusiasm. He might be several years older than Clemmy, but it reminded me somehow of my younger sister. I imagined she would be just the same in similar circumstances.

No doubt my family would be feeling Jasper's and my absence this Midwinter, but I knew they wouldn't begrudge it if they knew where we were and why. And I hoped that the joy of a winter free from Clemmy's usual run of illness was going a small way toward making up for their quieter holiday. Plus Jasper, at least, should have the chance to visit them after we returned and let them know where we had been.

The maid who helped with our hair was one of the few on their normal staff, and from the way she giggled and commented freely to Coralie, I got the impression there was something almost like friendship between them. Hardly surprising since the girl had apparently worked for Coralie's family since the age of ten and was a similar age to us. I suspected it explained something of why Coralie had been the most open to my presence at the Academy from the beginning.

A handful of other local mage families had been invited, along with the whole contingent visiting from the Academy and

University, so we filled out the available space comfortably. A group of local commonborn musicians had been hired for the evening, along with extra servers. I overheard Arthur talking about how they had all been paid with stacks of compositions to repel insects. I couldn't imagine Coralie's family would be wanting their illustrious guests to know as much, but I certainly wasn't going to tell anyone. It just made me glad I had helped out with everyone at the house that morning.

The dress Coralie had given me was gold, and I had experienced a brief pang of uncertainty when I slipped it on. It fit beautifully, but could I really attend wearing one of the royal colors? But another moment's reflection alleviated my fears. The tight bodice and full skirt were gold, it was true, but the highlights were in green, with creeping tendrils that looked like vines snaking up the sleeves and along the hems. It somehow not only brought out the green in my otherwise hazel eyes, but also made them look as though they sparkled with flashes of gold.

And, in truth, once it was on, I didn't know if I could have brought myself to take it back off. Coralie and the maid were both full of praises, and Coralie herself looked elegant and sophisticated in a wine red gown with accents of silver. She had clearly chosen both dresses to complement the color scheme of the party, and I only hoped none of the trainees said anything to shame her or her family. There was certainly no cause for shame that I could see.

To my relief, it seemed that the rules of hospitality overrode Natalya's usual petty feelings, and I heard nothing but a hint of gracious condescension from her upon her arrival. Perhaps she secretly enjoyed playing the great lady among lesser families when she had no other offer forthcoming.

Lucas I didn't see arrive, but he easily stood out among the crowd. He wore the same formal red uniform that he had worn at the Midwinter celebration at the palace the year before, complete with gold sash, tall black boots, and simple gold circlet. The same celebration that had marked his eighteenth birthday.

He should have looked out of place here, but his air of confidence carried it off. I wasn't sure if it was my imagination, but I thought his face looked more relaxed at this event than he had the previous year—less of his stiff court mask in evidence. I hadn't really thought about it before, but I wondered now if he actually enjoyed his birthday celebrations back at the palace. Was it possible he was truly happier here?

Even as I thought it, my feet carried me in his direction. He looked up and saw me but quickly looked away again, and just before I reached him, he turned to Dariela and asked her to dance. She nodded calm acceptance, and the two of them swept off, leaving me standing awkwardly on my own.

I ducked my head to hide my flush and hurried for the refreshment table where I found Jasper, Clara, and Edmond filling plates for themselves with aplomb. For the first minute, I answered at random, barely hearing their words while I fought the swirl of anger and humiliation. But gradually my insides calmed, and I even stole several delicacies from Jasper's plate.

"Are you all right?" he whispered to me. "You seem a bit…"

I quickly smiled. "I'm fine. Isn't the party beautiful?"

"Gorgeous!" Clara spun around taking in the decorations and the finely dressed guests. "Poor Jasper and I never get invited to things like this back in Corrin."

"Most of them aren't like this," Edmond assured us. "Dreadful, stuffy things, generally. But us youngsters seem to be in the majority this evening, and I sense it's going to be a jolly night." He winked at us and took off, weaving through the crowd. I hoped he was heading for Coralie and planned to ask her to dance. I knew she had dressed with him in mind and was hoping for several dances.

But when I caught sight of them moments later, Coralie was

already dancing with Finnian, and Edmond was bowing to a young lady I didn't recognize.

"Well, I certainly intend to have a jolly time," said Jasper with a twinkle in his eye. "As long as you'll agree to dance with me, of course, Clara."

She flushed and agreed, her response supporting my suspicions about her feelings for my brother. The two of them eagerly excused themselves, and I was once again left standing alone. Only this occasion held no pointed sting of rejection at least.

I selected a small pastry ball from the table and looked around for other friends. Surely they couldn't all be dancing. But the only person I could spot not doing so was Araminta, standing against one wall, watching the musicians.

I wandered over to her out of desperation, thinking she had never been unfriendly, even if we had never really connected, either. And we had been part of the same study group at the end of first year.

She greeted me warmly enough and complimented the room which made me feel even more pleasantly disposed toward her.

"I love music," she said, her eyes straying back to the musicians. "Too bad there isn't a discipline for that."

"You don't have to join a discipline, though, right?"

She shrugged. "My family can't afford for me not to. I just hope I can find one willing to take me." She glanced up at me and then down at her hands which had twisted into her skirts. "My father doesn't come from a rich family, but he was handsome when he was young apparently, and his parents hoped he might marry well. A girl from a great family even, perhaps."

"I'm guessing that didn't work out," I said softly, thinking of her struggles at the Academy.

She shook her head. "He fell in love and married a common girl. His family were horrified and almost disowned him. And they like me even less—I'm exactly what they were afraid of."

"What do you mean?"

"I'm weak. I mean, I'm a mage—I have enough control not to blow things up, and I can compose. But not strong compositions, or complex ones. And it doesn't matter how much I study, I'll never be able to. Not with a commonborn mother."

"You must have a very different sort of family," I murmured, trying to picture such a household. Did they have books? And what had her mother thought when Araminta had been taught to read as a child—a skill she didn't have and would never have?

"We keep to ourselves mainly." Araminta looked out over the dancers. "If I could marry someone strong, I could save things for the next generation, at least. But then, who would want to marry me?"

"Oh, I'm sure..."

She gave me a look, and my words trailed off. In truth it wouldn't surprise me if she was right. The great families, at least, seemed to place great stock in their positions and strength. It was hard to imagine any of them falling for someone like Araminta, let alone actually marrying her.

"Well," I said with a sigh, "no one's going to be exactly falling over themselves to marry me, either."

Araminta shot me a speculative look. "Really? I would have said..." But she let her own voice trail away, not finishing the thought.

After an awkward moment, she swallowed audibly. "I'm sorry, Elena. You probably despise me now."

"Despise you?" I turned to stare at her. "Because you're a weaker mage? Of course not. Why would you think that?"

"Not because I'm weaker," she said, still not looking at me, "but because I have a commonborn mother. I of all people should have been welcoming of you when you arrived at the Academy."

She sighed. "But I was afraid. I worried about passing the classes and about being accepted, and I thought if I aligned myself with you, I would have no hope..." She shook her head.

"But it was foolish of me. I had no hope of being accepted by the great mages in our class anyway."

"I don't despise you," I said. "No one could understand better than me about not fitting in. It can drive you to do things you wouldn't otherwise do."

She finally looked over at me, the warmth of gratitude in her eyes, and my mind swelled with guilt. She might not have reached out to me when I arrived, but I had done little to reach out to her since. She had spent her time at the Academy stuck between Natalya's group and mine, with only the abstracted Clarence for company. Whereas if I had never arrived, I could easily imagine she and Coralie would have spent more time together. I resolved to encourage Araminta to sit with us at meal-times, at least. And Clarence too.

Looking across the room, I happened to catch Coralie's eye just as Edmond led her toward the dance floor. I sent her a silent plea for help, inclining my head slightly toward Araminta. She followed my gesture and whispered something urgently to Edmond. He looked over toward us, too, and then flagged down a passing young man I didn't recognize.

The second man shrugged, grinned, and began weaving through the crowd toward us. A quick glance at Araminta showed her attention had returned to the musicians, much to my relief.

When he stopped in front of us and bowed, she started and looked at him in confusion. When he asked her to dance, her confusion deepened. But after a slight prod from me, she accepted with apparent pleasure, waving at me as they disappeared into the dancers.

I watched them go with a smile. I couldn't do anything about her future prospects, but that didn't mean she should spend the whole party lurking against the wall.

Of course, after another moment's reflection, I realized that I was once again standing alone—and this time it was entirely my own fault. I sighed. No doubt if I stood here long enough, one of my friends would finish their current dance and come and ask me for the next one. But I suddenly didn't feel in much of a dancing mood.

Long windows lined one wall, opening out to the gardens beyond. And with the mild weather, they beckoned appealingly. I would slip out for a short walk and clear my head. Hopefully by the time I returned both my mood and the availability of partners would be more conducive to dancing.

But I had barely started down the closest gravel path when I heard footsteps behind me. Glancing back, I saw who it was and sighed.

CHAPTER 14

"*A*re you following me?"

Lucas fell into step beside me, quirking an eyebrow. "What if I am?"

"Strange behavior for someone who couldn't run away fast enough earlier in the evening."

"You had that look on your face."

"Excuse me?" I turned more fully toward him. "What look?"

"The look that said you had something you wanted to talk about. And I thought it was probably better if you had your say—whatever it might be—without an audience. So here I am."

"Oh." A whisper of shame crept through me.

I had been approaching him to thank him, but that didn't seem to have occurred to him as an option. He might be arrogant at all times, and obnoxious at least some of the time, but he had helped me train back at the Academy, and now he had helped the people of Abalene. Was I really so harsh toward him?

Yes, came the whisper in my mind. *Yes, you are.*

"I wanted to thank you," I said. "That was all. I only just heard about what you did."

"Should I be alarmed?" He smiled down at me. "What did I apparently do?"

"No cause for alarm," I said stiffly. "I just said thank you, didn't I?"

"That's half the alarm." He chuckled, seemingly in a good mood.

"I meant about writing to your father. Getting him to put out a call for more healing compositions. I'm sure it's saved a lot of lives."

"Oh, that." He glanced down at me again. "You weren't supposed to find out about that."

I stared up at him. "Why ever not? Do you *want* me to always think the worst of you?"

He sighed. "That has certainly never been my intention." He paused. "I didn't think you'd be very impressed, to be honest. He only sent out a request, not a command, and not very many have chosen to respond. I didn't think it would do much to improve your impression of us."

I shook my head. "But some responded. And for every mage that did, more people are being saved. It's made a difference. You must have seen the empty beds."

"And all the full ones," he said quietly.

Another silence fell between us as I considered all those who had nothing to celebrate this Midwinter. And here we were dancing and partying. I ran my hands self-consciously down my dress. Had I become one of the people I railed against?

Lucas eyed my gown. "You look lovely tonight, by the way."

I looked up at him in surprise, my thoughts diverted, but I could see nothing but sincerity in his eyes. I flushed and looked away.

"I've been thinking about what you said." His stride didn't falter, but he looked uncomfortable.

My eyes flew back up to him. "Which thing?"

The ghost of a smile flitted across his face. "Yes, there are so many to choose from, aren't there? In this case I mean what you said when I found you at the healing tent. About how you just wanted to be consulted like an equal."

"Oh, right. That." Somehow here, walking through Coralie's garden in the soft light of lanterns strung from the trees, I couldn't call up the same anger I had felt then. Especially not in the face of what he had done since.

"It reminded me again, that you're new to this life," he said. "You're not used to how we operate, to the elaborate game we're all playing."

I kicked some gravel with my slipper, not liking where this was going. Whatever he thought, I was already all too aware of my deficiencies in that arena.

He sighed, looking carefully ahead and not down at me. "In the world I live in, we're not equal, Elena."

I flinched slightly, and this time he did look at me.

"Not because you're commonborn—although that is a factor, of course—but because I'm a prince. I'm the only prince, in fact. Apart from my parents and sister, no one is equal to me."

He came to a stop, and reluctantly I stopped as well, turning to face him.

"People don't expect me to explain myself, Elena. I don't have to consult with them. Not outside the Mage Council, at any rate. No one expects it except you." He shrugged. "You no doubt consider it arrogant and entitled of me—possibly it is—but in all honesty, the thought of consulting you as equal, of explaining my thinking fully, never even occurred to me."

"I...I see." I didn't know quite what else to say. His words made sense, and they made a lot of things clearer. But at the same time he was right. It was arrogant and entitled, and if he wanted me to smile and say it was quite all right for him to act like that, then he was going to be disappointed.

He did look a little disappointed at my flat response, but he pushed on with his explanation.

"That doesn't mean my family is free from considering the opinions of others. Keeping the kingdom on course is a finer balancing act than you probably realize. But we have to maintain the act—the superiority—it's part of how we maintain our authority. And without authority and leadership, everything would soon collapse into chaos. I told you once that my family makes it a priority to understand how each of the members of the Mage Council think. Well, they aren't the only ones. We spend a lot of time learning what everyone else thinks—and influencing their thoughts, where we can. But we don't consult with them. And when we speak, we don't explain ourselves, we just expect our words to be accepted. Even when we do need to convince them, we have to do it without letting them know we think they need convincing."

He laughed uncertainly and ran a hand through his hair. "That got a little convoluted. Did it make any sense? I *was* just saying that I'm not used to having to come straight out and explain myself."

"And yet you just did. For me." I spoke softly.

"Well, you're not just anyone. Are you, Elena?"

For a brief moment—a trick of the lantern light, perhaps—I thought he was leaning toward me, his eyes on my lips. And before I could think, I was swaying toward him.

The sound of laughter made us both jerk, our eyes turning toward the now-distant ballroom.

"Elena, I—"

"We should probably—" I said at the same time before stopping to give him a chance to finish. But he made no attempt to do so.

After a moment, I gestured back down the path, and he fell into step beside me. I wasn't sure what had just happened, but I was glad for the sound that had disturbed us. When a handsome prince looked at you in lantern light and said you were special, it was easy to get carried away. But I already knew I was special.

I was the Spoken Mage, and a great many people seemed to think I—or rather my abilities—had great value for the kingdom.

But that didn't make Lucas and me equals. He had used those exact words at the start of the conversation. Just as his actions had been saying it since the moment we met.

Clearly he had some interest in me—fascination, even. And while he might let highly charged moments like these scramble his brain, he would soon find himself returned to his usual mind-set. I had seen it all too clearly the one time I had let him kiss me. And I didn't intend to make the same mistake again.

Lucas was a prince of Ardann, and I was a commonborn curiosity. Even if my friend did sometimes dress me up and trot me out among fine company.

We didn't speak for most of the way back, but as we neared the ballroom, Lucas's steps slowed.

"I didn't contact my father for you. I did it because it was a good idea, and the right thing to do. The sort of thing we should have thought of for ourselves. But I am glad you approve. And I would like to be friends again."

"Friends?" My step faltered slightly. Had we ever been friends?

He chuckled, and when he looked at me there was a sparkle in his eyes. "Now I'm the one overreaching, I suppose. We haven't exactly ever been friends, have we? But perhaps we could be. Or, friendly, at least."

"Friendly." I rolled the word around my mouth. "I suppose we could give that a try."

"Thank you, Elena," he said, before slipping back inside, leaving me alone in the cool night air.

~

The next day Coralie and I both slept in. By the time we woke, much of the clean up had been done, but we helped with what remained, chatting about the success of the evening as we did so.

Coralie had danced half the night with Edmond, and even slipped out into the garden for a stolen kiss.

"Just like last year at the palace." She sighed dreamily, while I eyed her uneasily. I liked seeing her happy, but I didn't trust Edmond not to break her heart. He didn't seem like someone who took much seriously.

"And I'm not the only one who escaped into the garden." She gave me a significant look. "Don't tell me you got a stolen kiss, too! From Lucas!"

I shook my head sharply, fighting a flush as I remembered the way he had seemed to sway toward me.

"Of course not. Don't be ridiculous."

She giggled. "There wouldn't be anything wrong with it, if you did, you know. He's terribly handsome. And a prince!"

"Exactly!" I snapped. "Coralie, pull yourself together. A prince is not going to be interested in me."

"Why not?" She looked at me stubbornly. "You're one of a kind, Elena. You get to make your own status."

"Tell that to the great families." I gave her a pointed look before turning back to a garland I was unwinding. "And Lucas and I do not get along, anyway. Everyone knows that."

"I know you clash," she said slowly. "But sometimes I've thought…"

I turned toward her with narrowed eyes. "What? What have you thought, Coralie?"

"Nothing!" she said hastily, but I saw her fighting back a grin as she turned back to her own garland.

I sighed. Just what I needed. Rumors circulating about Lucas and me. I could only imagine how Natalya would react to that.

I hadn't spoken to Lucas again at the celebration, beyond wishing him a brief happy birthday after midnight struck. He had smiled and thanked me before moving on to the next person eager to congratulate him on attaining another year.

I was fairly certain I had imagined the special warmth in his eyes when he did so. Reflections from the nearby chandelier, no doubt. And I had no idea how to expect him to act when I returned to the campus building the following evening with Coralie.

But when we passed in the dining room, he smiled, nodded, and murmured a greeting before passing me to sit at his usual table. Weston watched the interchange with narrowed eyes, but no one exclaimed or questioned him when he sat down.

I took my own seat, relaxing a little. Friendly. This wasn't too dramatic a change. I could manage this.

Beatrice sat near me for the first time since the night of our arrival, and I frowned at her. She looked tired and drawn.

"Don't you have a babysitter on purpose to stop you wearing yourself out?" I asked, forgetting for a moment her rank and position. "Did you take a break at all over Midwinter?"

"I have no time for frivolity or celebrations," she said. "People are dying."

My stomach churned, and I pushed away my plate, no longer hungry. She was right, of course, although I had spent a lovely two days relaxing.

Her face softened. "I don't mean you all. You're doing what you can. And so am I."

I frowned. "But burning yourself out won't help anyone. I wish I could help."

I straightened, a sudden thought striking me. "Maybe I can."

Beatrice looked at me curiously, and I appreciated that her first thought wasn't to deny it. I leaned forward, full of eagerness.

"Honestly, without the ability to store compositions, I'm not much use trailing around with my year mates. Not when Acacia doesn't trust me to open my mouth anywhere near a healing tent."

"I heard about that." Beatrice raised an eyebrow, but she looked amused. "I wish I had seen it."

I grinned wryly. "I can follow instructions, I promise. That was a once off."

She raised her eyebrow again, and I grimaced.

"Mostly." I pressed on. "I just mean that if you let me work with you, I'll follow your instructions down to the last detail."

She looked apologetic. "I'm afraid you don't have the training to work with me, Elena. It's nothing personal, I promise."

"I know," I said. "I can't do anything to help you puzzle out the problem. But what I do have is raw strength. I've seen you at work. There's a lot of repetition as you test things with minute variances. I'm sure it's complex to set up and keep track of and analyze, but a lot of the compositions you're composing don't really take that much skill. Not individually. You could write them out on bound, safe parchment, and then I could read them out and add the power in. Then you can save your strength for analyzing the results."

As I spoke, Beatrice's expression had gradually shifted from apologetic, to interested, to almost hopeful.

"I don't want you exhausting yourself, either, Elena. You're only a trainee."

I brushed her words aside with a gesture. "But I'm not a normal trainee, am I? If I was, I wouldn't be stuck being useless all day. Let me help you. Please. I promise I'll let you know once I drain myself each day."

"Well…" She looked down at the table and then back at me. "You'd have to check with Acacia. She might not want you to put your other studies on hold, and we would need her agreement."

I leaped to my feet, my meal forgotten. "Thank you! I'm sure I can convince her. Just leave it to me."

It took me a little effort to track her down, but once I had fully explained my proposition, she put up less protest than I had expected.

"So you'd be under Beatrice's direct supervision the whole time? And you promise not to over-extend yourself?"

I nodded quickly.

"Then I think it's an excellent idea. It will give you the chance to get some real practice which you're not getting at the moment."

I embraced her enthusiastically, but she just chuckled and pushed me away.

"Plus it will get you out of my hair." She winked at me. "How could I say no to that?"

I grinned at her and flew back to the dining room, eager to tell Beatrice of my success.

We started the next day. Reese seemed torn about my inclusion, clearly not wanting to have an inexperienced trainee messing in their systems. But at the same time, his eyes lingered often on Beatrice's gray face. He was concerned for her, and he didn't have the strength to carry all the compositions on his own.

We soon fell into a rhythm. The most complex and delicate compositions were done by Beatrice, the more intermediate ones by Reese, and anything simple and repetitive by me. At first they both watched me like hawks whenever I composed. To check my work, of course, but also, I suspected, at least a little from curiosity.

But they soon grew used to me and began to trust that I could complete the compositions they assigned, reading them word for word and injecting a sufficient amount of power. It was obvious from the first day why Beatrice ended up exhausted. And why she had no doubt ended up exhausted and burned out on the front lines and been sent back to Corrin. She threw herself into her work with single-minded dedication and focus.

And Reese—for all I disliked him—wasn't much better. Once they got going, their work absorbed them fully.

It was a fortunate circumstance for me, since it saved me from constant pesky questions about my energy levels. In fact, it wasn't until the very end of the day that Beatrice looked at me, a crease between her brows.

"Elena. You're still here. Don't tell me we've overworked you on your first day. I could have sworn you promised to say something when—"

"Don't be silly. I'm fine." I smiled and jumped up from my chair, showing her through my energetic actions that I was far from drained.

"Oh." She looked a little taken aback. "Well then. That's excellent." She watched me curiously for another moment before Reese distracted her with a question about one of the records they had made. I could almost see her interest in me fading away as she considered the problem he was presenting.

But when I went to slip from the room, Reese stopped me.

"Thank you," he said, his voice quiet, and his eyes moving significantly to Beatrice.

I followed his gaze, and smiled. She had regained some of her color despite the long day, and she had a spark of energy in her eye that she had lacked at the meal the night before.

"Thank you," I said. "For letting me be helpful. I'll see you tomorrow." He nodded once, and this time I did manage to escape. I almost ran to the meal, my heart lighter than it had been since we arrived.

Finally I had found a way for my powers to be useful.

CHAPTER 15

I helped all the next day. And the next after that. The other trainees and students had been excluded from observing since Beatrice told Acacia she had reached a critical stage of her research and wanted no interruptions. I still couldn't really understand what they were doing, or the process they were using, but there was enough repetition in the compositions they called on me for that I became quite adept at them.

The workings themselves ceased to be a challenge, and I found my mind wandering to Lucas's nighttime lessons back in the arena. While Beatrice and Reese debated some complicated medical question, I considered how I could shorten the compositions I had done for them most often.

And without exactly planning to do so, the next time they called on me for assistance, I did exactly that. It worked—perfectly from what I could tell. But I still expected a reprimand. It never came. In fact, I wasn't sure they had even noticed.

And so for the rest of that day, and all through the next day and the next one, I kept practicing. Finally, on the sixth day, I managed one of the most common ones I had been doing with a single three-word phrase. After so much repetition it was easy to overlay the sense of the full words as I poured my power into the three words I pictured and spoke. The binding words made it longer, of course, but it still felt like a victory.

And for the first time, Beatrice glanced at me. She looked confused, her mind still half elsewhere.

"Did you just…?"

I grinned. "I did the composition you asked for. Is there a problem with it?"

"No. I just…It sounded like you…"

But Reese let out a triumphant cry, and she wheeled around, my composition forgotten.

"It worked! It worked!" he cried. "I think we've got it this time."

Beatrice responded calmly, carefully going over each thing he showed her. When she had finished, she looked at him, looked at me, and then sat down hard.

"Oh, thank goodness," she said, tears flowing silently down her face.

"We'll have to take it to one of the tents. It will take a few days to know for sure," Reese cautioned, although I hardly imagined Beatrice needed the reminder.

She nodded. "Yes, of course. We should leave immediately. Elena, you come with us. You've earned it, and you can probably help, too." For a moment her memory of our earlier conversation seemed to return, and she glanced with narrowed eyes between me and the parchment on the desk in front of me which held the words I had been supposed to say.

I grinned back at her innocently, and she shook her head and began to gather the necessary things.

She didn't tell me to go ask Acacia for permission, and I didn't suggest it. Better to ask for forgiveness later, if necessary. And, anyway, she had given me permission to work under Beatrice's supervision, which was what I was doing.

We started in the smallest of the tents, Beatrice and Reese

tearing the compositions they had just written, one per patient, and flicking the mist toward carefully chosen subjects. When they had ripped all except one, Beatrice glanced over at me.

"As we know, if left untreated, everyone will enter the second phase. But that phase will only be deadly for some. The whole point of this is to identify who will get through the second phase on their own. Those patients can be safely left unhealed, allowing us to focus our resources on those who would otherwise die," she explained to me, although after sitting with her and Reese for days, I didn't really need the explanation. I didn't interrupt, though, and she continued.

"So, these chosen test patients won't be healed unless the working indicates it's necessary. Since we might still be wrong, we want to pick the strongest of the patients. The ones who wouldn't have been chosen for healing anyway, so they have nothing to lose."

She held out the last composition to me and indicated the final patient. I ripped it, my hands trembling with excitement as I did so. If they were right, if this was it, we were so close to beating this epidemic.

It was something of an anti-climax to return calmly back to the campus building, but we had to wait for morning to see the results, they told me. The next day was a rest day, and we were the first three in the dining room for breakfast. Even Beatrice fidgeted slightly, a sight I had never seen before, and Reese could hardly sit still.

We hurried straight out to the healing tent we had visited the afternoon before. No visible change had occurred in any of the patients in relation to the disease itself, but then that hadn't been the purpose of the composition. Instead each patient now had an unnatural spot of color inside one of their wrists.

We moved among our test subjects, eagerly examining each wrist. Seven of them had green dots, three had purple.

"Purple means healing required," Beatrice explained, although

I already knew that too. I appreciated her desire to include me too much to protest her unnecessary explanations.

When she reached for her own ever-present satchel rather than calling for the tent's healer, I put my hand on her wrist to stop her.

"Please. Let me."

She hesitated and then nodded. "Very well."

I spoke the now familiar compositions over them to heal the necessary elements of the first stage infection. Each of the three healed patients—two women and a man—sat up almost immediately, asking for water or food or both.

The healer hurried over. "Oh. You've already done it." She examined each of their wrists and nodded in satisfaction. "How long will the color last?"

"A week, at least," said Reese. "We wanted it to last long enough that those marked green would stay marked through into the second stage. That way we won't be testing people twice."

The healer nodded, and Beatrice handed her an unused testing composition.

"The even more important thing is that we can see the test hasn't harmed any of these people," said Beatrice. "Of course, we won't know for sure if it works until these seven are allowed to run the course of both stages and emerge alive, as our test indicates they will. But I think it's worth testing the rest now. If we wait for the full results, too many of the current patients will already have passed through to the second stage."

The other healer nodded. "Even without complete testing, it seems as good a way as any for picking who should receive the healings. And far better than most. We've been groping in the dark up until now. You'll take copies to the other tents?"

She scanned the parchment she had taken from Beatrice, not waiting for a response. "This seems simple enough. One for each patient. I assume it doesn't require much power?"

"The tiniest dab," Beatrice assured her. "It was one of our

required parameters—otherwise we'd have the same problem we have now."

The healer nodded, already starting to walk toward a small desk someone had squeezed into a distant corner of the tent.

Beatrice hesitated and then crossed to me. She handed me one of the unused parchments. "Here, let me see you compose this. You can read it off here."

I almost asked her if she was sure before changing my mind and turning to the nearest bed.

The healer had been right. It was simple and required only a tiny expenditure of power. My voice would give out long before my power did.

And so it proved. Runners were sent to each of the other healing tents, carrying a copy of the composition and instructions on reproducing them so that the other healers could start manufacturing copies for their own tents immediately.

But even with the other healers working on the task, Beatrice and Reese and I still remained among the tents for the entire day. We visited several different ones, leaving each only once all the patients had received the test composition—either spoken by me or written by one of the healers.

In each tent, the healers were to be found at a desk or other flat surface, furiously scribbling. Beatrice and Reese would join them, while I began to roam up and down the lines of beds. I could move faster than they could, since reading took so much less time than writing, and I soon had a nurse assigned to do nothing but follow me around with a glass of water.

I grew weary from exhaustion—the regular kind—my eyes blurring and my steps slowing. Until at last, I looked for another bed and could find none. A scrap of material had been tied around the wrist of each tested patient, and I could see no more unmarked patients.

"Where's the next one?" I asked Reese.

He shook his head. "There are no more. We've tested them all."

I blinked at him, trying to process his words.

"No more? Are you sure?"

He nodded, something in his eyes that I didn't entirely like. It almost looked, the slightest bit, like awe.

"You've done this whole tent," he said. "The compositions we've been writing will be saved and distributed between the tents for new patients coming in tonight and tomorrow."

"Oh. Well. That's good."

"Yes, it is. It's time for us to get back now."

I nodded and followed him blindly. The evening meal was over by the time we returned, but someone had set plates aside for us.

Acacia came up behind me while I was eating and put a hand on my shoulder. I turned to grimace up at her.

"I'm all right," I said. "Just regular tired, not drained tired."

"I know," she said softly. "I'm a healer, remember. I can tell." She hesitated. "Well done, Elena. Beatrice says you've been a great help. That they couldn't have done it so quickly without you."

I flushed and looked down into my plate. "I had none of the skill or the knowledge required. They're the ones who did it."

She shook her head. "It's true enough. But I don't think you realize, Elena, just how unique you are."

I managed to find the energy to grin at her. "Believe me, that is one thing I do know."

"Do you?" She shook her head. "Well, sleep well, Elena. You can take tomorrow off."

I nodded, but it didn't stop me arriving in the dining room at the same time as Beatrice and Reese the next day. Once again we were the first three there.

Reese opened his mouth when he saw me, but closed it again at a glance from Beatrice.

"You look rejuvenated," she said to me, and I nodded, heaping my plate high.

"I had a very deep sleep." I laughed. "I imagine both of you did as well. It was a long day."

"But productive, I hope," she said, and both Reese and I nodded.

We had eaten and left before anyone else appeared. When we visited the first tent, we discovered the first of our original batch of test subjects had recovered from the first stage and had just entered the second stage.

"No blood in sight," the healer in the tent assured us. "Although it's early days yet."

"Please keep us informed," Beatrice told her.

We had brought a fresh batch of healing compositions, both from my year mates and from a messenger from northern Ardann who had arrived the night before. We used them on those who now had a purple dot, Beatrice even allowing me to compose a handful of the healings.

As we moved from tent to tent, we found some already cleared out of purple-dot patients, while others had barely been touched, depending on their existing supplies and the strength of their healers. We noticed something of a trend, with the more vulnerable—the elderly, the young, the frail—more often coming up purple. But some surprised me. One wiry little girl, horribly tiny in her stretcher, showed up stubbornly green, while the brawny young man beside her showed purple. It took some self-control not to heal the girl anyway, but I knew I needed to trust Beatrice's research.

"She's only just come in," a nurse whispered to me, as I tore myself away from her bed. "She still has time…if the first test cases prove a failure."

I nodded my thanks to her, somewhat relieved as I progressed to check the next patient.

We didn't make it through every purple-marked sufferer that

day, but the vast majority had been healed and sent home by sunset. The others would have to wait for the arrival of more compositions. I had been sorely tempted to heal them all myself, but Beatrice had expressly forbidden me from any more healings for the day, and I didn't want to be locked up in the campus for disobeying. I could tell from the way my head spun that she was right, too. I was reaching my limits.

The nurses had assisted by sorting the patients, so that those with purple dots who would have to wait for healings, had time left in the first stage to do so. And the empty beds of those already gone beamed back at us like a victory.

I just wished those with the ability to survive didn't have to suffer through the remainder of their illness. But there was no other way. How quickly the patients' hopes had changed from wishing to be one of those able to survive, to wishing to be one marked for death, with the surety of first stage healing that now provided.

Acacia greeted us on our return with the firm instruction that we were all three to take a rest day the next day, whether we wished to or no. I spent at least half of it in bed.

When I passed Lucas in the corridor in the afternoon, I nearly looked the other way. But at the last second I remembered, and nodded to him instead. He stopped and gave me a long, level look.

"There are rumors spreading about you. And no doubt they'll grow to include things that can't possibly be true."

I had learned enough to read the warning in his eyes. I was too unique. I had been served best so far by secrets and silence and not drawing attention to myself.

I grimaced but then shrugged. "Unfortunate. But it was worth it. So many lives are going to be saved, Lucas."

He sighed. "Yes. I thought you would say that."

When he didn't say anything else, I resumed my progress

down the hall, but I only made it several steps before he called softly after me.

"Congratulations, Elena. You've done incredible work here."

I paused mid-stride. "Thank you." I continued on without turning. I didn't want him to see the flush of pleasure on my face.

But the next day, when I visited the tents again with Beatrice and Reese, all color drained away. I looked around at the overflowing space, every cot full and some sitting in the aisles.

"I don't understand. I thought we were getting on top of it."

"We are." Beatrice was still smiling. "This was to be expected."

I frowned at her, but a nearby nurse nodded at us both.

"Word's getting out. All those holed up in their houses are coming to be tested. It's a good thing. Because we still can't do anything for them if they don't come in until the second stage."

It was still hard not to be discouraged to see the tents overflowing again, but the mood was soon raised significantly by the piece of news we had been waiting for. All seven of our first batch of test subjects had recovered—or very nearly—from the second stage of the fever. The test had been a success.

I returned to my year mates after that. The work in Abalene was far from over—new cases needed to be tested, purple dots needed to be healed, and green dots needed to be nursed through days of hideous illness. But the test had changed the balance. The healers could now control the infection instead of drowning helplessly. It was easy now to see why Beatrice had been commanded not to use her considerable skill and strength on healings. It had taken a long time, but her efforts had been better spent on the test.

∾

A week after that, Acacia announced our return to Corrin. We had learned all we could from the epidemic, and they no longer needed our help, either. It was time to return to our regular training at the Academy.

Driving back into the Academy courtyard felt both familiar and strange. The sense of homecoming hit me more strongly than I had expected, and yet at the same time there was a strangeness in re-entering ordinary life after being so immersed in the bubble of Abalene and the epidemic. While we had been there, the rest of the kingdom had faded away. Now I suddenly remembered that it had continued to roll on without us.

We arrived in time for the evening meal and said goodbye to the University students before heading straight into the dining hall. I usually had so little interaction with the trainees from other years that I was halfway through my plate of food before it sank in that something felt different.

I looked around at the other three rows of tables, but the numbers seemed about right. I looked at the others at my own table and saw a crease between Finnian's brow, and Saffron's attention focused on something at a fourth year table.

"Is something going on?" I asked. "It feels...different."

We had been away for a while, I knew, but the tense atmosphere definitely hadn't been present when we left. The low buzz of voices sounded different, too, and a sudden raised voice from the far row of tables only confirmed it. The tone sounded angry, although I didn't catch the exact words, and one of the trainees from that row got up and left the room in tears, two more trailing after her.

I glanced down my own row and noticed a significant absence.

"Lucas isn't here," I added. "It looks like he never came in from the carriages."

Finnian stood up. "I'm going to find out what's going on."

He wove between the tables, heading for the fourth year row, and we all twisted in our seats to watch him. A third year hailed him before he reached his destination, however, and he stopped to talk to him. As the third year spoke, Finnian's face hardened and tightened. He looked almost…angry. Far from his usual good humor.

The third year made a final comment, and Finnian's face changed. Was that grief? Coralie, Saffron, and I exchanged worried looks.

Slowly Finnian made his way back to our table. He had reached us, but not sat down, when Calix approached us.

"What's going on, Finnian?" he asked. "Lucas got called away before he even made it into the building. Something's happened, that's for sure."

Everyone at our table—which now included both Araminta and Clarence—had fixed their full attention on Finnian, obviously eager to hear the answer. And from further down the row, the rest of Calix's group watched as well, despite being too far away to catch any words.

Finnian shook his head. "It's not good. Word only reached the capital this afternoon, apparently. Kallorway launched a big offensive at the border, a surprise attack overnight."

Calix fell back a step, more shaken than I had ever seen him. "Don't tell me they managed to push through?"

Finnian shook his head. "Not that, thank goodness. Our troops managed to hold them off. Just. But it came as a total surprise, and several units were taken unawares. We've had losses. Heavy ones."

I bunched my hands into fists, thinking of Torkan and all the ashes ceremonies to come for other families, but Finnian wasn't finished.

"They lost five of the most recent graduates."

Saffron gasped. "Five? In one day?" Her lip trembled, and her voice dropped to a whisper. "Who?"

Finnian listed off five names I didn't recognize, as I belatedly realized he meant Academy graduates. Five young mages had been killed.

Saffron gave a small shriek at the last name on the list and burst into actual tears.

"I'm sorry, Saffron." Finnian sat back down and put his arm around her shoulders. She turned her face into him, hiding her continued tears.

Glancing over at Coralie and me, Finnian's face looked pulled and tight. "A Callinos. A first cousin of Saffron's. They were close as children."

"Oh, Saffron! I'm so sorry." Coralie looked over at me, and I shrugged slightly, equally helpless. There was nothing we could do and nothing we could say to make something like this better.

Calix had already disappeared, taking the news back to his own table, and I soon heard cries of outrage from them as well. Dariela stood up abruptly and strode from the room, although I could see no sign of tears. I wondered if one of the other names had been an Ellington.

I looked around the room again. It was easier to identify the underlying emotions now. Some looked almost numb, eating quietly, while others talked energetically with those beside them. For these people, anger seemed to dominate. I could only imagine they were cursing Kallorway and planning all sorts of counter-attacks and revenge.

And it was no wonder the fourth years looked the most shocked. Not only had they been closest in age to those who had been lost—most of them likely knew each other and had probably been friends—but they also faced joining their number in less than a year.

I shook my head. All I saw was death. Everywhere I looked. First in Abalene, now at the front lines. And while the room full of mages mourned the five of their number who had been lost, I sat in silence and mourned alone for all the nameless common-born who had died beside them.

CHAPTER 16

Speculation about further offensives and counter-offensives gripped the Academy for at least a week. Lucas showed up at breakfast the next morning, but he wasn't answering any questions about the front lines.

At least that was what I heard. I didn't approach him myself. Abalene already seemed far away and distant.

I had half-expected Thornton to put our arena bouts on hold —surely our simulated battles were too close to home for the current rawness of grief. But instead the opposite happened.

Thornton was gripped with an intense focus—although he seemed neither grieved nor angry—doubling our bouts in our first week back. The other year levels were apparently being put through the same thing, rushed through their bouts so that twice as many could be crammed into each day.

And yet, despite that, my name wasn't called. When I commented on it to my friends, a shadow crossed Finnian's face.

"It seems even the instructors have lost interest in harassing you in the face of a real threat. I'm sorry to say that dueling you isn't much practice for anyone, Elena."

"A real threat?" I glanced between him and Coralie. Saffron

trailed several steps behind us, withdrawn as she had been ever since the news. "The Kallorwegians haven't made it past the border, have they?"

"No, it sounds like things have been quiet since the big attack. I don't mean an imminent threat, exactly. More of a reminder, perhaps. Thornton is angry, and he's working twice as hard because of it." He grimaced. "Or rather, we are."

"Angry? Is that him angry? I couldn't tell."

"He takes every loss at the front lines personally," said Finnian.

Every mage loss, you mean, I interjected in my head, but I didn't interrupt aloud.

"He trains us to survive, and for some of the graduates at least, his training wasn't enough. Now he's angry and worried. He's training us harder—doing the only thing he can to try to prevent further deaths."

"There are some situations no amount of training can get you out of," said Coralie quietly.

Finnian grimaced. "Try telling that to Thornton."

"It does seem strange," I said, dropping my voice. "That they were able to keep such a large offensive a secret. Did we really have no warning?"

"None apparently." Finnian eyed me thoughtfully.

"But surely we have warning systems in place. Spies, compositions..." I frowned as I tried to remember what I had so far learned in my armed forces studies. "I'm sure we do."

"Yes, of course," said Finnian. "But so do they. And ways around our detection systems, apparently. General Griffith will be scrambling to get new ones in place, no doubt."

"No doubt," I murmured and let it drop, but I couldn't help wondering. How had they done it?

The ashes ceremonies for the killed mages happened gradually over the space of the following week, and the dining hall looked half-empty for much of that time as trainees attended the ceremonies of those mages they had personally known.

With the ceremonies completed, and as the days passed without any further news of a continued push from Kallorway, life at the Academy slowly drifted back toward normal. I still sometimes passed trainees crying in odd places, and Thornton continued to work the senior students twice as hard, but otherwise classes resumed their usual rhythm.

Since we had spent the time in Abalene focused entirely on our healing studies, the second years were excused for a time from the healing assignments in discipline studies and instead all focused on our second area of study—making up for lost time and missed essays. When we were given an individual choice assignment for armed forces, I chose attack detection methods, and challenged myself to think of ways that Kallorway might have circumvented them.

And while I no longer snuck out to the arena to train with Lucas, I continued to work in the privacy of my room using much simpler compositions. It was a far cry from a true attack situation, but I still made progress, especially after my breakthrough while working with Beatrice.

Since I could safely practice a shield in even a confined space, I focused on perfecting my shielding composition in particular.

By the time spring set in, I could bring it into life with only the binding words and the phrase, "Shield me with limits." And after a great deal of practice, I could overlay a whole variety of limitations to the words "with limits" without having to slow myself down with too much thought. Each one—or any combination—came almost as naturally as any other. It was necessary preparation since speed was my goal.

Soon I could choose to pour most of my power into my shield to allow it to withstand almost any attack, or limit it to a single powerful blast—after which it would collapse—or even give it just enough strength to last through a sustained assault with smaller force. That one was the most fun to practice, since I had to simultaneously compose a hailstorm of rocks to rain down on me while I monitored how long the shield lasted.

And, inevitably, the day came when Thornton once again called on me in the arena. Whether his frenzied need to train the others harder had dimmed somewhat, or whether Lorcan had intervened, I didn't know. But I was ready to test myself in a bout again.

Of course, I wouldn't have chosen Weston as my first partner, but I was hardly surprised at Thornton's choice.

Coralie winced when my name was called, but I gave her an encouraging smile. I hadn't spoken to my friends of my private training—a leftover legacy of secrecy from my training sessions with Lucas—so she didn't know that I actually welcomed this opportunity. Better to practice here against my fellow trainees—however much they disliked me—than to wait to be tested against the Kallorwegians.

Because I hadn't forgotten what spring meant. Soon I would turn eighteen. A day I had long both dreaded and hoped for. Much to my surprise, I had come to like my life at the Academy, and I was in no hurry to see it end. But I also knew that as soon as my mark hit that enlistment roll, Clemmy was free. And every day that passed before then was a day that something could happen to prevent me enlisting.

As I walked down through the seating to the arena floor, my eyes caught on Lucas. He gave me a small nod and even smaller smile, and I felt my back straighten. I might not be able to win this bout, but I would not be utterly crushed as I had been in the past. I was determined.

I faced Weston, my sword gripped in my hand, and my body already tense and alert. He, on the other hand, looked relaxed and confident. My best strategy was to move fast and take him off guard. He was better than me with a sword, but if I attacked strongly enough, it might keep him occupied long enough for me to rush off a composition.

As I looked at his smug face, I decided on a rain of rocks. I had perfected the composition while testing my shield, and I knew none of them were big enough to kill or even do serious damage. I had taken one to the head often enough when my shield gave way—thus giving me the opportunity to practice my healing compositions as well.

I was allowed to use three compositions, so if I kept the shield one in reserve, that would still leave me one more to try to strike a winning blow. Hopefully the rocks would keep him occupied long enough for me to manage the perfect one.

But as soon as Thornton called for a start to the bout, my plan began to go wrong. I lunged rapidly, but Weston easily blocked, his own initial composition somehow appearing in his hand as he did so. I rushed out the words to mine, and the first rock hit him, but he had already ripped his.

I had no time to compose a shield, even with my new finesse, so I was thrown to the side by a large buffet of wind. I had barely regained my footing when a crack gave me just enough warning to throw myself back down as a streak of lightning tore through where I had been standing half a breath before.

From the ground, I saw Weston dodge my rocks. He looked surprised that I had managed to complete a composition at all, but when he took two steps to the side, the rocks didn't follow, continuing to rain down on the spot where he had been standing, uselessly draining my energy.

I mentally kicked myself. In my rush I had failed to modify the parameters of the composition to attach to him rather than remain stationary. It hadn't been an issue in my training.

Smiling again, Weston pulled out a second parchment. I didn't wait to see what this one would unleash, already stumbling over the binding words.

"Shieldmewithlimits.Endbinding," I rushed out, hoping I spoke clearly enough.

As a rush of unknown power surged toward me from Weston, a shield of my own energy sprung up around me. Whatever it had been, the attack bounced harmlessly off, and Weston's eyes widened, his smile dropping away.

I let myself remain on the ground, taking a few moments to breathe and consider my next move. Without knowing what attack was coming, I had put only broad limitations on the shield and, on top of that, my rocks continued to rain uselessly down, another drain of my strength. If I spoke a new composition to stop them, I would have used up my three. I needed to do something—but I needed to do it quickly.

Weston reached for his sleeve but hesitated, raising his sword instead of drawing his final composition. As he stalked toward me, I tried to remember if I had limited my shield to magical attack. Would his sword be able to pass right through? I couldn't be sure.

Scrambling to my feet, I pulled up my own sword. But I couldn't beat him in a straight sword fight, especially not with two constant drains on my energy.

I considered the broad incapacitation composition I had used when under attack before, but I still didn't know what it actually did to the victim, and I suspected using it would bring down Thornton's ire.

I called the binding words in front of my mind's eye and spoke them without thinking, my mind racing to compose the next words in preparation.

As Weston stepped almost within reach, I rushed out the words I had decided on. An untested composition, but at least a more limited one than amorphous incapacitation.

"Bind the legs and arms of my opponent, so that he cannot move, for the span of one minute. End binding."

Weston's sword pierced through my shield, just as I finished the final word. A look of shock twisted his face as he stumbled, his legs and arms freezing, and toppled over to lie flat on the ground. It had worked.

I took a shaky step forward.

"I heard what you said," he snarled, his tongue and throat unbound. "I'll be free in one minute, and you've used up your—"

I pressed my sword tip to his throat, and his words cut off.

"Yield," I said quietly.

He glared at me silently.

I pushed harder, a trickle of blood sprouting from my blade and trailing down his neck.

"Yield," I said, loudly this time.

Still he said nothing, but Thornton called out on his behalf from the stands. "Weston yields."

I immediately pulled my sword away and stepped back. But I kept my eyes on him, in case he was too angry to play by the rules. But although my binding composition had dissipated, he merely stood up, wiping at his throat, and stormed off toward the stands.

With the bout over, I quietly spoke a new composition, ending the useless hail of rocks. My shield had given out on its own since I had thankfully retained the sense to place my stepping out of it as a condition of ending the working.

I looked up at the stands, swaying slightly with exhaustion but still firmly on my feet. All eleven spectators watched me, their expressions varying widely.

When I reached the first level of seating, Thornton met my eyes.

"Your first victory." He paused, and I waited for him to add some sort of congratulations, as he had done on occasion with the other trainees. But instead, he said, "Some lessons for you in there."

My shoulders slumped, and for a moment weariness nearly

overwhelmed me. But then I met Lucas's eyes where he sat just behind our instructor. I straightened again.

"Yes," I said. "And I will certainly be noting them."

Lucas's mouth twitched, as if he were suppressing a smile, and I nodded to him as I climbed the stairs past his seat, hoping he read my thanks for his training in the acknowledgment.

I had done it. I had won. Barely, and with far more expense of energy than should have been necessary, but still—I had done it. I had proven to myself that I could. Now I just needed to get better.

As I sat down among my friends, who all showered me with exclamations, praise, and congratulations, I was already considering Thornton's words.

There had been lessons for me in that bout, and I needed to ponder them. Even Weston himself had pointed out a weakness I hadn't sufficiently considered—unlike with a written composition, my opponents could hear my words if they were close enough. All the more reason to build as much control into as few words as possible.

Already new ideas for training exercises were springing to my mind, and suddenly I couldn't wait to try them. I looked down at the trainees below me in the stands. Let them consider today a warning. One day soon I would be able to beat them all.

CHAPTER 17

I beat Araminta next, and then Clarence. Neither were a big challenge for me now, and I didn't like doing it—especially against Araminta. I kept my compositions as gentle as I could, and I heard Saffron afterward reminding the other girl that I had beaten Weston, so she had no reason to be so downcast.

I winced and turned away, knowing I was the last one she would want to see in that moment. But I had spent far too long at the bottom of the class not to sympathize.

Coralie at least seemed pleased that Thornton was no longer pitting me against only the Devoras and Stantorn trainees, but Finnian seemed less impressed.

"Cowards, the lot of them," he said. "Now that they've seen you can win, they don't want any part of it."

Whatever the truth, I itched to test myself again against a more difficult opponent. Because as the days ticked past, my life at the Academy was drawing all too swiftly to a close. Not mentioning it to my friends was increasingly difficult, but I had long ago decided to tell no one about my plans to enlist. It seemed all too likely that Lorcan would find some way to forbid it—and never mind the price to my family and sister if he did so.

Coralie had discovered the date of my birthday during first year, thanks to an unexpected birthday visit from Jasper, so I knew I wasn't going to be able to avoid her making a fuss over it this year. Not when I was turning eighteen.

And, sure enough, she started making hints at least two weeks out. Of course, when I dutifully inquired after her cryptic comments, she refused to answer. The game amused me more than I thought it would, and I found myself appreciating her enthusiasm more than I had anticipated. Perhaps because I was finding it increasingly difficult to sleep as the big day approached. For far too many commonborn, an eighteenth birthday was something to be dreaded and feared. But no such stigma clouded the day in the minds of the mageborn, and their excitement was hard to ignore.

Coralie herself wouldn't turn eighteen until just after she returned home for the second half of the summer, and she had already begun planning her own celebration. When Jocasta had arrived back at the Academy with the news that the epidemic was officially over and Abalene free of green fever, Coralie had thrown herself into the plans with even more enthusiasm. When she insisted I come for the event, I hedged, not wanting to make a promise I couldn't keep. But she assured me blithely that one way or another she would send a carriage for me.

I woke with a jolt on my birthday, unable for a brief second to remember why the day felt so significant. Then memory came surging back, and I just lay there, trying to take it all in. My original plan had been to leave the Academy on my birthday, not risking even a day more than I needed to. But if I wasn't going to be able to say goodbye to my friends, I at least wanted to leave with good memories. And disappearing before whatever celebration Coralie had planned didn't seem like the actions of a friend.

Honesty also compelled me to admit that I wanted a single

day to celebrate before reality hit me with deadly force. I had started to hope that my training at the Academy might keep me alive on the front lines for the three years of my term, but the five mage deaths at the end of winter had been all too sobering. If fully trained mages with four years at the Academy behind them could die in this war, then it would be all too easy for me to do so. Especially when I had enemies on my own side who might go out of their way to ensure it. Once I left the safety of the Academy, everything changed.

But I had one day left, and I meant to enjoy it.

I entered the dining hall for the morning meal, already mentally practicing my surprised response. But no cake greeted me as it had done the year before. My friends, already seated, greeted me as they normally did, Coralie merely pausing briefly as she spooned porridge into her bowl.

"Oh yes, and Happy Birthday, Elena."

Finnian and Saffron immediately chimed in with their own birthday wishes, and then everyone returned to their meal. I slid into my seat, trying not to feel disappointed. None of them owed me anything.

The day progressed from there as it always did. Thornton didn't call on me in combat, and lunch also held no surprise birthday delicacies. All in all, the day was proving an unexpected disappointment.

Even Jasper failed to appear. After his visit for my seventeenth birthday, I had thought his attendance on my eighteenth guaranteed. After all, he was the only person in Corrin who knew what today really meant for me.

I held out hope all through composition class and then through discipline studies in the library that the cake would appear at the evening meal. And since it was not only my birthday, but my last day at the Academy, I gave myself permission to spend the library study session just browsing through the shelves. In my year and a half as a trainee, I had lost much of my initial wonder at this unimaginable collection of words, but every now and then I liked to take a moment to bask in it again.

All of these shelves, shelf upon shelf upon shelf, all filled with books and even scrolls. All holding words that I could now understand, mysteries there ready for me to explore. I hoped I never entirely lost the wonder of it. I closed my eyes and listened with something other than my ears. Listened for that elusive siren call of the letters. The one I barely felt now that I had discovered how to unlock their power.

But I hoped I never forgot. No matter what happened to me from here, no matter how long I had left to live, I had felt a feeling no one else had ever felt. I had opened my mouth to speak and felt my words bend and shape reality. Felt the rush as power shaped itself to my spoken will.

My eighteenth birthday had always meant the Armed Forces. And now that I had safely made it, gratitude filled me that I had been able to experience this first. How much fuller and stronger I felt now than if I had never left Kingslee.

The evening meal brought no special surprises, although Coralie led my friends in a quiet chorus of happy birthday. I thanked them with tears in my eyes. Somehow the disappointment from earlier had faded away, and instead I could only remember that this was my last meal with them. I hadn't expected on my arrival to make friends at the Academy that it would one day pain me to leave.

I lingered at the table, unwilling for the meal to end. Eventually, however, I was the last one left, my friends having drifted away with murmured good nights. Finally I hauled myself to my feet and slowly left the hall.

The closest barracks of the Armed Forces wouldn't be open now until first light, but I couldn't imagine being able to sleep. My steps dragged as I took in every aspect of this place that would soon no longer be my home.

So distracted was I, that I almost didn't see a shadowy figure waiting for me in the corridor. When he stepped forward, I started, pressing my hand to my heart.

"You scared me. What are you doing lurking in the dark like that?"

Lucas smiled, a half-quirk that was dangerously alluring. "Waiting for you."

"For me? Whatever for?" I frowned at him suspiciously.

"I heard a rumor. That it's your eighteenth birthday today."

"Oh, that. Yes, it is."

"Happy Birthday."

"Thank you."

I waited, but he neither moved nor said anything else. Instead he calmly stood there, his eyes fixed on me, as if he had all the time in the world.

"Was there anything else?" I asked eventually.

"Yes, I want to show you something."

I raised both brows. "Show me something?"

He nodded. "It's just up here." He gestured toward the stairs before leading me in that direction.

I followed behind, uncertain but too curious to refuse. Before I could demand to know what he wanted to show me, he spoke again.

"I don't think I ever congratulated you, by the way. On your wins in the arena."

I flushed, although hopefully the darkness hid it. "Thank you. You can claim some of the credit, you know."

"Can I?" He paused, seeming to find this idea amusing. "Then I will. Although you seem to have improved since we stopped our lessons."

I shrugged. "I practiced in Abalene."

He looked back down at me with a raised eyebrow.

"Oh, not with combat compositions, of course. But just on my finesse. I had lots of chances to practice picturing and speaking the necessary words while maintaining a secondary overlay of meaning."

He nodded, his face approving, and I reminded myself that this was supposed to be our new normal. Friendly. My heart didn't seem to have received the message, however, and was racing far too fast. Would this be the last time I ever saw Lucas?

I tried to think of something significant to say but could think of nothing.

He led me down the corridor, not continuing up to the next floor where his own suite lay as I had half expected. We didn't go far, however, stopping in front of a closed door that I was fairly certain led into an unused classroom.

He turned the door handle and then looked back over his shoulder at me.

"Happy Birthday, Elena."

"You already said that."

His smile sent shivers down my spine. "Did I?"

And then he pulled the door open, placing a hand on the small of my back and propelling me inside.

"Surprise!" yelled a chorus of voices as I blinked in the bright light of many candles.

"Happy eighteenth birthday!" Coralie bounced over and gave me a hug. "Are you surprised?"

I looked around again, still trying to take it all in. Flowers and garlands hung everywhere, and a table to one side held an enormous chocolate cake along with several other small delicacies. Another table held a small pile of presents, and people seemed to be everywhere.

Slowly my eyes picked out each of them. Coralie, of course. Finnian and Saffron. Araminta. Walden, and his assistant librarian, Jocasta—although the latter didn't look much like she wanted to be here. Acacia. And, even more surprisingly, Jasper, Clara, and Edmond. I glanced back at the door again to find it closed now with no sign of Lucas. He hadn't stayed. I shouldn't feel so disappointed.

Jasper strode over to envelop me in an enormous hug, holding me for so long that tears sprung into my eyes. He knew. He understood. When he stepped back, he shook his head at me.

"Tonight is for fun only."

I nodded and smiled back, surreptitiously wiping my eyes.

Clara was next. Then Finnian and Saffron, and even Edmond. The sudden sound of strings filled the room, and a fiddler in the corner nodded and winked at me.

"Coralie!" I shook my head at my friend. "This is outrageous!"

"Well, are you surprised?" She grinned at me. "I've been bursting all day!"

"You did a good job of hiding it."

"I know. Didn't I? I couldn't believe you would think I didn't have anything planned, though. It was a stroke of genius to ask Lucas to bring you here. I knew if I tried anything like that, you would have been onto it in a second."

I shook my head again. "It really is outrageous. But also incredible. And amazing. You're the best friend."

She squeaked and pulled me into another hug before pulling back and winking. "Just wait until you see my eighteenth."

She dashed off suddenly in the direction of the cake, calling an instruction to someone, and my eyes moistened again. I wished I was going to be around to see her party. But then I firmly banished the thought. Jasper had been right. I was able to be here for my birthday party, at least, and tonight was for fun.

We proceeded to dance and eat and talk and dance some more until far too late into the night. At some point, Coralie insisted I open the presents, although I protested the whole time that it was just too much.

I received a fan from Finnian and Saffron, and a bag of my mother's homemade cookies from Jasper. He watched me open them with a twinkle in his eyes, and it warmed me to know he had somehow made it home since Abalene.

Clara and Edmond had gone in together on a beautiful shawl, and Coralie had outdone herself, giving me a small book of fairy stories. I gaped at it for a full minute, stroking its leather bindings. A book. Of my own.

She looked utterly triumphant, so I couldn't refuse, although it seemed too rich a gift.

Only one package remained after that, but it wasn't marked with a name and no one present would own to it. When I opened it and shook out the contents, I gasped. A warm cloak unfolded, made of rich material but in a practical design of deep forest green.

It was far finer than anything I had owned, finer even than the clothes and robes the Academy had provided. Again I pressed everyone, especially Jasper, but they all assured me it had not come from them.

"I wish I had the coin to buy you such a thing," Jasper said wistfully, rubbing his fingers along the hemline.

I could think of one person with plenty of coin to spend, but I quickly squashed the idea. *Friendly* didn't cover such a rich and thoughtful gift, and I couldn't—shouldn't—let myself wish for anything more than the friendly we had agreed on. He hadn't even stayed for my party, after all.

The group broke up after that, Coralie helping me carry my gifts up the stairs to my room. Once we had dumped them all on my bed, I gave her a lingering hug.

"Thank you, Coralie. For everything. I don't know if I would have survived at the Academy without you. You're the very best friend I've ever had."

Coralie smiled, her own eyes misty now. "And you're the best friend I've ever had. What would I do without you? The Academy would be far too boring." She chuckled, and I shook my head. I knew where the true burden of gratitude lay.

When she left, I sat on my bed for a long time, remembering and treasuring each memory from the party. Then I made myself get up and sort my things, carefully selecting what to take and what to leave. My Academy clothes and robes would have to remain, of course. But it was cool enough still overnight and in the mornings that I could wear my new cloak. I hoped they would let me use it on the front lines, where I could only imagine its warmth would be more than welcome in the colder months.

The cookies fit in one of the cloak's inner pockets, and for a long time I held the book, telling myself I could take it too. But I knew I couldn't. I couldn't remove my ability to read just because I was returning to the world of the commonborn, but neither could I justify taking any writing with me. If it didn't bring the Grays down on my head, it might well bring them down on one of the other recruits.

The shawl and fan I also reluctantly left. I would have no use for such items in the Armed Forces.

Finally there was nothing more to be done, or even to pretend to be done. I made myself slip into bed, and surprised myself by waking several hours later. I hadn't thought I would sleep at all.

Dawn was about to break, and I stood at my window for the last time, watching as the Academy grounds and the river beyond slowly lightened from gray, the first fingers of orange appearing.

Then I dressed in my own clothes from Kingslee, wrapped myself in my new cloak, and stole silently from my room.

CHAPTER 18

*W*hen the Academy doors closed softly behind me, it felt more final than anything before had done. I paused for a moment on the top step, looking down at the courtyard and the fountain. How grand and foreign it had all looked the day I arrived.

Dawn still hadn't truly arrived, and everything around me was dim as I made my slow way across the courtyard, my feet dragging.

When I heard the doors behind me open, I jumped and spun around. Lucas almost slammed them closed behind him, running lightly down the stairs toward me.

I stared at him. "What are you doing here?"

He jerked to a halt and stared back at me, his eyes running up and down my new cloak. A slow smile spread across his face.

"It looks good on you."

I froze. "Is…Is this from you?" Had I been right, after all?

He nodded and closed the distance between us. "It was your eighteenth birthday. I wanted to give you something practical."

"Practical?" I shook my head, still trying to gather my

thoughts. "It is, of course. But it's also beautiful. And far too expensive for me."

He shrugged. "I have plenty of coin."

"I suppose you do," I said, my feelings souring somewhat. "And you haven't answered what you're doing here at this hour."

"The real question, is what are *you* doing here."

I raised my chin. "I don't have to account for my movements to you, Lucas."

His eyes narrowed. "I thought you seemed a bit strange last night. What are you planning, Elena?"

I stared back at him, defiantly silent. A sudden thought shook me.

"Did you follow me out here?"

He looked away and shifted slightly. I leaned forward.

"*Lucas.* Did you follow me out here?"

I saw the briefest flash of guilt before his court mask descended.

"So what if I did? You're clearly about to do something stupid. You need to be protected from yourself. You always have."

"Wait a minute. What do you mean I always have?"

His eyes widened slightly, and I realized he had let something slip he hadn't meant to. I pounced on it.

"Last year. There was that day I visited Jasper at the University. And the day I went exploring in the city. Both times you were there."

"And a good thing, too," he said. "If you remember, you needed protecting both times."

I shook my head, my eyes distant as I raced through my memories. "And when I was abducted during the final exams. My friends said you disappeared just as the commotion was breaking out. Almost as soon as it happened. And you can't have gone to Lorcan because he would never have let you pursue me on your own. Yet you were the first one to get to me."

I fixed him with a hard stare. "And then in Abalene, when I

slipped away from the group. You knew where to find me. And now here you are. Why are you following me, Lucas?"

I quickly shook my head. "No, never mind that. *How* are you following me?"

A slight tinge of color crept up his cheeks, and he wouldn't meet my eyes. I stepped closer.

"Tell me the truth. I'm sick of deceptions and half-truths and never knowing what's really going on. How are you following me?"

"It's a composition." His words tumbled out in a rush. "One I designed myself. It lets me know where you are. Basically it alerts me if you start to leave the Academy. I probably wouldn't have noticed this morning until you were further away, but I was already awake. Awake and alert because I suspected you had some foolish scheme."

"You put a working on me? A constant one? *You're tracking me?*" My voice rose in volume with every question, and he winced.

"I only did it to protect you. Since you didn't seem overly interested in protecting yourself." He shook his head. "Almost every one of those excursions was poorly thought through. And I would have thought you would be glad to have someone tracking you when you were abducted."

"Are you serious? You expect me to be grateful? First I learn you had someone secretly watching me the whole summer, and now I learn you've been watching me at the Academy. Are you mages ever going to trust me?"

"I don't know, Elena. Are you ever going to stop doing foolish things? Like right now. You still haven't told me where you're going."

"And I don't intend to. Certainly not until you remove that tracking composition." I put my hands on my hips.

He sighed. "Elena. Please. Be reasonable. I've already said, I'm only trying to protect you."

"You really don't see it, do you?" I shook my head. "How condescending that is. How arrogant. Did you ever once consider talking to me? Asking me to tell you before going somewhere?"

"Would you have?" He pinned me with a stare.

"In all honesty?" I paused. "I don't know. Because you never asked."

He ran a weary hand over his face. "I never seem to get things right with you. No matter how hard I try." He stepped toward me, closing the last of the gap. "And I do try, Elena."

I swallowed, all too aware that enough of the dawn had crept in to give me a clear look at his straight, strong features, and the breadth of his shoulders.

"Do you?" I asked, the question coming out as a whisper. "It's hard to tell."

The ghost of a smile crossed his eyes. "It's all that ingrained princely arrogance, remember?"

And then his arms reached out, and before I quite knew what was happening, I was pressed against him, our hearts beating against each other. He leaned down and rested his forehead against mine.

"I try harder than you realize."

"Oh."

"And I'm trying now."

"To..." I stopped and licked my dry lips and tried again. "To do what?"

"Not to kiss you."

I froze.

"Tell me not to, Elena, and I won't." He was still whispering.

I opened my mouth to say the words, but nothing came out. My mind had betrayed me, instead reliving the burning warmth of the one kiss we had previously shared. I had been denying it to myself all year, but I couldn't now open my mouth and deny out loud that I wanted to feel his lips against mine again.

"Oh, good," he said when my silence stretched out. "I've been waiting all year for this." And then he crushed me against him, his lips meeting mine in an explosion of heat.

I responded instinctively, my arms twining around his neck, and my fingers pushing up into the perfect waves of his hair. I stood on my tiptoes, reaching up to meet him, and somehow his arms tightened even further around me.

For a long moment there was only us. And then he pulled away and placed his forehead against mine again, his breathing now ragged.

"Where are you going, Elena?"

And without thinking, my mind still spinning, I opened my mouth and replied.

"I've turned eighteen. I'm going to enlist."

"What?" He almost yelled the word, thrusting me away from him.

I staggered backward, barely managing to keep my balance at the sudden loss of his support.

He stepped forward quickly again, gripping my arms. "No, Elena, you're not. You're a second year trainee at the Academy. You can't enlist. Lorcan would never allow it. *I* don't allow it."

I was shaking now, not even attempting to stop the tremors racing through me.

"You don't allow it? Why, because you're royal? Because you're a prince? Because I'm only commonborn, and therefore you have the right to order me around and control my life?"

He groaned. "Because I—" But he broke off abruptly before finishing the thought.

"Well, you are a prince, Lucas. But tell me this. Do you have the power to protect Clemmy?"

"Of course you're doing this for her," he almost snarled. "I should have realized. But I thought I'd taken care of that. I never thought...It never occurred to me, you might..." He let go of me and ran a hand through his hair, turning as if to stride away before turning back again.

"Might think what? That my family had to sacrifice one child to conscription? I wonder where I got that idea? But you haven't answered my question. Can you protect Clemmy? If I don't enlist now, can you change our family's status? Can you make it so my service after I graduate counts for my family's enlistment?"

Lucas's face twisted. "I could try. I could talk..." His voice trailed away, but I stared at him expectantly.

"The royals have no role in such administrative matters," he said with a sigh. "We could request from the relevant head, negotiate, possibly even order. But there are things going on right now. It isn't a good time. Maybe later in the year...You just need to wait. Don't do anything rash."

"General Griffith."

My words stilled him.

"The relevant head—the Head of the Armed Forces—is General Griffith. Natalya and Calix's father. The one whose efforts to have me executed were blocked by your family and the council. The one who just lost an untold number of soldiers to a surprise attack he didn't anticipate. Do you really think he's going to give me a free pass on enlisting? Can you guarantee me that you can convince him? That your family will consider it enough of a priority?"

"You are a priority, Elena. Never doubt that."

"Oh, my abilities are of great interest, I'm sure. But can you promise me that if I wait, Lorcan and your father won't see an easier option? One that doesn't involve approaching General Griffith at all?"

Lucas looked at me warily. "What do you mean?"

"Oh come on, Lucas. One thing you're not is stupid. The minute you report my intentions, they'll forbid me from stepping foot outside the Academy. Find some way to forcibly prevent me, no doubt. They just have to wait until I turn nineteen, after all, and then all inducement for me to enlist disappears. Problem solved." I took a shaking breath. "I may be of interest, but my twelve-year-old sister is not."

I could see from his arrested expression that this possibility had genuinely not occurred to him. But it had occurred to me. I had long ago thought it through from every angle. And now that I had planted the idea, I could see in his eyes that he considered it all too likely.

He ran another hand down his face, and I began to mutter as quietly as I could.

His brow creased. "What are you—"

But I had already finished the binding words. "Bind Lucas in stillness and silence until I put my mark on the enlistment roll. End binding."

His eyes widened as I spoke, but I had caught him off guard. He had no defense ready. As my power hit him, his whole body froze, and he fell, landing hard against the ground.

I knelt down and rolled him over onto his back. His eyes pleaded with me, but his mouth didn't move, bound shut by my power.

"I'm sorry," I whispered. "But I have to do this."

CHAPTER 19

$\mathcal{I}$ ran through the streets, afraid that at any moment someone might discover Lucas's prone form and release him. And then they would come after me.

Plus, just the thought of him hitting the ground, lying there helpless, made my heart seize. If no one found him, then the sooner I put my mark on that paper, the sooner he would be free.

At least I hadn't been called on for any great use of power the day before, and my energy levels were at full strength. Still, I ran as fast as I could, the cobblestones flying beneath my feet. And my mind raced equally quickly—too many thoughts to keep track of spinning on an endless loop.

I had just assaulted a member of the royal family. The very thing General Thaddeus of the Royal Guard had always claimed I would do if given the chance. Would I ever even reach the front lines? Or would I be executed first? At least if I was, my last act would have been protecting Clemmy.

But not even fear could drive away a stronger memory. Lucas's lips against mine. His arms around me. He claimed he had been waiting to do it, and if I was honest, I had been waiting for it as well. But then he had pulled back and asked me where I was going. Tricked me into answering while I was dazed and distracted. Had that been his purpose all along? How could I be sure?

My mind replayed the scene, remembering how he had thrust me away from him. The anger in his eyes. He hadn't even hesitated at the mention of my sister, not even a trace of confusion. Earlier memories sprang at me from the distant recesses of my mind.

Of Finnian apologizing, telling me he hadn't sent Beatrice. That he hadn't even known I had a sick sister.

Of me and Lucas in the library in first year when I had thrown the issue of conscription in his face. When I had also mentioned my chronically ill little sister.

And of his words in the dawn. *Of course you're doing this for her...I thought I'd taken care of that.*

I stumbled, regaining my balance and rushing on through the early morning. Powerful friends. Of course. Lucas had sent Beatrice. I should have guessed it. Even more emotions coursed through me.

Gratitude.

Disgust at the thought that he had done it just so she could go and fight on the front lines.

Confusion. How was it possible to feel so many emotions toward one person?

And then finally I reached the barracks. I stumbled through the doors, letting them bang behind me. Reaching the desk, I leaned against it, regaining my breath.

"I'm here to enlist."

"Well there's no need to get excited about it," said the young man manning the desk. His gray uniform proclaimed him a commonborn soldier. "We're here all day."

"I'm in a hurry."

He raised an eyebrow. "That would be a first."

Far too slowly for my taste he drew out a sheet of parchment.

I looked back toward the door for any sign of pursuit. When I turned back to him, he was watching me with curiosity.

"You look like you're expecting someone to appear and drag you away. It's usually the opposite, you know." He pulled out a shallow tray with a black sponge sitting inside it. "I suppose you must be a conscription case. Doing the noble thing are you? Who disapproves? Your parents? The sibling in question? We did once have a full brawl in this very receiving room. Some seventeen-year-old trying to stop his brother making the sacrifice. More excitement than we usually get, I can assure you."

I cut through his chatter. "What do I do?"

"Put your thumb on the ink and then make your mark on this page. Once your thumbprint's on here, there's nothing the king himself can do."

He grinned at me, and a prickle ran down my neck. I knew it was a saying, that he didn't mean the words literally, but they fell all too close to the truth.

Taking a deep breath, I pressed my thumb into the black sponge, pulling it away covered in ink. With a single firm movement, I pushed it down against the parchment. I lightened instantly as the drain on my power broke off. Lucas had been freed.

Only when it lifted did I even register its presence. I should have known no one was following me since as long as the power continued to drain away, Lucas remained bound and unable to report my departure. But now he was free. It was too late, though. I had made my mark. I had enlisted. My family had fulfilled its conscription responsibility.

It took me a moment to realize the soldier was still speaking. He directed me to go through a wide door and down a corridor until I found an office marked with a silver star.

"That's the symbol of our mage officers," he told me. "You'll learn it soon enough. And come to recognize their silver robes even quicker. The mage in the office will take down your name and family and record it against the register. Whoever you're protecting is free now."

He smiled at me, and I managed a shaky smile back. Clemmy was free. And she'd been healed—whatever Lucas's intentions. Her whole life was before her now.

I managed to propel myself into the corridor and find the marked door. The mage inside seemed even more bored than the soldier had initially been. But he dutifully wrote my name, and the name of my family and of Kingslee. My eyes followed his pen until he looked up, and I quickly looked away. It was hard to remember I was a commonborn and no longer a trainee. I was a mage, of sorts—but did the freedoms of a mage still apply to me now? I couldn't be sure.

He regarded me with narrowed eyes for a moment, before scanning a full shelf of books behind him. He pulled out a fairly slim volume with Kingslee marked on the spine. Flipping through it, he found the record of my family and drew a line through it.

I let out a breath I hadn't even realized I was holding.

"This is the central training barracks," he told me. "All new recruits are sent here from the other enlistment centers. And all records are kept here as well. Don't think there's any chance of wiggling out of your enlistment now."

I shook my head. "No." Then added quickly, "Sir. I mean, My Lord." I bit down on my clumsy tongue. I had grown too used to the relaxed ways of the Academy and couldn't even remember the proper forms of address now.

He just rolled his eyes. "You're in the Armed Forces now, girl. All officers, male and female, are to be addressed as sir."

I nodded and then belatedly added, "Yes, sir."

The mage picked up a small silver bell from his desk and rang it.

"Sir!" A young girl who didn't look like she could possibly be eighteen popped into the room and saluted energetically.

"We have a new recruit," the mage said, gesturing at me.

The girl didn't look my way, merely saluting again. "Yes, sir!"

She turned and left the room, holding the door open behind her. When I didn't move, she finally looked my way.

"Well? Are you coming?"

"Oh." I rushed to follow her, but as I passed through the doorway, she gave me a loaded look, her eyes flicking to the mage behind us.

Belatedly I spun around and gave a clumsy salute. "Sir."

The mage nodded without looking up from his desk, and the girl closed the door behind us.

"Phew, that was a close one." She grinned at me, looking me over curiously for the first time. "They're big on protocol here, but you'll learn soon enough."

She started further down the corridor, and I trailed behind her. I could already tell the protocol was going to chafe. When had I started to view all mages as my equals?

"That's a nice cloak you have. Come from one of the rich families, do you?" She sounded like she felt sorry for me. "It'll be an adjustment, but we're not such a bad lot." She grinned over her shoulder at me. "I'm Leila, by the way."

"Elena." I didn't bother to correct her assumption about me. It was certainly a much simpler explanation than the truth.

She led me into a supply room where I was measured and given two gray uniforms. The clerk in charge of the stores looked at my boots and declared them fit for purpose before adding a supply pack to the stack in my arms.

"That's your water pouch and such," Leila told me as we returned to the corridor. "You won't need that stuff here, but you're expected to keep it in good condition anyway. They do random equipment checks."

I nodded, still not contributing to the conversation. My brain was struggling to process my new reality. Too much had happened and too much had changed in the last few hours for me to take it all in.

"We shipped out a whole batch to the border only yesterday, so there are plenty of bunks in my dorm," Leila continued on. "You should be able to nab yourself a bottom one."

We exited the main building, the full light of dawn having now arrived and showing a number of training yards not dissimilar to the ones at the Academy. A small group jogged around one, but no one else was in sight.

"The early birds," said Leila, nodding toward them. "Sickens the rest of us." She winked at me.

"You're up early yourself," I pointed out.

"I'm on officer babysitting duties this week and managed to pull the night shift." She wrinkled her nose. "So it doesn't count."

"You are eighteen, then?" The question popped out before I could stop it.

She just laughed. "Nineteen, in fact, if you can believe it. Most people can't."

"But you're still here at the training barracks? I thought training only lasted a few weeks."

She grinned. "Oh, I'm not a new recruit. We don't all do our full term at the front lines, you know. The majority do, of course, and the rest of us will cycle through for at least a year's posting at some point. But there are other duties in the Armed Forces that need doing. I've been given a year's posting here. I expect I'll be off to the front lines after that." Her face remained cheerful, but I thought I detected a hint of fear in her voice.

She shook her head. "There are exceptions, though. There was a boy from my street who enlisted at the same time as me. He got recruited straight after basic training into one of the special squads that work with the Grays, if you can believe it. A whole three-year posting, too. If there's one thing the mages take as seriously as the war, it's reading!"

I frowned. It had never occurred to me that not all recruits would spend their three years at the front lines, but I supposed it made sense. As she had just said, the seekers had their own special squads of soldiers, plus we had soldiers posted all over the kingdom.

"So don't despair, Elena," Leila continued as we approached a long, low building. "You might get lucky yet."

Her words jarred me from my thoughts. If only she knew the truth. I was already as different from a regular recruit as it was possible to be. I just didn't know what consequences that was going to have yet.

She pushed open a plain wooden door and led me into a room lined with bunks.

"Ah-ha! There's a bottom one." She pointed at a stripped bunk. "Put your things in that metal locker at the end. The one on the left. The other one is for the top bunk. And then you'd better make the bed right now, so everyone knows it's taken. Sometimes the new recruits come all in a rush, it's the strangest thing."

She chattered on as she helped me to make the bed with the clean linens folded neatly at the foot.

"The dorms for the boys are all on the west side of the building, and the girls are all here on the east. Us girls only have two rooms since we don't exactly get equal numbers of recruits." She smiled, not seeming to mind in the least. "But don't expect any special treatment from the officers, we're all soldiers here." She gave me a stern look. "So you just watch for any of the boys getting saucy, and let them know what for. A good wallop over the head will tell them to keep their distance."

I tried to imagine this tiny girl walloping one of the recruits we'd seen out in the yard and couldn't help a smile of my own.

"There you go!" she said. "It's not all bad here, I promise you. And talking of things which are a great deal better than they might be, you get yourself into one of your uniforms, and we'll take ourselves off to breakfast. The latest batch of cooks posted into the kitchen actually make a decent meal."

I changed as quickly as I could, depositing my own clothes and my cloak in the locker. Leila flitted around me, straightening my uniform, before declaring me ready to go. We could smell the food before we reached the mess hall—as she called it—and she was right. It did smell good. Better than I had expected.

She introduced me to several other new recruits, as well as some soldiers like herself who were posted to the training barracks, but I didn't absorb any of the names. Somehow I did manage to eat, though, despite my roiling stomach. The food even helped to settle it.

"Good timing on your arrival," said a new recruit who sat with us at the meal. "They only start basic training in batches every few days. And we all started yesterday. Means you'll get to laze around for a few days before they start cracking the whip."

I tried not to look dismayed. The last thing I wanted was to be left alone with my thoughts for days on end.

"She enlisted before dawn," said Leila. "I don't think she's the lazing type. Right, Elena?" She smiled at me.

"Jason had the night shift on the front desk," said the boy across from the new recruit. I seemed to remember he was one of those posted to the barracks, like Leila. "Told me she looked like she was enlisting against someone's wishes. So maybe early mornings aren't her usual style."

He looked at me questioningly, but I just shrugged.

"She's a silent one," Leila said. "But you'll open up eventually, Elena. We're like a family here."

"Sorry," I said. "It's all just a bit...much." And I was afraid if I opened my mouth they would all quickly realize I didn't belong.

The boy laughed. "That's the Leila effect."

She made a face at him and threw her fork toward his face with deadly aim, prongs first. He laughed and caught it deftly before it made contact, sliding it back across the table to her.

She shook her head and polished off the last of her food, standing swiftly. "Well I'm off to get some rest. Longest night shift of my life until Elena here arrived. Nothing but fetching old silver robe endless cups of tea as he got grumpier and grumpier. It's a wonder I didn't fall asleep and get myself cleaning duty."

She turned to go and then paused. "You coming, Elena? You could do with some rest, too, I'll bet. After your early morning."

I nodded and stood. If the other recruit was right, and I wasn't to start training today, then I didn't exactly have anything else to do. We wandered back toward the barracks together, until the group we had seen jogging earlier strolled past on their way to the mess hall.

One of them called to Leila, and she crossed over to talk to him, laughter drifting back to me, although I couldn't catch their specific words.

"A new recruit, hey?" One of the other young soldiers stopped beside me. The smile he directed at me was pleasant enough, but I didn't like the glint in his eye when he looked across at one of his friends who had also approached us.

"I'm Tobias. You just let me know if you feel lost. I'll be more than happy to show you around. Any time." He winked at me, and I shifted away, even more uncomfortable now.

"Thank you, but Leila's already given me the tour," I said.

I stepped away again, but he followed me. Slinging a heavy arm around my shoulders, he dropped his voice into what he clearly thought was a sultry tone.

"Yes, but Leila's only good for some things." He winked. "If you know what I mean."

I didn't think, my body just reacted to eighteen months training at the Academy. Grabbing his wrist, where it hung over my shoulder, I slipped out from under his arm and twisted it up behind him.

He yelped and tried to pull free, but I just twisted it tighter. He stilled.

"Don't touch me," I said, my voice coming out strong and authoritative. "And you can let your friends know the same thing. I don't like being touched."

"I was only trying to be friendly," he said.

"Well don't. I'm not the friendly type."

"Obviously," he muttered, and I let his arm go.

He stepped away from me, shaking out the limb, while everyone around us stared at me. I looked around at them and swallowed. Had that been the wrong way to handle the situation?

A whoop sounded across the yard, breaking the moment, and Leila hurried back toward us, laughter now shaking her.

"That was smooth, Elena! I'd apologize for not paying more attention, but you can clearly look after yourself." She put her hands on her hips and glared at Tobias.

"And let that be a lesson to you, Tobias, not to try the moves on every new recruit we get. You should know by now that I tell them all to give you a good whack."

"I'm not doing any harm just asking a question," Tobias said, with a sour look at her and a suspicious one at me.

"Well I have a question for you," she said with narrowed eyes. "Would you like my foot up your—"

"Officer in the yard," said the soldier behind her quietly, and she broke off abruptly.

All of them sprang to attention and saluted, so I did the same as best I could. The silver-robed figure moved swiftly past us, her eyes traveling over us without really seeing. The sensation of being invisible felt strange. I had thought I hated so often being the center of attention at the Academy, but now that my status was gone, I was ashamed to find I missed it.

As soon as the officer had disappeared, they all relaxed.

"I don't know about you lot, but I'm off to get some breakfast," said Tobias, stalking away from the group. The rest of the joggers followed him, many casting final glances at me. Only the one who had been talking with Leila hesitated.

"Nicely done, new recruit," he said with a grin.

I couldn't help but smile back at him, and he gave me a mock salute before hurrying off after the others. But his words gave me a pang. He spoke as if I was one of them, but I had seen the looks the others had given me. It wouldn't be long before someone discovered just how much I didn't fit in here at all.

"That was…unexpected," Leila said as we continued on toward the dorm. "You should have seen your expression. I'll be honest, I wasn't sure you'd be able to handle yourself, but I can see I was wrong."

She looked at me with a calculating expression, and I quickly looked away.

"There's something different about you," she said when I didn't respond. "You don't carry yourself like any other recruit I've ever seen."

I bit my lip, still remaining silent. I could hardly explain to Leila that I had spent too long now turning myself into a mage to slip comfortably back into my old commonborn self. And once the officers realized what had happened and who I was, I couldn't even imagine what they would do.

When we reached our dorm, Leila dropped straight to sleep, despite the light pouring in the windows. I tried to do the same but only succeeded in tossing and turning in my bunk. Eventually I gave up and got out of bed, straightening out my covers. I ate one of the cookies from home, but the familiar taste brought tears to my eyes, so I put the rest away.

The hours passed painfully slowly, but I didn't want to go wandering around the training grounds in case I ended up somewhere I shouldn't be. I tried not to make any noise to disturb Leila, so when she suddenly swung her legs out of bed, I jumped.

"Sorry…" I started, but she shook her head.

"It wasn't you. It's just time for lunch."

I stared at her. "But you were dead asleep. How do you know that?"

She winked. "You learn all sorts of skills in the Armed Forces. First among them is to never miss a meal."

Together we started back toward the mess hall. I watched her out of the corner of my eye as we walked. She seemed a lot more cheerful than I had imagined for a soldier. Was it because she hadn't been sent to the front lines yet or just her natural personality? I still couldn't believe she was nineteen. She looked more like fifteen, and it was almost impossible to imagine her charging a line of enemy soldiers.

If that was what they even did on the front lines.

I had saved Clemmy, and I had been working for months to develop the skills to save myself. But confronted with Leila, I realized that would never be enough. I couldn't save myself and leave the soldiers serving around me to die. But then how much could one person do—even if that person did have the powers of a mage? I had managed to make a difference in Abalene, but I hadn't done any of it alone. If my magehood was now to be rejected, and I was to be abandoned among the commonborn, even my power would prove unequal to the need around me.

I had fought so hard to become a mage, but conscription had undone it all. The commonborn soldiers would soon realize I didn't belong with them, but neither would the mage officers welcome me to their ranks, I was sure. I would be stuck endlessly between the two groups, impotent despite what I had learned at the Academy.

And all of that was assuming I wasn't executed for attacking Lucas.

We ate the midday meal with an entirely different batch of soldiers, although I recognized one from the front desk. Jason, I think the other soldier had called him.

He greeted Leila and me with good cheer, looking a great deal more lively than he had on my arrival. No doubt he had spent the morning sleeping, as well. When we finished eating, the three of us left the hall together, the two of them discussing their plans for the afternoon—which included some combat practice, apparently—and their upcoming night shifts.

When a flash of silver emerged from the main building, however, they both snapped to attention, falling silent. I followed a beat behind.

This time the mage officer strode straight toward us.

"You. New recruit. Elena." It was the man who had taken down my name earlier. "Come with me."

Leila raised both eyebrows and exchanged a look with Jason that told me this wasn't normal. My stomach dropped into my feet.

CHAPTER 20

$\mathcal{T}$he mage started back toward the building, and I followed reluctantly. Had the Royal Guard come for me then? Was I about to have the shortest ever enlistment in the Armed Forces?

As we entered the main building, the mage gestured for me to hurry up, eyeing me with mild annoyance and a great deal more curiosity than he had done when I first arrived.

"The colonel has asked to see you," he said as he led me up a flight of stairs. "Asked for you by name. Can't say that's ever happened before in the time I've been serving here."

I bit my lip. Excellent. I really was setting a record.

The colonel's office was at the top of the stairs, marked with a large silver star. The officer with me rapped at the door once and then opened it without waiting for a response. I followed him inside, trying not to let my knees shake.

I still hadn't recovered the energy I spent binding Lucas, and it had been a long day after little sleep. But it seemed it was about to get longer.

An older woman with silver hair that matched her robe

looked up from her seat behind a large, solid desk. She had a lined, no-nonsense face, and she didn't look pleased to see us.

My eyes raced around the room, but no one else was present. Not a single red or gold robe, or even red or gold uniform, in sight. I told myself not to feel relieved. They had probably just sent instructions for the Armed Forces to deliver me to them.

"Elena of Kingslee?" she asked, her voice rough and weathered.

I nodded.

She narrowed her eyes, scanning me up and down before nodding a dismissal to the mage who had brought me. He left, casting a reluctant glance at me as he did so. I could feel the curiosity radiating off him, but he didn't question his superior's orders.

When we were alone, the colonel leaned back in her chair and stared at me for a silent moment.

"I would say this is unusual," she said at last. "But the truth is that it's unprecedented."

I swallowed.

"We have never had a new recruit assigned to a post before completing basic training."

Wait. What? I blinked at her, trying to comprehend her words. Had she said a post?

"However, I am assured—and from the highest levels—that your skills are already sufficiently advanced to render basic training unnecessary."

We stood in silence again while she continued to survey me. After a long moment she shook her head.

"I can't say I'm surprised. Not once I heard your name. My second lieutenant clearly hasn't heard of you, but I am a great deal more senior than he is, Elena of Kingslee."

I shifted uneasily, wondering what family she hailed from. What exactly had she heard about me?

The colonel sighed, her manner turning suddenly business-like.

"Elena of Kingslee, you may now consider yourself a full private in the Armed Forces of Ardann. You are to take up an irregular posting at the Royal Academy of the Written Word under the immediate command of the Academy Head. Your posting there will last until further notice."

My mouth fell open, and I gaped at her. She was sending me back to the Academy? I felt nothing but a tingling numbness. This day had taken so many turns I had apparently lost the ability for emotional response.

When I neither spoke nor moved, she raised an eyebrow at me.

"You are dismissed, private."

I jolted and began to move toward the door before remembering and turning back.

"Yes, sir," I said, but I still hesitated. "Should I...leave for the Academy immediately?"

She shook her head. "That is the usual response to my orders, certainly. I assume you don't need an escort to find your way."

"No...sir."

"Oh, and private? Do not forget your new rank. You will conduct yourself at all times as is befitting a member of the Armed Forces and obey all orders given to you by your new commander as well as any other officers you may encounter. Do you understand?"

I nodded, then quickly added, "Yes, sir."

She regarded me for a final moment and then looked down at her desk as I rushed from the room. As soon as the door closed behind me, I leaned against the wall and closed my eyes. Could it really be true? I had been here for only half a day, and already I was to return. Clemmy was free, and now so was I. I was to continue studying at the Academy.

It seemed too good to be true.

Sudden energy filled me, and my feet were racing down the stairs before I knew what I was doing. I sped across the training yards, bursting into the barracks.

Leila started at my abrupt arrival before rushing over to my bed. She looked as if she had been lingering, waiting to see if I would return.

"Elena! You're back. I wasn't sure…" When I said nothing, she continued. "Well? What did he want?"

I pulled open the locker and threw my cloak around my shoulders. Bundling my clothes into my arms, I turned to face her.

"It was the colonel, actually."

"The colonel?" She stared at me. "The colonel wanted to see *you*?"

I nodded. "I've received a posting. I'm to leave immediately." I paused. "But thank you for showing me around. I appreciated it."

"Leave immediately?" She was still staring at me. "But you haven't even completed basic training. You can't be posted yet."

I shrugged. "Apparently I'm already sufficiently trained." I hesitated. "I don't know how long my posting is going to be, but I hope we cross paths again, Leila, and that you don't end up at the front lines."

"I…" She spluttered, seemingly too confused to question me properly.

I smiled at her and took the opportunity to escape. I could only imagine the rumors that would soon spread through the training facility. But it didn't matter. Because I was going home to the Academy.

I walked this time, instead of running, but somehow the journey seemed to take less time. Long before it seemed possible, I stood in front of the Academy gates. I paused for a minute, just staring at them. I hadn't expected to ever see them again, and now here I was less than a day later.

The courtyard was deserted, as I would expect at this time of the afternoon when the trainees would all be in class. I passed the fountain and slowly mounted the stairs. It suddenly occurred to me that I didn't know what to do now. Should I just join class as if nothing had happened?

But as soon as I entered the building, I found Damon waiting for me.

"I'm glad to see you made it back, Elena."

I eyed him warily despite the smile spreading across my face. "Me too, Damon. Me too."

He shook his head. "I've been instructed to take you straight to Lorcan the moment you arrive."

My smile fell away.

"Yes, exactly," he said. "And don't expect to find him in a good mood."

I winced and fell into step beside the head servant as he crossed the entrance hall and started down the corridor toward Lorcan's office. I should have seen this coming. Lorcan was not going to be pleased.

But at least it hadn't been Lucas waiting for me. Or General Thaddeus with a squad of the Royal Guard.

When we reached the waiting room of Lorcan's office, Damon gestured for me to stay put as he knocked on the internal door before poking his head into the office.

"She's here."

I couldn't hear Lorcan's response. Damon pulled his head back out and crossed over to me.

"You can go in now." He held out his hands. "But why don't I take those? I'll send them up to your room."

I started. I had forgotten all about the bundle of clothes still clutched in my arms. I handed them over to Damon and reached up to straighten my hair before deciding I was only procrastinating and pushing through the door into Lorcan's study.

Lorcan watched me in silence as I entered, the expression in his gray eyes harder than I had yet seen from him. His lean frame radiated both power and authority, a reminder that he was more than just the absent-minded academic he so often appeared. As the Head of the Academy and a member of the Mage Council, Lorcan was a powerful and important person in Ardann.

For the first time since hearing he wanted to see me I felt truly nervous.

"I am disappointed in you, Elena," he said. "Most disappointed." He spoke quietly, but the words held more force than if he had shouted. "You arrived at this Academy—a commonborn girl in a more than unusual situation—and since then I have exerted my utmost influence and power to keep you safe. To keep you sheltered within these walls."

His eyes pierced me, and I pulled up an image of Clemmy's face to bolster me. Whatever he thought, I knew I had done the right thing.

"And now I discover that you have flouted me. Rejected my protection completely and left the Academy before your training is completed. A thing that is forbidden."

"Here I am back again," I said weakly.

His expression only grew more stormy. "Yes, thanks to the very great forbearance shown by Prince Lucas." He shook his head. "I know he would never have let you leave willingly—he understands the stakes even if you do not. And I could feel your power lingering on him. You're fortunate indeed he didn't report whatever you did to Thaddeus. Which is just what we would have needed—yet another discipline getting involved."

He paused, but I could think of nothing acceptable to say in my defense. I knew he cared nothing for my younger sister—that had been the problem in the first place—and would find my reasons less than convincing.

"And if it hadn't been for the prince's quick thinking, who knows what situation you would be in now? I hope you realize the depths of your indebtedness to him."

I frowned across the room at him, and he raised an eyebrow.

"Who do you think had the idea to have you posted to the Academy? A neat bit of thinking. Outside the usual procedures but just close enough to be quickly pushed through before the general caught word of your foolishness."

He paused to take an angry breath.

"You have no concept of the attempted interference I have protected you from. And all because I had the authority to do so. You were a trainee under my discipline. And now look at you." He gestured at me, and I looked down to see my cloak had fallen open, revealing the gray uniform I still wore underneath.

"Now you are a trainee, of sorts, but you are also a private in the Armed Forces. You fall under the authority of two disciplines, and we can only guess at what consequences that might have."

His words were true. But I also knew I had been left no other choice. Of course, that didn't stop me wondering uneasily just what sort of interference he had prevented.

I bit my lip, but I couldn't keep the words inside.

"You're the Head of the Academy. I'm sure you're not used to consulting with your trainees." Lucas's words at Midwinter rang around in my head. "And yet you said yourself that I'm an unusual case. About as unusual as they come. And I know you have some experience with making exceptions for unusual cases. You certainly seem to consult more with Lucas than with any of the rest of us."

His eyes narrowed, but I took a deep breath and pressed on.

"Perhaps if you had ever considered talking to me, I might have made a different decision. Perhaps if you had told me of this attempted interference, I might have been able to make a more informed decision. I might have consulted you in return before acting. But the truth of the matter is that I did what I did not for you, or for Ardann, and certainly not for myself. I did it for my sister. And unless you could have guaranteed protection for her —something not even Lucas could do—then I would almost certainly have made the same decision."

I looked him squarely in the face. "And I don't regret it. Whatever the cost may now be."

He shook his head slowly, letting out a long breath.

"I only hope you don't change your mind about that, Elena. Because you haven't just committed yourself to any discipline. You've committed yourself to one run by a Devoras."

A shiver ran down my spine. General Griffith.

Lorcan sighed again. "You're dismissed, private. You can resume classes in the morning."

CHAPTER 21

Coralie teased me over the evening meal, clearly under the impression that I had taken an unexcused day off after my birthday celebrations the night before. It soon became apparent that none of the other trainees knew what had really happened.

None except Lucas, anyway. And after my attack on him, it seemed that we had returned to not speaking to one another.

I had to admit I was glad for it. Several times I tried to steel myself to approach him and thank him—both for getting me posted back here and for not reporting my attack on him—but somehow my feet always led me in the other direction whenever I got close.

Perhaps it had something to do with the fact that I couldn't see his face without remembering how his hair had felt under my fingers and how his lips had moved against mine. And then quick on the back of that thought always came the memory of his subsequent betrayal.

I couldn't turn off my emotions where he was concerned, and if I was honest with myself, I had never been able to. But I could remind myself of how he had played with me, using those emotions against me. I might be learning to fight as well as one of them, but I would never match the sophistication with which he played *the game*—as he called it.

But I was determined to master the fighting, at least. I threw myself into my training with more focus than ever. With Jocasta returned, Walden offered to tutor me again, but to my own surprise, I turned him down. I had grown used to training on my own, and I suspected he might not approve of my focus on combat compositions.

I just wished I could practice in the arena where Thornton continued to pit me only against the weakest members of our class.

A week after my enlistment, Natalya strolled past Coralie and me as we all finished combat class on one of our regular sparring days.

"Nice work, *private*," she said, her tone making it clear she considered the title humiliating.

Coralie frowned. "What's she talking about?"

Natalya tittered. "Don't tell me you haven't told your friends about your new rank?"

"Oh shut it, Natalya," I said loudly. "You really think you're better than me? Then prove it. In the arena. I could beat you with my eyes closed."

She swelled up, her eyes growing huge as I stared at her with a challenge on my face.

"We'll see about that," she managed to spit out before storming off.

I looked across at Thornton, the challenge still in my eyes. He looked from me to Natalya, his face thoughtful.

"Good to see that turning eighteen hasn't sobered that ready tongue of yours," said Finnian, wandering over. "I think I would miss your little outbursts."

"Oh that wasn't an outburst." I smiled cheerfully at him. "That was entirely calculated. I've just been waiting for her to take a swipe at me."

He raised an eyebrow. "You fill me with curiosity."

"Just you watch," I said. "I'll bet Thornton starts mixing up my opponents in the arena now."

"Ah. I see." Finnian bent slightly in my direction. "I bow before your mastery."

I rolled my eyes. "I'll never be as good at all this underhanded stuff as you lot, but I'm trying to learn."

"Elena." Coralie's voice sounded slightly high-pitched. "What did she mean by calling you private?"

"What's this?" Finnian looked between us, frowning.

"Natalya," Coralie explained. "She called Elena private. That's what started it." She stared at me. "Where were you the day after your birthday?"

I grimaced. There was no avoiding it now.

"I may have gone down to the barracks and enlisted in the Armed Forces."

"What?" shrieked Coralie. "How could you do that? And how could you not tell me?!"

"I knew you would try to stop me. You all would have. But I had to do it. If I didn't enlist at eighteen, then my sister would have to. You know how conscription works."

She stared at me, true hurt in her eyes. "And afterward? You couldn't even tell me afterward?"

My heart sank. I hadn't meant to hurt her by keeping it to myself.

"I guess I just wanted to forget all about it. As much as I could, anyway. There didn't seem to be anything to be gained by talking about it."

Finnian frowned and slung an arm around Coralie's shoulders.

"Poor form, Elena."

I bit my lip. "I know. I guess I can see that now. And I'm sorry. I truly am. Next time I'll tell you, I promise."

"Oh, you're planning to sign up for a second term at the end of this one, are you?" Finnian couldn't seem to resist turning it into a joke.

"Absolutely, definitely not." I shook my head as fast as I could. "If I make it through the next three years, I want nothing to do with the Armed Forces ever again."

"Except you'll be a mage in three years," he reminded me. "And only just started on a different sort of term at the front lines. I don't think you'll get out of that one. I suspect avoiding a term with the Armed Forces is the sort of thing you only get to do once."

"Well, I haven't exactly avoided it," I said.

When they both gave me confused looks, I hurried to explain.

"I'm still a soldier. That's why Natalya called me private, I assume. I've just been posted to the Academy under Lorcan's command. And he's commanded me to continue my studies…"

I trailed off at Finnian's disbelieving look.

"That sounds like getting out of your term to me." His eyes followed Lucas who was walking back toward the Academy building. "And I suspect I know who managed to organize such a thing."

I flushed.

"I can't believe you would do that," said Coralie quietly.

I looked over at her. "You would do the same, Coralie. I know you would. If it was your family on the line."

Her brow creased as she considered that, and I held my breath, waiting. Finally she looked over at me and sighed.

"I suppose I might. Just promise me you won't hide something that big from me again. You could have trusted me, you know. I wouldn't have told anyone."

I hugged her, murmuring another apology. She returned the embrace but didn't regain her usual bubbly good cheer until the following morning when she demanded a full description of my brief stay at the training barracks.

I gave it to her between mouthfuls of breakfast, faltering only once when I recounted my run-in with Tobias. An angry hiss made me pause and glance behind me in time to see Lucas—who seemed to have stalled just behind me—start moving again toward his own table further down the row.

Coralie followed my gaze, so I quickly resumed the story, distracting her by describing being called before the colonel.

"You are so fortunate it worked out as well as it did," she said when I finished.

"I know." I inhaled the last mouthful. "Believe me, I know. I thought I was never going to see the Academy again."

Her face fell at that, so I quickly changed the subject, musing instead on who might battle who in the arena that morning. It was the second year arena day, and I had high hopes of being assigned a good fight.

And when we arrived at the arena, it seemed my words had achieved their aim. Natalya and I were called for the first bout.

My chances came thick and fast after that. For the following three weeks, I battled Lavinia, then Calix, then Weston again.

And I won. Every time. Each week I pushed myself to learn from any mistakes, and to tighten my control so I could compose a greater variety of workings in ever shorter phrases. Coralie started to complain that I did nothing but study, but I couldn't explain to her the fervor that drove me. At first I had only wanted not to be last anymore. But now I was determined to come first. I would keep pushing myself until I could defeat them all, without fail.

I fought Finnian next and lost. He helped me to my feet after I yielded, his usual grin in place.

"Good bout," I managed to wheeze out, still regaining my breath after his winding.

He shook his head. "You should have won it. You know you should."

I just shrugged, but Thornton eyed me disapprovingly when I returned to the stands.

"Sloppy, Elena, very sloppy. You should have had him more than once. He may be your friend, but you can't afford to hesitate. Not for anything."

I climbed slowly back to my seat. I *had* hesitated, reluctant to hurt Finnian. And though he told me I should have won now, I could have sworn he had given me a pleading look down there in the bout.

I glanced across at his twinkling eyes and wanted to kick myself. Of course he had. No doubt on purpose. I might never be called on to fight my friends in the real world, but Thornton was still right. I couldn't let myself hesitate. Who knew what distractions I might face on the battle field.

I didn't lose to any of my friends again.

Two weeks after that I fought Dariela for the first time. When my barrage of raw power broke through her shield and she shouted, "Yield," I barely had time to invoke my pre-set limitations and break it off before it slammed into her.

When I left the arena floor, I was greeted by total silence. I kept my eyes on the ground as I climbed back to my seat. Whatever was on their faces, I didn't want to see it.

For the next week, I found it hard to focus, and every single one of my friends commented at least once on how jittery I seemed. But I couldn't help it. There was only one bout left. The one bout I didn't want to ever face.

Sure enough, when we all took our seats in the arena the following week, Thornton called my bout first.

"Elena and Lucas."

I forced myself to stand and walk down the steps to the arena floor. I couldn't even face him to speak to him. How could I fight him?

All too soon we stood a short distance apart, both of our swords gripped ready. How long ago our training sessions felt. We had stood across from each other many times then, but it had been different in the darkness, without an audience.

Immediately I thought of how the moonlight reflected and enhanced the intensity of his green eyes, and how utterly black the waves of his hair looked at night. And then I remembered how it felt to stand so close I could feel his body heat, and the shape of his arms around me, his body pressed against mine.

I thought of how much I owed him, and that he had done none of it for me. He was the prince of Ardann, and I was the Spoken Mage. It had always been what defined our relationship, and it always would be.

I barely heard Thornton call the start of the bout. My distraction delayed my defensive parry, and Lucas faltered slightly, caught off guard by the weakness of my response to his attack. But his surprise lasted less than a breath, and I had to stumble backward out of range in order to recover myself and prepare my own attack.

The force of Lucas's compositions made even Dariela's seem weak by comparison. I suspected he had also known who he would face today since I couldn't imagine he poured such strength into his workings every week.

I had to devote far too much of my energy to my shield, and by the time he had used all three of his workings, leaving me still with one final composition to go, I could feel the exhaustion setting in. I composed quickly, cutting off my shield as soon as I heard him yield.

I swayed slightly, and for a second I thought he meant to cross over to offer me the support of his arm. But the moment passed, and he returned to the stands, leaving me to trail behind.

I expected a reprimand from Thornton for pushing myself so far, but when my eyes caught his, he said nothing. I swallowed, something in his face making my feet move slightly faster as I hurried to get up to the top row of seating.

As I glanced away from him, my eyes fell on Calix instead. He shook his head, something almost like wonder in his eyes, and I turned my face from him as well.

If only I could have avoided fighting Lucas forever.

~

The next day was a rest day, as it always was after our arena day, and for once I didn't study. And I was glad I had chosen to laze in my room after lunch when a knock sounded, and an unexpected visitor appeared.

"Jasper!" I threw myself at my brother.

"It's a nice day," he said. "You can tell it's almost summer. Shall we walk in the gardens?"

I nodded, holding back my questions until we had left the building and walked alone through the shrubs.

"All right, what are you really doing here?" I asked. "Because I haven't seen you since my birthday. Plus, I've seen the gardens you have at the University. You didn't come here to stroll through a small patch of greenery with me."

He sighed. "I should have come before now. I wish I could get away more."

"No, Jasper." I put my hand on his arm. "I didn't mean it like that. When do I ever get over to the University to visit you? You're working hard for the sake of our whole family, and you already spend enough time worrying about your little sister."

He bit his lip and glanced over at me. "I do worry about you. And I'm not the only one."

I frowned at him. "What's that supposed to mean? Have you been back home again?"

He shook his head. "I don't mean Mother or Father, although

I imagine they worry enough about both of us." He hesitated, and I stopped, pulling him to a stop as well.

"What is it, Jasper? What's going on?"

"I had a visitor this morning," he told me. "At the University. A most unexpected visitor."

I stared at him as he paused to clear his throat.

"It was the prince. Prince Lucas himself came to visit me at the University." He pinned me with a penetrating stare. "For some reason he seemed to think you wouldn't listen to him if he talked to you directly. Despite his being royalty and all. He seemed to be laboring under the delusion you might actually listen to me."

He rolled his eyes. "Naturally I disabused him of that notion, but I promised to try anyway. So here I am. Under royal orders, you might say."

My lips compressed into a thin line, and I started walking again, marching faster than I had before.

"I can't believe he went to my brother," I muttered to myself, before rounding on Jasper.

"And did His Royal Highness say what exactly he's so concerned about? Other than my failure to give his royal self proper respect? I suppose I was expected to lose to him yesterday."

"You beat the prince? In combat, you mean?" Jasper's eyes flew over my head to the arena in the distance behind us. "Then it's as bad as he said. Elena, what are you doing?"

My steps slowed again, and I let him pull me to another stop. But when I looked up at him, I knew my eyes were defiant.

"I'm becoming the best," I said. "Isn't that what training is all about? To be the best we can be? Well, it turns out I can be the best."

He shook his head, and it was hard to keep meeting his eyes, given the worry reflecting back at me.

"Elena, we've talked about this before. It isn't a wise idea to draw so much attention to yourself. To be so open about what you can do. There have already been rumors swirling since Abalene. You wouldn't believe the number of people at the University who asked me about it."

"Jasper." I paused before going on. "That's exactly it."

"What's it?"

"Abalene just proves my point. I've tried holding back, hiding my strength. But it didn't do any good. I just end up forgetting myself and doing or saying the wrong thing. So now I'm trying the opposite. They'll have to acknowledge me as one of them eventually. Once I've made myself so strong no one can ever touch me."

"Oh, Elena." He looked sad and utterly weary. "You know that much strength is impossible."

I bit my lip and looked away. "I have to try something," I whispered.

Jasper wrapped his arms around me, and I let my head rest against his shoulder in silence. A long time passed before I sighed and pulled back.

"I was surprised to hear the rumors about your wins at the Academy," he said. "I thought, after your birthday..." He looked away. "Well I thought you wouldn't be here. That you were planning to conscript straight away. Not that you can't change your mind...Clemmy has been healed now, after all."

"That doesn't matter," I said. "I already told you. I would never abandon her."

"No, I didn't think so." He looked at me. "You've still got plenty of time, I suppose. You won't be nineteen until next year."

"I couldn't take that risk," I said. "I enlisted the day after my birthday. Our family is free, Jasper. I saw the mage cross our names out of the records myself."

"But I don't understand. You're still here?"

"They intervened," I told him, not able to bring myself to

specify who. "They had me posted here to the Academy. But, officially, I'm Private Elena."

He slowly shook his head. "Do you mean it? Really?"

I nodded.

"Remarkable. Truly remarkable. We never could have guessed it would end up like this." He reflected silently for a moment, and I could almost see a visible weight lifting from him. He had always hated having to leave our family's burden to me and Clemmy.

"But this is amazing news, Elena. Far better than any of us could have hoped for." He looked down at me and seemed to deflate a little. "As long as you don't go and get yourself killed some other way."

I chewed on my lip. "And that's why I need to make myself strong, Jasper. I still have nearly three years of my term. Anything could happen. And if I do find myself on the front lines, I have every intention of surviving. No matter what they throw at me."

He shook his head, wonder in his eyes. "I almost believe you could do it, too."

"Good," I said. "Now I just need everyone else to believe it."

CHAPTER 22

The week after that, on the second year arena day, Thornton called my name twice. He had returned to his usual practice of only one bout per person per week some time ago, so I wasn't expecting it.

Unlike the others, I had never fought twice in one day. And also unlike the others, I couldn't prepare my compositions across the whole week. With a limit of three per bout, they only needed to prepare one a day to cover two bouts. And many of them used composition class to craft them.

For me, on the other hand, two bouts meant I had to produce six workings within the one session. Six workings strong enough to either break through or withstand the stored strength in the workings of my year mates. And that was after producing yet more all week in composition and my own training.

I wasn't prepared for hearing my name a second time and had expended too much energy winning the first bout.

The second was against Weston, and though it galled me, I had to yield. It was either that or push myself dangerously close to the edge. After nearly two years at the Academy, I should be so accustomed to their gloating that it wouldn't even register.

But I did feel a pang as I traipsed back up to my seat, Weston already having sat down to the gleeful congratulations of his friends. Never mind that it had been Weston's first bout of the day, and he had been using stored compositions.

"Always expect the unexpected, Elena," Thornton said as I passed him.

I wanted to snap at him, but I knew he was right. Out on the battle field, my fights wouldn't come in neat bouts with limits and set numbers of compositions. Already I found my mind turning over the first bout, considering how I could have won it with less energy.

And the next week I was ready. I won both bouts.

Thornton called me twice every week after that. At first Coralie grumbled on my behalf, complaining that it wasn't fair, but Finnian just shook his head.

"Thornton doesn't care about being fair. He cares about pushing us. About giving us the skills to survive."

And when I continued to win even Coralie stopped grumbling.

I noticed the third and fourth year students watching me in the library and the dining hall, but I did my best to ignore them. They hadn't been interested in me when they thought me weak, and their interest didn't matter now.

I did appreciate it when Walden stopped me one afternoon in the library to congratulate me, though.

"I can see my tutelage wasn't needed," he said with an encouraging smile. "From what I hear you've outdone yourself. You're outshining them all."

"I don't know that I'd quite say that. But I'm doing my best."

"And what a best it is!" He patted me on the shoulder. "No one could ask more, Elena, no one could ask more."

He turned to go before swinging back around. "Oh, did Lorcan and Jessamine find you? He was saying something about needing you for testing earlier…"

When I shook my head, confused, he shrugged.

"Ah well, he is the head, after all. I'm sure he'll track you down if he needs you badly enough. I suppose Acacia might have left by now, anyway. I heard her talking about having to take a short leave of absence from the Academy."

"Acacia? What does she have to do with it?"

"Oh, to draw the blood, of course." He smiled cheerfully. "I suppose they didn't get what they needed from the last batch."

Another student called for him, and he hurried off, waving farewell as he went. I remained where he had left me, trying to make sense of his words. Jessamine. Testing. Acacia. The last batch? Of what? My blood? But they had never taken my blood for testing.

A creeping cold crept over me. They had never taken it that I knew of. But I had been unconscious in Acacia's rooms for two days at the end of last year. And she herself had admitted to keeping me that way with a composition.

Another memory surfaced, and I had barely registered it before my feet were carrying me out of the library and toward Lorcan's study. Clementine. Reese had taken Clementine's blood after they had healed her, and Beatrice had looked confused, as if it was not, in fact, normal procedure.

As I strode across Lorcan's waiting room, I heard the indistinct murmur of voices from inside his office. Walden had been right, the University Head was here today.

I didn't pause or even knock, bursting in on them unannounced. They sat one on each side of his desk, their heads bent over something between them. Both jerked at my arrival, looking over toward me.

"Elena." Lorcan frowned. "I didn't send for you."

"No, you didn't." I looked between them, unsure how to proceed now that I was actually here. "I came to ask you a question."

Lorcan exchanged a look with Jessamine.

"Well, then, what is your question?"

I drew a deep breath. There was nothing for it but to ask straight out.

"Did you take my blood? Last year, while I was unconscious. Without asking me or even informing me?"

Despite my fears, I had half expected a denial. But none came. Instead Lorcan exchanged another loaded glance with Jessamine and then instructed me to close the door. I did so with hands that trembled.

"Sit down," he said.

I remained standing, staring at him defiantly.

"Oh, sit down, Elena," said Jessamine, fixing me with her keen eyes.

I sank into the closest chair, but my hands balled into fists.

"Were you the ones who instructed Reese to collect my sister's blood?"

Lorcan actually looked guilty this time. "We heard about Beatrice's task, and it seemed too good an opportunity to miss. There were things we couldn't learn from your blood alone. We needed a close relative…"

His voice trailed away as he took in my expression.

"Come now, Elena. Reese didn't do her any harm by taking it. In fact, from what I hear, he and Beatrice did her a great deal of good. It was a small price in exchange."

"Perhaps," I said. "Although surely that depends on what you wanted it for. And nothing could excuse stealing it in such a manner."

"Surely you must have known that we were studying your origin," said Jessamine.

I stared at her. "My origin?"

"Yes, of course." She looked impatient. "My dear girl, you are something entirely new. We must discover how you came to be. And whether your unique abilities can be replicated." She looked across at Lorcan. "Whether, perhaps, they already have been."

"Other spoken mages," I breathed.

Lorcan nodded. "Yes, of course. Surely it has occurred to you what an enormous coincidence it is that you discovered your powers at all. How many more of you might exist out there, undiscovered due to illiteracy?"

Of course I had considered the possibility of other spoken mages. And I had known it would be a matter of interest to others. I didn't know why I hadn't thought about the inevitability of Lorcan and Jessamine investigating it. I jumped to my feet.

"Have you tested any others? Shown them a written word and had them speak it?" My eyes grew wide. "What if all common-born can—"

"Yes, of course we have tried," said Jessamine. "And you can rid yourself of that notion. We have run a number of tests on random subjects. No one else can replicate your ability. Not even the slightest whisper of power."

I wasn't sure if her expression was relieved or disappointed.

"And so we were forced to turn back to investigating you, specifically," Lorcan said. "We began examining your blood over the summer and quickly realized we would need something to compare it with."

"Of course you did," I muttered to myself, sinking back into my seat. I looked up at them. "And what did you find?"

They exchanged yet another look.

"You're talking about me," I snapped. "My life. My origins."

Lorcan nodded once. "It appears from certain markers in your blood and that of your sister that you have at least some ancestry from outside Ardann."

"Outside Ardann? From where?" I stared at him. I didn't know what I had expected to hear, but that hadn't been it. Kallorway had been enemies with Ardann for as long as anyone could remember. And the Sekali Empire had been uninterested in the "southern savages" for even longer. Where could such an ancestor have come from?

"That is what we are trying to determine. And it is not the only thing. There are curious markers in your blood. Ones we can find no sign of in your sister's. Further study is needed."

He frowned at me. "But our work must be done under the utmost secrecy."

"Secrecy?" I scoffed at him. "Don't try to tell me that none of this has occurred to anyone else. I'm sure the king is greatly interested in my origins."

"Naturally we are not keeping our discoveries a secret from the royal family," said Jessamine stiffly. "But there are certain factions…There is a delicacy to how we release certain details…"

The royal family? So Lucas knew they were investigating me in secret. Of course he did. I tried to focus on Jessamine's words.

"Yes, I know," I said impatiently. "Devoras, Stantorn, executing me. I am aware that some of those in power would rather see me dead than alive."

Lorcan frowned. "Perhaps that was true last year, Elena, but times change."

I stared at him. Wasn't he the one who had lectured me only weeks ago about all the protection he had given me? And while it was true that no one had yet attacked me this year, I hadn't forgotten that a Stantorn—or one of their servants—had attempted to abduct me last summer and had gotten away with it entirely.

"What do you mean? They don't want me dead? But after I enlisted, you said—"

"There have been developments even since then," Lorcan interrupted. "The tide is always changing. And you can hardly claim to be unaware of your recent feats in the arena. Well, others are also aware of them. And there are an increasing number who believe you have been here long enough to prove you are not some rebellious commonborn who will attack at the first opportunity."

I snorted.

"We have suffered some devastating losses at the border this year," Jessamine continued for him. "And not just among our commonborn troops. These things are always about timing, and you have managed to gain attention at just the right moment. People are looking for hope. And then come the stories of you. Your power, your strength, your control. First in Abalene, where they say you held back the tide of an epidemic with the words from your mouth, and now in the arena, where you have only to speak to blast away any opponent."

I stared at her, my mouth falling open.

"I most definitely didn't turn back any epidemics on my own," I started, but she cut me off.

"The truth is not important here, Elena. It is the perception. You are protected here within the walls of the Academy, so you do not hear the stories circulating at court or feel the turning of emotions. Our kingdom needs hope. And you have arrived in the nick of time."

Lorcan leaned toward me. "And so, you see why this would not be an opportune moment to announce that you may not be Ardannian at all. Or at least, not completely. The seeds of doubt about your loyalty might once again start to flourish. And the king does not wish to see the tide turn back toward fear—not toward you nor in regard to the war."

"It makes it all the more important," said Jessamine, eager again, "that we acquire some more samples of your blood. With further study we may be able to determine exactly…"

Her voice faded from my hearing as I reeled under their revelations. But one thought pushed its way to the fore. If I hadn't pushed my way in here demanding answers, I would still know none of this. They had been wanting more of my blood, but it didn't seem to have occurred to them to share any of this with me. To simply ask for a sample.

And Thornton's continued pushing of my limits now took on a more sinister note. If I had been determined to beat Weston, that first week when he called me for a second bout...If I had pushed myself too hard and collapsed, how convenient for them it would have been.

I leaped to my feet again, and this time began pacing the room, unable to remain still. Jessamine had earlier referenced the other commonborn test subjects, and that was the root of the problem.

"I don't know why I'm surprised. At either of you." I paused mid-stride to glare at them both. "You've been the same ever since I arrived. I'm nothing but a test subject to you. Well, you're wrong. I'm a person. And I deserve the same respect and consideration as anyone else. Would you draw Lucas's blood and study it without his knowledge? Or Finnian's? Or one of the twins? Would you keep information like this from them? When it related to them personally?"

Neither of them said anything.

"Well? Would you?"

"Of course we would not," said Jessamine. "The circumstances..."

"No!" I said, slicing at the air with my hand. "There is no difference. Some things are going too far. No matter what. Did it ever even occur to you that I might assist you willingly if you only asked?"

Jessamine leaned toward me. "Would you? Assist us? This is an important line of study, more important than perhaps you realize."

I stared at her, slowly shaking my head.

"Do you even hear yourself? Either of you? What am I? The hope of Ardann, or a test subject without rights or even basic consideration?"

She froze, something passing across her eyes I couldn't read.

"You're right," said Lorcan, and I was the one to freeze. "We should have consulted you before now."

I blinked at him. "I...I am?"

"Of course." He nodded. "You have more than proved yourself a mage. The time for doubt is passed. You are one of us and should have been afforded the same privileges and courtesy as one of us." He gestured across the table at his counterpart.

"Jessamine and I are both academics. Sometimes we can become so focused on the details that we forget the big picture. You have proven yourself in two disciplines now, and Walden assures me of your intelligence. We may not have cracked your origins yet, but one thing we should not have overlooked is your position among us as a mage."

Jessamine slowly nodded, her eyes fixed on him.

"I hope you will accept our apology and consider working with us fully to move forward our understanding of the great power to be found in words."

He sat back, and they both fixed me with identical looks of hope.

I stumbled back to my seat.

At the end of last year I had decided to embrace my position as a mage. And I had spent this year striving to win a place among them, to win a voice among them. And here I was with two of the most powerful mages in the kingdom talking to me almost as an equal. Asking me for my help. Telling me that I was one of them. No—that I was the hope of Ardann.

All I had to do was say yes. Yes I would help them.

I could stop hiding, stop playing games with my power and true abilities. I could join them and actually be their hope rather than just the empty promise of one.

But even as I thought it, I felt a phantom weight in my arms. A small girl's eyes looked up into mine, suddenly clear of infection, as she told me she was hungry. And the ghost of a laugh sounded in my ears, coming from a girl who looked far too young to be facing the front lines next year.

They called me the hope of Ardann, but they meant I was the hope of the mages. And if I looked past the flattered feeling that wanted to simply accept his words, Lorcan had entirely missed my point.

I deserved respect and consideration because I was a person, not because I was a mage. And if I lost sight of that, how quickly would I lose the essence of myself as well?

Somehow I had been placed here, in the midst of these mages. And the combined efforts of two of their most intelligent researchers hadn't been enough to work out why or how. Not in nearly two years of study. And yet here I was.

I was in a unique position to push for change. To keep reminding them at every turn that they weren't the only ones in this kingdom. That a vast number of commonborns shared it with them. People who might never be able to read or write, but who still deserved consideration.

I hadn't turned back an epidemic—and certainly not alone. Beatrice and Reese would have made their breakthrough without me. And they would have subsequently treated the patients without me, too. Just a little more slowly.

But how many more would have died in that time? How many had been saved because Lucas had listened to my suggestion, and his father had requested assistance from the mageborn outside the healing discipline?

It shouldn't have fallen to me to make such an obvious suggestion. And yet it had. Not because I was more intelligent than the rest of them, but because I saw things from a different perspective.

And if I wanted to become one of them, I would have to give up making such suggestions. Because the more I pushed, the more uncomfortable I would make them. And the more uncomfortable I made them, the less stable my position would be. I couldn't have it both ways.

And it didn't take much reflection to realize which person I wanted to be. How could I ever return home and look my family in the eye if I chose now to embrace only my magehood? No.

Somehow I had to learn how to be both mage and common-born. And the rest of the kingdom would have to learn to adjust along with me.

I suddenly realized Lorcan was still waiting for an answer. I sighed and looked across at him.

"I accept your apology, of course. And I will give you whatever blood you need because you're my commanding officer, and I am bound to obey your directives. But my full attention and energy are needed elsewhere."

"Elsewhere?" Jessamine frowned. "What could be more important than unlocking the mysteries of how to control power?"

I shook my head. "A great many things, Jessamine. In my opinion, of course."

I stood up and crossed over to the door. "I heard Acacia is away. Have her find me when she gets back, and you'll get your blood. Oh, and this year is nearly over. Since I am a soldier under your command, should I be expecting to go home over the summer at all?"

Lorcan cleared his throat. "It should be possible to arrange a short visit at least. And I have already had an application from the Cygnet family for you to be given leave to attend some sort of celebration at their home in Abalene as well. Naturally I agreed."

A small smile crossed my face. I should have known Coralie would leave no detail of her birthday unaccounted for.

"Thank you." I paused. "I assume I will be assigned watchers again for these excursions. Please let them know there is no need to skulk around in hiding. I won't confront them or make a scene."

Neither of them said anything, so I walked out of the room.

CHAPTER 23

I left Lorcan's office with a heavy weariness, but I soon felt my energy returning. I had made the right decision, and the knowledge gave me a new buoyancy.

Final exams were nearly upon us, and this year I didn't fear failing them. I now led the class—alongside Dariela and Lucas—in both combat and composition. And I had already completed all of my healing and armed forces assignments for discipline studies.

Naturally Araminta didn't share my confidence, and Coralie and I spent hours assisting her in study. Finnian excused himself from these study sessions, having no need of them himself, but Saffron often joined us. Whether for her own sake or to help Araminta I wasn't sure.

But even with the extra study, the exams seemed to race upon us with much greater speed than the year before. I blinked and found myself trooping out to the arena with the other second years. We had to wait this year for Thornton to finish the first year exams, but since we would be the first year level to be examined in the arena, we all waited there.

Many of the other students fingered something hidden in

their sleeves and robes, and I wondered what compositions they had chosen to prepare. I didn't ask any of them, though, not even my friends. None of us knew who we might face today, and no one wanted to give up the advantage of surprise. I also imagined they had each poured as much strength into their compositions as they were able.

I felt no concern over failure, however. Today, at least, we would each only participate in one bout. And despite my speed disadvantage, I had a flexibility the rest of them lacked. I hadn't had to choose my compositions in advance.

In reality we didn't wait long, but the minutes still seemed to stretch endlessly. My mind wandered to Lorcan and Jessamine's studies. Had they found anything in the new vials of blood I had given them? Had they unlocked the secrets of my history?

Coralie had said I had permission to leave with her directly after exams, but perhaps I could find a moment to ask them before then. Or should I trust they would come to me if they made any breakthroughs? I wanted to, but I still wasn't truly sure I could.

The sound of feet made all twelve of us sit up. Only Lucas looked as calm as ever, his court mask firmly in place.

But the boots sounded too numerous for Thornton and Lorcan, our two combat examiners from first year. Were there to be extra judges this time?

When our two instructors came into view, they did indeed have a small entourage. General Griffith in his glittering silver robe strode beside them, three other silver-robed officers trailing behind.

For a moment I sat frozen before remembering to clamber to my feet and salute. The general smiled at his children, sitting in the first row of seats, and then looked up at me and nodded.

I took the gesture as permission for me to resume my place and did so.

"The general has honored us with his presence," said Lorcan.

"He wishes to observe his two children complete their first arena exam today."

But his eyes flicked up to me as he finished speaking, and they held a message I couldn't read. When the general also turned several times to look up at me, including once during the first bout between Clarence and Araminta, I realized something at least of Lorcan's message.

General Griffith wasn't here to observe his children. He was here to observe me. The private under his service. The apparent hope of Ardann's war effort.

A small prickle of sweat broke out beneath my collar. What consequences might come from this? I couldn't even begin to imagine. I had begun to feel more hopeful about my enlistment since Lorcan had told me that the great mage families no longer wanted me dead. But I should have known the situation would be more complicated than that.

What exactly was the general thinking? Should I put on a spectacular show or downplay my strength? I still hadn't made up my mind when Coralie was called, facing off against Saffron, thankfully for them both. But I barely registered their bout, or the following ones, my gaze constantly straying to the silver-robed officers sitting at the front of the arena. And then I heard my own name called.

I sat frozen for several seconds of confusion. Was he calling me? I couldn't be sure because he had called too many names.

"I repeat," said Thornton, his voice carefully blank, "the next bout will be Elena against Lucas and Dariela."

"What?" said Coralie as a ripple spread among the other students. "But..."

Thornton fixed her with a stern stare, and her words trailed off. When he turned his stare on me, I somehow lurched to my feet.

I walked down to the arena floor in a daze. If Dariela and Lucas were equally surprised, they hid it better. They also moved

224

into the arena, heads bent together as they whispered—about strategy no doubt.

I looked across at our audience and detected a gleeful gleam of anticipation in General Griffith's eyes. Of course. No doubt this change had come from him. I glanced over at Lorcan, but his face was as carefully blank as Thornton's. Had the Head of the Academy been unable to refuse the suggestion from the general because of my status as a private?

And did the general just wish to see me pushed to my limits? To my limits and most likely beyond since they had chosen not just two opponents, but the two strongest in the class. I had never fought against two at once before, and both Lucas and Dariela had no doubt brought their strongest compositions.

Or did he intend for me to lose? An ordinary trainee who failed their exams was locked away somewhere where they could not access written words and thus risk losing control of their power. It was why the exams were usually fairly easy. No one wanted the trainees to fail.

But I had always been a special case. Failure last year would have meant my execution since I could not safely be contained. And that had aligned perfectly with the agenda of far too many on the council. But Lorcan and Jessamine had assured me things had changed. Surely they did not want to execute their hope of turning the tide in the war effort?

I watched the light on General Griffith's face and had another thought. If one exception could be made for me to the normal consequence of imprisonment, could not another one also be made? One in the opposite direction?

What if the price of failing now was that I would be expelled from the Academy, leaving me no other option but to transfer to a regular Armed Forces command? One, no doubt, on the front lines. Perhaps even under General Griffith himself.

I looked over at Lucas's dark head still bent toward Dariela's fair one, and my heart sank. I thought I had escaped my fate of enlistment. I thought I had won freedom at the Academy. But I wasn't really free. And if I couldn't defeat the two best trainees in our class, I would discover just how little freedom I really had.

I changed my sword into my left hand, so I could wipe my sweaty right palm against my robe before transferring it back. I only had one option. I had to win.

I tried to think quickly as they separated, walking slowly toward positions on either side of me. With two of them working together, one of them could keep me occupied with the sword, while the other released one of their compositions. I would have to move fast—faster than I'd ever moved before—if I was to have any hope of not going down in the first minute.

And there was only one way to move faster. I needed to drop the binding words. Which meant I needed to overlay all my controls over a single word. I had never even practiced it before, and I wasn't sure I could do it. But I had to try. And I couldn't make it an unlimited composition either. Because with the amount of power shared between these two, I'd burn myself out all too quickly if I did.

Both of them raised their swords. I was out of time.

At least I wouldn't have to worry about needing time to visualize the words. Not with only one.

I raised my own sword.

Thornton called for us to begin.

Lucas lunged toward me as a scrap of parchment appeared in Dariela's hand. Just as I had predicted.

I ignored the incoming sword and put every ounce of my concentration into my composition.

"Shield!" I screamed, my power rippling to life around me a bare half-second before Lucas's sword plunged toward my heart. It bounced off the shield just as a huge jolt hit me from behind.

The entire ground shook, and I staggered inside my bubble. I had limited the shield to protect me only from debilitating blows, thus why I still shook from the after effects of whatever that composition had unleashed.

But even with the limitations, the shield had already drawn a frightening amount of power. I could only hope Dariela had started with her strongest composition.

The two of them circled me slowly, shock in their eyes that I was still standing after their two-pronged attack. But I could see the calculation behind their emotion. Exchanging a glance, they each pulled out a parchment.

They must have heard my single word. Did they think I had erected an unlimited shield? Perhaps they thought to drain me. I held myself ready on the balls of my feet, my sword held loosely, and my eyes on their hands.

The second they ripped the paper, I let the sword drop and launched myself forward onto the ground, rolling into a tiny ball. The smaller I made myself, the less of a target I became—and the more my shield could safely let through.

Something huge and hard hit the shield and bounced off, draining more of my power as it went. But several smaller weights passed through, one glancing off my shoulder, sending a sharp pain searing through me.

I grunted but held my position for a moment longer before cautiously raising my head. Both of my opponents were staring at me, once again thrown off.

But these two weren't the pride of the mageborn for nothing. They paused for only a second. Then, exchanging a glance, they both raised their swords and advanced on me. I leaped to my feet, scrambling to place my hand on my own sword.

I felt dangerously weak already and couldn't afford to leave it to my shield to deflect all their blows. It wouldn't anyway, I realized with a jolt. Only the debilitating ones, like the lunge at my chest that Lucas had tried earlier.

I pulled my sword up in time to parry an attack from Dariela. Lucas attempted another lunge while I was distracted, but my shield again deflected him. I wheeled, taking several steps back to keep them both in sight.

I could see Lucas's narrowed eyes passing between his own sword and Dariela's as he worked out why hers had passed through and his hadn't. He was smart. Too smart. He would work it out quickly enough. And then he could wear me down with a hundred tiny cuts.

I went on the offensive myself, trying to distract him as I desperately tried to come up with a composition that would incapacitate them both. He blocked my attack, countering with a lunge. I whipped my sword up to meet his, feeling my shield deflect a blow from Dariela that I hadn't even seen coming. I fell back again, and we all circled each other warily.

Their compositions weren't draining them which gave them an undoubted extra advantage in the sword play. Both of them could keep this up a lot longer than I could, which meant I had to end this. And end it soon.

I needed something I had used before, something I knew worked. I whirled suddenly and directed my next lunge toward Dariela, whispering the binding words as I did so. This time they wouldn't hear what was coming for them.

"Bind Lucas and Dariela in stillness until they yield. End binding."

I gave an unstable lunge toward Dariela as I said the final words, distracting her with its wild aim as much as the attack itself. She stepped back, countering me neatly, but in doing so she had failed to notice my composition.

The stream of my power hit her hard, and she fell, arms and legs stiffly held in the positions they had occupied when my composition hit her. I could do no more than hope Lucas had gone down as well as I leaped forward and pressed my sword tip against Dariela's throat.

"Yield," she said quietly, and I didn't pause to hear anything more.

Whirling, I looked for Lucas. He was charging toward me, a shimmer of his own power around him. Without my attack to distract him, he had managed to unleash his own shield in time to protect himself.

The drain of power holding Dariela bound had dissipated when she yielded, but my own shield remained active, deflecting another lunge from Lucas as I stumbled backward away from Dariela's still prone body.

I kept moving backward as Lucas prowled toward me. He still had one composition he hadn't used, and he now had both a shield and energy to wield his sword. I, on the other hand, had already used a significant proportion of my reserves.

If I had any hope of defeating him, I needed to break through his shield. Which meant I needed to put every drop of remaining power into my final composition. And to do that I had to lose my own shield.

I continued to back away as fast as I could go, murmuring quietly to myself. I let myself take the time to build the composition properly, attaching its release to an action rather than the end of the binding.

Lucas continued to pursue me, although he came more slowly than I would have done in his place, seeming to think he had the upper hand. Even so, he managed to close the gap just as I said, "End binding."

When he attacked, my shield deflected it. I took a moment to prepare myself for my final desperate move, and he attacked again. As his sword glanced up and away, deflected by the curve of my shield, I whipped my arm back and threw.

I didn't worry about aim, leaving my now released composition to guide the sword forward as it flew through the air. At the moment my hand left the sword, my shield dropped, every bit of my strength pouring into the force of my projectile.

It hit Lucas's shield and pressed against it, hovering in mid-air, before an audible pop sounded, and his power dissipated, having reached whatever limit he had set. My sword flew forward, still guided by my power, as it followed Lucas's movement.

He had recovered from his final failed attack more quickly than I had anticipated, and already he had launched another. And now I had neither shield nor sword to protect me.

At the last second, I threw myself to the side, and his sword slid deep into my shoulder, scraping along bone.

I screamed and felt my power waver. But I gritted my teeth and threw everything I had into holding on. For just one more minute.

My sword hovered in the air as I had directed it, its tip now pressed against Lucas's throat. He had frozen still lunged forward —his own sword still lodged in my shoulder—his eyes wide as my sharp tip nicked his skin.

Our eyes met, and I managed to grind out a single word.

"Well?"

His eyes flashed to my shoulder, and he swallowed. The tiny movement made my sword nick him again.

"Yield," he said, a fresh droplet of blood blooming against his neck.

As he spoke the word, my sword dropped away, my composition released. The drain on my power abruptly cut off, and the pain of my shoulder rushed forward to take its place, swamping me.

I swayed and fell.

CHAPTER 24

*a*s I dropped, Lucas ripped his sword free of my shoulder, letting it fall beside him. Taking a single step forward, he caught me before I hit the ground.

I looked up into his white face, the smears of red stark against the skin of his neck.

"I thought your shield would—" He didn't finish his sentence.

I shook my head, unable to take in his words. Everything spun around me as blood poured down my shoulder. I needed to stop the bleeding now.

The bout was over, I could use a fourth composition. I opened my mouth to begin the binding words, but Lucas clapped one of his hands across it. Somehow he knew my intentions.

"No," he said. "Let Acacia do it."

Acacia? I looked around feebly and spotted a blur of purple racing toward us. Oh, good.

I let myself relax a little, already anticipating her cool mist against my burning skin. If she said anything, I didn't hear it, but my anxious ears heard the clear sound of ripping parchment.

I gasped and then sighed as her power settled over me, and the pain subsided. I felt the rush of blood slow to a trickle and then stop as the wound healed. I took a deep breath, shook my head, and then struggled out of Lucas's supporting arms.

For a moment he tried to hold on but then seemed to think better of it, abruptly releasing me. I swayed slightly as I took my weight on my own feet, but then I blinked several times, and my head cleared.

"A nice clean wound, at least," said Acacia with a look of sympathy.

"Were you truly going to attempt to heal it yourself?" Lucas asked me in a low voice.

I gave him a confused look. "Of course."

"But you must be close to burn out. Surely."

"I could have stopped the bleeding at least. I think. But better to try than bleed to death."

He shook his head. "This wasn't a real battle, Elena. We wouldn't have let you bleed to death."

I stared at him for a moment as a creeping feeling of foolishness washed over me. He was right, of course. I had let myself get swept up in the stakes of the exam. And then in the pain and exhaustion I had forgotten that with the bout over someone else would heal me.

I flushed and then shrugged, too tired to work out if I should thank him for stopping me. Given he had been the one to injure me in the first place. Except that had been during the bout. I shook my head and started back toward the stands.

In the heat of battle, I had forgotten our audience. To a person they stared at me in total silence. I swallowed and tried to keep from swaying as I walked. When I placed my foot on the first step, the silence broke.

"Incredible," said General Griffith, his eyes on me, but his words seemingly directed at Lorcan beside him. "You told me… But I didn't think." He shook his head. "Incredible." A greedy light lit his eyes, and I shivered.

Whatever it had cost me, that victory had been worth it to

keep myself out of his grip. But when my eyes skipped over Lorcan and landed on Thornton, I nearly stumbled. I couldn't mistake his expression this time. It was awe. He clearly hadn't expected me to win.

I turned away from all of them, but my eyes only landed on the trainees filling the front row of seats on the other side of the stairs. And Calix was looking at me with just as much wonder in his face as Thornton.

First my instructor, and now one of my enemies. I didn't look at anyone else, hurrying up the stairs and taking the first seat I could find on a higher level.

Only when my heartbeat had slowed and calmed did I look around. I had expected my friends to rush over to me as soon as I sat, but none of them had moved. Every one of them—even Coralie—was looking at me with something in their eyes that I didn't want to see there. I looked away.

If there were more bouts after mine, I didn't absorb them. I did hear Thornton announce that everyone had passed and managed a moment of relief for Araminta. And when everyone rose to clear the arena for the third years, I stumbled to my feet to follow them.

The general and his entourage remained, talking quietly with Thornton, and I averted my eyes, walking quickly past. But Lorcan called out to me, so I reluctantly stopped.

Coralie cast me a hesitant look, but I gave her a slight shrug, and she kept walking.

"The other trainees will complete their composition exams after the midday meal," he said, and I stared at him in dismay.

The composition exam. How had I forgotten it? And how would I ever complete it now? After everything I had just done, I was going to fail second year after all.

But he kept speaking. "Every few years the suggestion is made that the composition exam is unnecessary for the second years and above since they demonstrate compositions in their combat exam. But those compositions used in combat were prepared previously, and not necessarily under instructor supervision. We still need to observe them as they compose. That is not so in your case."

He gestured to where Griffith and Thornton were still talking. "Two instructors and two members of the Mage Council just witnessed you compose three separate workings. You may consider yourself to have passed second year entirely." He dropped his voice. "Well done, Elena."

I managed to smile, relief washing over me. So I *had* done it. And now I would get to sleep. My bed had never been more welcome. I nodded at him and continued on my way toward the exit, not wanting to get caught in any sort of interaction with the general.

As I left the arena, the third years filed in, looking at me curiously as they passed. Apparently the general had decided to stay and observe the efforts of the upper year levels as well.

The last of them passed me just as I stepped out into the open air. I remembered that unlike after a normal class, it would still be some time before the meal. The third and fourth years needed to bout first.

I immediately resolved that food could wait. My pillow called to me.

But a low voice murmuring my name stopped me in my tracks. I turned slowly to find Lucas waiting for me in the shadow of the arena wall.

My feet took me over to him of their own accord, drawn perhaps by his pale color and the note of desperation in his voice.

He gripped my shoulders and examined every inch of my face.

"You're all right? You're truly all right?"

I nodded. I had never seen him so shaken, and it temporarily drove away my exhaustion, sharpening my mind.

"Oh, thank goodness." He pressed his lips together and swallowed. "When I felt my sword slide into your shoulder…"

His hands tightened convulsively, and he looked almost as if he was going to be sick.

"I thought your shield would block it. I only meant to tire you further. And then your sword meant I couldn't even draw back. The feel of my blade, held there…" He shook his head. "I let myself get caught up in the bout, but I would never knowingly…"

"Lucas. It's all right. I'm fine. Truly." I managed a smile. "I even won."

A slow blaze lit his eyes. "Yes, you did. I didn't think it was possible. I wanted to refuse when Thornton announced the bout, but it was an exam. That would have done neither of us any good. But I was so angry. Surprising you with something like this. And against Dariela and me. If I could have softened my compositions —but it was too late for that. And then the bout started, and I forgot for a moment…"

"You mean you didn't cheat in an exam and let me win?" I shook my head. "I would never expect such a thing. Truly it's all right, Lucas."

"No," he said. "It's not. Some things are more important than winning. Even when you're a prince."

"Are they? Are you sure?" I tried to inject a lighter note into the conversation, but his eyes remained serious.

"Yes. Some things—or rather some people—are more important. *You're* more important, Elena. More important to me."

My head spun, but not with exhaustion this time. I could not be hearing these words from Lucas of all people. From Lucas who had always put his interest in the kingdom above me. Perhaps it was all some fever dream, a wish conjured up by my tired brain. Perhaps even now I was lying unconscious in Acacia's rooms, recovering from burn out, and everything since the end of the bout had been a dream.

But his arms gripping my shoulders felt real and steady. And his eyes burning into mine lit an answering fire inside me.

But I had been here before. I tried to find the strength to draw back.

"You kissed me at the end of first year exams," I told him, "only to go straight back to ignoring me. And then you used my feelings to try to stop me from saving my sister. How can you say now that I'm more important to you than anything?"

"Used your feelings?" To my astonishment it was hope that sprang into his eyes. "For nearly two years I've been tormenting myself wondering if you had any feelings at all for me beside resentment and anger."

He shook his head. "At least whenever I wasn't reminding myself that as a prince I shouldn't have feelings for you myself. At least not outside of interest in the Spoken Mage and the asset you could be to Ardann. And yet everywhere I turned there you were. Braver, more caring, more resilient, more full of fire than I could possibly have hoped. Nothing has beaten you down. No matter what you face, you rise from it, stronger than ever."

His voice dropped to a whisper. "More beautiful than ever. So tell me, Elena. Do you have feelings for me?"

"I...I can't," I whispered back.

"Can't have feelings for me or can't tell me?"

I swallowed as I tried to gather my whirling thoughts.

"You tracked me," I said at last. "You kept secrets from me, you ignored me, you watched the other trainees beat and harass me. I suppose...I suppose I can't *trust* you."

But even as I said it, my heart screamed at me to give a different answer. Because there was another side to this prince. He had protected me, spoken up for me, sought me out, trained me, challenged me. Again and again. In Abalene he had even listened to me and taken action, risking his family's ridicule.

An anguished look crossed his face. "I've made so many

mistakes where you're concerned, Elena. If I had only been open with you from the beginning. If I had only trusted my heart." He stared into my eyes, begging me to hear him. "But as a prince I was never taught to listen to my heart, only my head. And it seems with you, my head has too often steered me wrong. But my heart..." His voice dropped low. "My heart has remained steady, Elena."

When he spoke of his heart, my own heart took over, unable to resist his nearness or the allure of his words. I didn't speak, instead tilting up my face to his in a silent invitation.

With a soft sigh, he pulled me into his arms and pressed his lips down against mine.

New strength flowed into me, rejuvenating my tired body. I responded eagerly to his embrace, giving myself over to the feelings I had been denying and fighting and ignoring for so long. For an endless moment, there was nothing but Lucas. Lucas and his fire, and the wonder that, despite everything, he truly cared for me.

When he at last drew back, his breathing uneven, I let myself stare in wonder at his perfect features and brilliant eyes. It all seemed surreal. Lucas was a prince. He had no business caring for someone like me.

I jolted, pulling back slightly as the thought triggered an unpleasant memory.

He frowned down at me in quick concern.

"You said you have no business listening to your heart," I said, "and you're right. Didn't you tell me once that as royalty you can only ever marry someone from one of the great families? The purity of the blood line and all that."

He bit his lip, a shadow crossing his eyes. The silence lengthened, and he made no effort to deny it.

This time I pulled back fully, dragging myself from his arms.

"So what is this to you? A dalliance? A temporary distraction?"

He shook his head quickly. "No. Never. I want to be with you, only you."

A new fire of hope lit inside me. But caution still held me back.

"You want to fight then? Fight for change?" Some of my excitement tinged my voice. With Lucas by my side, perhaps I could take my place as a mage and still push for change, after all.

"Changing the laws about royalty could only be the beginning. We could do so much good, Lucas. Just think of what we could accomplish together—just like in Abalene. Together no one and nothing could stop us."

But I hadn't even finished the last sentence when I saw something in his eyes that killed my fire. I didn't need to hear his answer.

"You're not going to fight for change," I said, my voice dull even to my own ears. "You're not even going to fight for us."

He tried to take my hand, but I pulled it out of his reach.

"It's not that I don't want change." His eyes pleaded with me. "And it's certainly not that I don't want you. I've never wanted anything more. But Kallorway is on the move. They haven't made a push like this since before we were born. Ardann can't afford to be divided right now. We can't afford to focus anywhere but on the war effort."

"The war effort?" I shook my head and stumbled back another step. "Then that means I will be nothing but a weapon, and we can never be together."

"After the war—"

I laughed, the sound grating against us both. "The war has been going on for thirty years, Lucas. If you won't fight for change until it ends, you may never have the chance."

He stared at me, and I could see the struggle raging behind his eyes. I willed him on, desperately telling myself it wasn't too late. He could still choose us.

But I saw the moment my battle was lost.

My shoulders slumped, and the exhaustion came crashing back in. "Go," I said, not giving him the chance to speak. "It seems there is something more important than me, after all."

"Elena," he murmured my name, his voice desperate and his arms reaching for me.

I shook my head. "No. It's all or nothing, Lucas. If you won't fight for me and with me, then we can never be together. It seems your head had the right of it all this time. Your laws are clear. I am not a suitable choice."

A tiny spark of hope still lived in me. I waited to hear his voice deny my words. Hear him say that he would see the law changed or an exception given. That he would find a way. But he said nothing.

"Just go," I repeated. And this time he obeyed me.

For a long time I stood alone outside the arena. For one brief, shining moment, I had let myself believe. I had opened the door and let in every feeling that I never should have had. And now it had been ripped away, and the pain felt far greater than his sword in my shoulder had done.

It took a long time to remember how to breathe. And even longer to remember how to walk. And then, when my head hit my pillow, I could remember nothing but how to cry. The tears poured out of me for a long time, and then sleep claimed me.

CHAPTER 25

I slept all afternoon and all night. Only the breakfast bell the next morning finally woke me. For a moment I tried to remember why I felt so groggy and stiff, and then it all came crashing back.

I groped at the healed skin on my shoulder, feeling for a reopened wound before I realized the pain I felt was in my heart. I lay back and took long breaths until it subsided.

I had never had Lucas. I had never thought I would. One dizzy moment of wild hope didn't change anything. And I would keep telling myself that until my heart believed it.

Slowly I dragged myself out of bed. I hadn't spoken to my friends since the combat exam, and they would no doubt be worried. Plus, I wanted to hear how their composition exam had gone.

Slowly I descended the stairs, my mood at odds with the light-hearted chatter all around me. Exams were over, homes beckoned, and the sun outside shone brightly.

I entered the dining hall, my eyes seeking out Lucas's table before I could stop them. He wasn't there. I didn't know whether I felt more disappointment or relief.

I took my own seat, and Coralie greeted me with a tentative smile.

"I didn't know whether to knock on your door or not. I wasn't sure how much sleep you would need after yesterday…" She peered at me with cautious concern.

"Stop." I held up my hands and glared around the table at all of them. "Yesterday was exams. Nothing else. I don't want any of you treating me differently or tiptoeing around me. I couldn't bear it."

"You do realize what you did was unheard of, though, right?" said Finnian. "People tell stories about mages who can do a controlled working with a single word. And none of them were trainees."

I held up my hand to stop him from saying anything further.

"I passed my exam. That's what I did. That's all I did. I made sure I would get to be a third year with you crazy lot."

He grinned, looking more like his usual self. "I can understand how that prospect would be enough to motivate anyone to epic feats."

Coralie gave me a sudden hug. "I'm just glad you're all right. I thought for a minute there…"

"What about you?" I asked quickly. "How did the composition exam go?"

"Easy enough," said Saffron. "Even Araminta passed without trouble. Coralie cornered Lorcan afterward, and he said you'd passed yours in the arena."

I nodded. "Sorry if I worried you all. After I heard that I'd already passed, I headed straight for bed and crashed. Hard. I'm fine now, though." I glared at Coralie who was looking teary again. "Truly."

"Well that's good." She smiled properly for the first time since I had entered the dining hall. "Because my parents are sending a carriage for us today. And we wouldn't want to delay our departure and lose any party preparation time."

I brightened. I had almost forgotten Lorcan had given me leave to travel to Abalene. Being with Coralie would be many times better than remaining alone at the Academy, no doubt pressured into helping Lorcan and Jessamine with their investigation. I resolved not to approach Lorcan before I made my escape, after all. There would be time enough for questions when I returned.

And he had said I could visit home as well. Perhaps for Midsummer, if I was back in time. I might even be able to convince Jasper to come with me. All together again. It had been far too long since we had managed that.

My eyes strayed across the room, but Lucas still hadn't appeared.

"Everyone seems to be leaving fast this year," said Saffron.

"Well, we didn't have any crazed abductors storming the Academy this time around," said Finnian. "So excitement levels are a little low."

"Lucas disappeared as soon as he passed his composition exam," said Coralie. "Someone saw him leaving the Academy. I guess that set the tone, and now the rest are scrambling off as fast as they can go as well."

So Lucas had left. I wouldn't be seeing him again until next year. I tried to remember that was a good thing, but a pain had started up again near my left shoulder.

I glanced around the dining hall, in an effort to distract myself. It did look half empty.

"Have you heard the rumor?" Araminta slid into an empty seat at our table. We all stared at her blankly, and she grinned.

"This is great. I'm never the one to hear things first."

"Come on, spit it out," said Finnian good-humoredly.

"Well, as you know General Griffith came to watch all the arena combat exams. I can understand his interest in the fourth years—they'll all be traveling to join him at the border in a couple of weeks. But rumor says he had a special interest in the second and third years too."

She paused dramatically for a moment, and I could only hope she wasn't about to say anything about me.

"Well, apparently with Kallorway on the offensive, and with all those deaths earlier this year, he's been arguing that it will do the trainees good to be exposed to the front lines before they graduate. The rumor is that next year the third and fourth years will be heading for the border for at least a month. Not to fight directly, of course. But to see it for ourselves. To study the war effort like we did the epidemic. To get practical, on-the-ground training."

She shivered, and I couldn't tell if she was excited or terrified.

The other three peppered her with questions and exclamations, Saffron sounding as horrified as Finnian was interested. But my mouth seemed to have stopped working.

I had passed. I was supposed to be safe for another year. And yet somehow General Griffith had found a way to get me to the front lines after all. Oh, the third and fourth years wouldn't be fighting. Of that I had no doubt.

But upstairs in my wardrobe, I had a stark gray uniform. I wasn't just a third year, I was also a private. A member of the Armed Forces under Griffith's command. I had seen the greedy light in his eyes after my bout. Once he got me to the front lines, what would he order me to do? And would I survive it, whatever it was?

I forced myself to take a deep breath. I was still better off than if I had lost the bout. I would travel to the border as a trainee, and surely some at least of our instructors would accompany us. Even Lorcan himself, perhaps. I would not be entirely outside of his protection.

Someone called to Araminta from the entrance hall, and she leaped to her feet, giving hurried farewells to us all as she took off. Coralie stood as well, dragging me with her.

"We need to pack, or we won't be ready for the carriage when it arrives." She fixed the other two with a stern glare. "We'll see you at my party, right? You won't forget?"

Saffron rolled her eyes. "Of course we won't."

A sunny smile broke across Coralie's face, and somehow a little of its warmth crept into my own heart. The four of us would be together again soon. With no responsibilities for a little while except to celebrate Coralie and enjoy ourselves.

Autumn would come soon enough, and all its problems with it. I would have to face Lucas again. And, sooner or later, I would have to face the front lines.

But I had survived everything thrown at me so far. Somehow I would find a way to survive those hurdles as well. Dwelling on them now wouldn't help.

I smiled at Coralie and then across at Finnian and Saffron.

"Let's make this a good summer," I said. "One to remember."

Finnian raised his glass of juice in a toast. "A summer to remember."

We all echoed back the words, and then Coralie dragged me from the dining hall. Our summer was waiting.

NOTE FROM THE AUTHOR

Read *Voice of Dominion*, The Spoken Mage Book 3, to follow Elena and Lucas to the front lines in their third year at the Academy.

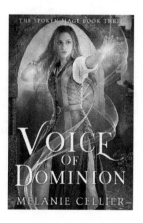

To be kept informed of releases and of bonus shorts in the Spoken Mage world—including an exclusive bonus chapter of Voice of Power, retold from Lucas's point of view—please sign up to my mailing list at www.melaniecellier.com.

Want more fantasy, romance, adventure, and intrigue while you wait for the end of Elena and Lucas's story? Try *A Dance of Silver and Shadow,* the first book in my *Beyond the Four Kingdoms* series in which twelve princesses must do a lot more than just dance when they get caught up in a dangerous and magical competition.

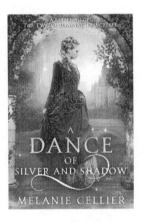

Thank you for taking the time to read my book. I hope you enjoyed it. If you did, please spread the word! You could start by leaving a review on Amazon (or Goodreads or Facebook or any other social media site). Your review would be very much appreciated and would make a big difference!

ROYAL FAMILY OF ARDANN

King Stellan
Queen Verena
Crown Princess Lucienne
Prince Lucas

MAGE COUNCIL

Academy Head (black robe) - Duke Lorcan of Callinos
University Head (black robe) - Duchess Jessamine of
    Callinos
Head of Law Enforcement (red robe) - Duke Lennox of
    Ellington
Head of the Seekers (gray robe) - Duchess Phyllida of
    Callinos
Head of the Healers (purple robe) - Duke Dashiell of
    Callinos
Head of the Growers (green robe) - Duchess Annika of
    Devoras
Head of the Wind Workers (blue robe) - Duke Magnus of
    Ellington
Head of the Creators (orange robe) - Duke Casimir of
    Stantorn
Head of the Armed Forces (silver robe) - General Griffith of
    Devoras
Head of the Royal Guard (gold robe) - General Thaddeus of
    Stantorn

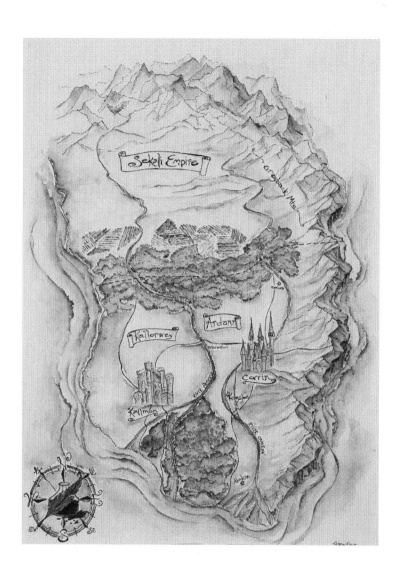

ACKNOWLEDGMENTS

Elena and Lucas still have a long way to go, and there are still lots of corners of the Spoken Mage world to explore, but I enjoyed expanding their world at least a little in Voice of Command. I also enjoyed dreaming and planning where their journey will take them next. Writing a series that follows the same characters and working on arcs that will require multiple books to pay off has been a new experience for me. And I'm grateful to everyone around me who has listened to me think, scheme, and stress aloud, and to those who have dived into the world with me to make sure that it's coming together in the way it needs to.

My family—Marc, Adeline, and Sebastian—deserve the same praise as always for both bearing with me and keeping me going. I've greatly enjoyed the extended break with you that was my reward for finishing the edits on this book. I look forward to both many more books and many more breaks shared with you in the coming years.

My beta readers never cease to astound me. And their support for this book has been an encouragement when I really needed one. Thank you Rachel, Greg, Priya, Ber, Katie, Marina, and Casey.

Kitty, Kenley, Shari, Aya, Brittany, Diana, and Marina—your friendship means a great deal to me, and I hope 2019 brings new heights and new joys to all of our writing journeys.

Thank you to my editors, Mary, Dad, and Deborah, for keeping me consistent and helping me to bring this next chapter of Elena's story into its final form. I can't wait to discuss all the ins and outs of books 3 and 4 with you!

Further thanks also to my cover designer, Karri, for taking Elena to the next level. It continues to be a pleasure to work with you.

And to God, whose voice is the first and only true source of power—thank you for giving us words and creativity and the chance to explore what we can do with them. May we always choose to follow in your footsteps and speak life rather than death.

ABOUT THE AUTHOR

 Melanie Cellier grew up on a staple diet of books, books and more books. And although she got older, she never stopped loving children's and young adult novels.

She always wanted to write one herself, but it took three careers and three different continents before she actually managed it.

She now feels incredibly fortunate to spend her time writing from her home in Adelaide, Australia where she keeps an eye out for koalas in her backyard. Her staple diet hasn't changed much, although she's added choc mint Rooibos tea and Chicken Crimpies to the list.

She writes young adult fantasy including her *Spoken Mage* series, and her *Four Kingdoms* and *Beyond the Four Kingdoms* series which are made up of linked stand-alone stories that retell classic fairy tales.

Made in United States
Troutdale, OR
12/21/2024

27112880R00162